MOSES' CHISEL

MOSES' CHISEL

BY
STEVEN LOWELL-MARTIN

Everlasting Publishing
Yakima, Washington
USA

Moses' Chisel
by
Steven Lowell-Martin

ISBN: 0-9852739-5-X
ISBN-13: 978-0-9852739-5-8

This novel is a work of fiction. Names, characters, businesses, places, events and incidents are either the products of the author's imagination or used in a fictitious manner. Any resemblance to actual persons, living or dead, or actual events is purely coincidental. Everlasting Publishing does not necessarily endorse or support the theories and/or ideas presented in this novel.

First Edition
Everlasting Publishing
P.O. Box 1061
Yakima, WA 98907

To Phyl and Larry Martin

No finer parents could anyone have.

MOSES' CHISEL

MOSES' CHISEL

Steven Lowell-Martin

Manastash Ridge. National Security Agency listening facility — outside Ellensburg, Washington: 0700 Hours.

Air Force Staff Sergeant Jacob Knapse sipped from an oversized mug of sugar-laden mocha as he seated himself in front of his console. His piercing blue eyes bore intently into the unique hardware assembled before him. The Sergeant's greenish- blue full dress uniform was spotless and neatly pressed, as always. The computer multi-colors illuminated the handsome man eerily. The silence and subdued lighting of the workplace always reminded him of a submarine. The clouds of sleep began to abate as he began his daily routine. He was relieved to have not fallen asleep during his morning hour-long drive to the remote federal facility, via winding and steep foothill roads. The central Washington State sagebrush and dirt-brown rolling hills had provided little stimulation along the way, on a bleak February morning. Neither did the five minute subterranean elevator ride, far below the earth's crust.

Agency upper managers began to gather around the Sergeant as he logged into the system. Numerous unfamiliar suited men blended into the dimmed background, arms crossed, leaning forward intently.

The Sergeant said, "Don't bill me if this new over-priced system goes up in smoke." He entered a magnetic key into the elaborate console as a humorless technician inserted a counterpart beside him. Six three-dimensional monitors instantly sprang to life, filling with iridescent scrolling numbers and symbols. The Sergeant felt strangely uneasy to have several sets of high-ranking eyes following his every typed letter and number. He was relieved to tune them out while affixing his headphones. He could focus on his extraordinarily sensitive hearing.

At a mere 26 years of age, the Sergeant was a rising star within the United States Air Force. His test scores had highlighted an exceptional aptitude for computer sciences with military applications. His innate powers of observation, near photographic memory, and foreign language skills had been equally noted. He had thus quickly become recruited and absorbed into the intelligence community and a valued member of "the company". He was flattered to have been chosen to test the most advanced listening software in human history.

The High Yield Digital Radio Analysis, or "HYDRA" for short, was the brain-child of three Nobel-Prize winning physicists, IBM's brightest minds, and scant few others. Beneath the small gathering stood a 22,000 square foot warehouse of one hundred eighty 64 core IBM power 1500 Express servers. The vaunted system wielded 104 Terabytes of memory, designed to parse all human speech in nano-seconds. The algorithm capacity of the first-ever specific form of artificial intelligence was believed to exceed that of NASA by roughly a thousand times. The multi-billion dollar ultra-secret system was known by few, and understood by even fewer.

Three mammoth parabolic listening dishes carved into the barren mountains relayed what they "heard," via underground cables, a half-mile to the technological wonder that was HYDRA.

The Sergeant slowed his breathing and heartbeat in order to listen intently…

"Four score and seven years ago our fore fathers brought forth on this continent a new nation." The message was as clear as if the orator were seated next to Knapse.

The Sergeant shook his head disapprovingly. He re-calibrated the computer program, designed to sort thousands of conversations virtually instantaneously, and attempted to listen again. He heard a replication of the first relayed sets of words.

The Sergeant said loudly, "Is this some kind of joke?" He pulled his headset away from his right ear and leaned backward toward the surrounding assemblage of brass. The unsmiling directors and generals stepped to the rear and away from Knapse. They blended somewhat into the darkness of the room. Their conversations were muted, yet animated.

The Sergeant entertained himself by listening to additional bizarre conversations and typing rapidly upon his keyboards. He glanced at the reflection of the small group of suits on his computer screen. They continued to argue heatedly amongst one another. He withdrew a platinum alloy advanced thumb drive from the system and secreted the recording into his right sock. Curiosity was already gripping him.

The NSA Director approached the Sergeant and smiled benignly. The dignitaries grew quiet. The distinguished man clearly wielded a command presence. Many guessed him to be Native American. Others thought he was Hispanic. During his days of espionage, he had earned the nickname "the chameleon" because of his ability to blend into any ethnic setting. In actuality, Director Michael Portworth was one quarter Vietnamese. The Caucasian genes seemed to account for his six foot two stature. He placed a hand upon the Sergeant's shoulder.

The Director spoke to the Sergeant, "Obviously we have run into some glitches in the HYDRA, Jake. Go ahead and unplug and we'll put our techies on it. Let's move you to another console and get you working those conversations in Yemen."

Staff Sergeant Knapse protested, "But sir, I've already run diagnostics on this, it is functioning per-"

"Staff Sergeant, you have your orders," the Director whispered abruptly. The Director looked behind himself toward the dark figures in the background. He quickly unplugged the Sergeant's headset and walked him by the elbow from the room. Two persons unfamiliar to the Sergeant immediately seated themselves at the console and began to type.

The Director leaned through the doorway and said, "Staff Sergeant, might I remind you of the special clearances afforded you for this assignment?"

The Sergeant answered, "Understood, sir. But may I ask when I can begin work again on HYDRA?"

The Director said, "I believe the people of this great country have just wasted a lot of tax dollars on this former experiment, Sergeant."

Knapse realized that the conversation was clearly ended…

Jacob Knapse's day eventually ended as drearily as it had begun. The sun had begun to rise again over the Manastash ridgeline as he began his drive homeward. He realized that a day had come and gone without his recognition. As usual, he had been totally immersed in his duties within the dark and eerie vault of security. He thought about the bizarre segments of recorded conversations he had retained on his thumb-drive. He had noted seemingly biblical wording, big business discussions, and high-level political orations. He reached downward at the hard object tucked within his sock, needing reassurance that he had daringly retained custody. Theories swirled in his mind as to the nature of such recordings. Computer anomalies? He thought not. Radio "skips" often prone to occur in the mountains from distant radio stations? Maybe, but he thought the equipment far too sophisticated to be so deceived.

The Sergeant sought to concentrate on his driving, as the sheen of the pavement was glistening beneath his headlights. Beautiful crystalline granules of snow began to fall and coat the lonely roadway. He was grateful that the drive home from "the middle of nowhere" was actually not unmanageably distant to the verdant agricultural valley of Selah, Washington. As he rounded the curve of the two-lane state highway, he could see the faintly twinkling lights of the town below, some eleven miles further south. He instructed his cell phone to dial home with his voice command and heard his wife's voice in the vehicle console. He could hear his two young sons playing in the background. They were early out of bed and being prepared by their mother for school.

Knapse said, "Hey there lady, I hear two men in my house with you... you running around on me?"

His wife responded, "That depends on how many hours you keep putting into that bloody job of yours, sir!" Alisson Knapse rubbed her ample belly, knowing full well that another boy was on the way.

Sergeant Knapse laughed and said, "OK, fair enough, well I'll be home in ten minutes to check up on you. I can drive the boys to pre-school and kindergarten. By the way... what the HELL?"

Blinding lights from behind appeared out of nowhere and Knapse had a mere instant to react. He was jolted violently backward in his car seat and his ears rang from the sound of crushing metal. He could taste his own blood, as his vehicle rose and lurched quickly toward the passenger side. He could hear the sound of peeling guardrails and then all was black and silent, almost peaceful.

The car belonging to Staff Sergeant Jacob Knapse plunged silently off of the Umtanum Ridge Bridge of Washington State Highway 82. The remote stretch of roadway harbored no witnesses, as the vehicle plummeted for 6 seconds to the floor of a deep and barren canyon. A ball of flame below gave proof that the vehicle had found its final resting place. A widow and fatherless children would be left to grieve.

The White House phone rang only twice.

"It's done," uttered the nondescript voice. The White House disconnected.

Chapter 2

Palo Alto, California

Professor Gordon Huard stood behind a maple podium. An Italian racing bicycle leaned against the lectern, seemingly pleading the speaker to end his lecture and ride away. The Professor was a tall and fit blonde man in his late thirties. He was wearing a red Nike jogging suit over riding gear, complete with riding shoes. He looked as if he would have preferred to be breaching the summit of a mountaintop on his bicycle in one of his beloved triathlons, or playing a set of tennis on-campus. Yet, he spoke with passion toward the 150 intrigued students within the lecture- hall of Stanford University.

The Professor pointed upward animatedly and said, "My friends, the very words I have just uttered to you have now been etched on an infinite easel." He stood with his arms crossed against his chest and smiled, looking bemusedly at the perplexed gathering of students. He paused for several seconds for effect.

Professor Huard continued, "A fellow by the name of Albert Einstein already proved the endless nature of sound waves some fifty years ago. But, as usually happens with great thinkers… no one listened. But even old Albert was not the first, nor the last to hypothesize on the very nature of sound waves, and how our universe houses them. As early as 1820 a so-called crackpot of an English scientist by the name of John Herapath opined that sound was a kinetic catalyst of sub-atomic molecules, whose gaseous signature could be measured for amplitude and duration. But no one listened."

"Only gradually over the generations have theory

and practical application proven that sound waves have a shelf-life of at least 100,000 years. My good friend at Oxford, Doctor Hawking has quantified such facts. He and I agree that sound wave infinity is a very real probability."

Huard continued, "Yet, Herapath and Einstein's theories were limited by the knowledge derived from the technologies of their respective eras. Today, with the advent of innumerable satellites, space shuttles, and our beloved Hubble telescope, our knowledge of our cosmos and our lovely little planet have increased exponentially. Whereas Einstein once believed that sound traveled endlessly throughout the vast reaches of our curved universe at some 333 meters per second, destined to return in millennia, we have recently learned that the planet had a better idea. In actuality, the marvel that is earth provided a sanctuary for all sounds that have emanated from this little blue marble. Our beloved mesosphere, designed by some great engineer to protect us from cosmic radiation, meteors, and the like, is comprised of nitrogen, oxygen, argon, and even water molecules. These molecules are all perennially excited in their protective chores. Yet a strange and wondrous byproduct of this shell occurred. The speeding sound waves, rocketing into the dark beyond, leave a modulating fingerprint behind, within this shell." Many of the students appeared to be lost.

The Professor stepped forward onto the stage, clasped his hands and smiled mischievously. "In other words, if we develop the right listening device, we could someday listen to a tyrannosaurus fart." The hall erupted in laughter.

An attractive Asian female student in the front row raised her hand and asked, "Professor, how could any listening device conceivably find such a phantom recording out there in outer space? Have you been watching too much Star Trek?" The audience snickered.

The Professor placed his hands in his pockets, walked toward the student, and looked downward. He replied, "The technology might already exist. Think about it….when some bomber in Syria calls his buddies to plan an act of terrorism, several American and possibly other government computers immediately start the recorders running. I know that for a fact. I once worked for such an agency, before opting for the higher-paying educational endeavors. We are paying billions for the technologies and millions for the personnel to listen to any and all spoken words, whether over phone lines or other means. We have satellites and parabola ground listening dishes, two blocks in circumference, on every corner of the earth. I assure you, boys and girls, if you call your classmate on your cell phone right now… now DON'T DO THAT, (more laughter) and utter words such as Missiles, Rocket, Israel, or Obama, you will be recorded and listened to more often and intently than Lady Gaga. A project called Echelon."

A pensive male student in the third row spoke up, "So what are you saying, Professor, that we could someday listen to the party conversation at the last supper live?"

The Professor said, "Absolutely. The technologies may already be here, given advances in sound and word decryption. Computerized word recognition is now child's play. When our computers decipher the language of the humpback whales, we may very well sort that harmonious web of human speech." In fact, our own university has two professors working in conjunction with the folks at M.I.T. to develop such an application.

I believe many of you know Professors Steinberg and Bontrager. In your lifetimes, I am confident, every uttered human word will be collated for review." He seemed to smile excessively.

The Professor closed by saying, "So, be vewy vewy caofuw what you wabbits say. See you tomorrow, scholars." The classroom was again filled with laughter.

The students, clearly enamored with their charismatic and fascinating professor, filed out of the classroom. Their young faces were replete with smiles and lively conversation. One unfamiliar "student" remained in the rear of the classroom, near an exit. A muscular man in his thirties wearing a black baseball cap pulled nearly over his eyes stared intently at Professor Huard. The Professor felt an immediate sense of foreboding. He did not recognize the man. He wondered if he were one of the occasional students auditing the class for entertainment.

Shrugging, Huard wheeled his bicycle to a side exit. He looked backward a final time and saw the figure slowly slide out the exit door, his steps measured and graceful. Huard immediately recalled the stealth personnel at the NSA, where he had performed a "side job" until recently. The men had always given him the creeps, as they reminded him of sloths in a dark jungle. Yet, he quickly discarded his senses as absurd paranoia. The pleasant Central California sunshine immediately diffused his sensation of dread. The Professor was quickly engrossed in his daily ride toward evening dinner and beverages with his nearby peers. They would all meet and exchange information regarding the project upon which they had devoted their lives in recent months. They were all incensed at being denied the promised access to the very product they had helped design.

Chapter 3

Ellensburg, Washington

Kittitas County Sheriff's Deputy Joe Phewell began an arduous early morning climb into Umtanum Ridge Canyon, just south of Ellensburg Washington. Earlier, he had been patrolling his vast county "sector" when he noted the telltale signs of doom on the snowy roadway of Washington State Highway 82. He had actually arrived at the obvious fatality only a few minutes after the crash had occurred. He made a mental note of two conflicting sets of tire tracks. His innate suspicion was immediately on high intensity. Phewell was a bespectacled man of 50 years of age. He stood some six feet two inches tall and was as thin as a reed. Meticulously clean-cut, as always, he was nicknamed "the professor" by his peers. Deputy Phewell always displayed a thoughtful and articulate demeanor that only served to enhance his reputation. He held a master's degree in mechanical engineering and had recently picked up a second master's in computer science "for something to do."

Phewell's peers often wondered why he had opted to become a low-paid county deputy. But he loved the work, and a considerable inheritance had negated any impetus to concern himself with income. He was also known by his peers for his tendency to study the intricacies of any police investigation ad-nauseum. Supervisors often told him to "get on with it." Jealous peers would refer to his basic cases that morphed into the complicated as "Phewell injected." But he consistently found leads that others over-looked, regardless of how miniscule or seemingly trivial. He had a reputation with state and federal law enforcement peers for possessing unrivaled powers of observation, and an eidetic memory to match. Phewell's tireless work filled prison cells with sophisticated criminals whom had once thought themselves too clever for discovery. By the same token, he had set a number of wrongly convicted individuals free — sometimes drawing the ire of local prosecutors.

With Deputy Phewell stood fellow deputy Jessie Lee Leslie, who had arrived shortly thereafter. Considering the budget issues and expansive geographical reaches of the county, the proximity of a peer was cause for celebration. It was clear that Deputy Leslie lacked the physical attributes to make the steep and treacherous ascent into the cavernous rocky canyon below. Deputy Leslie's ample belly hung over his leather gun-belt conspicuously. He stood with his thumbs jammed inside the belt and smiled. Leslie wore his "Smokey the Bear" hat cocked to the side and rocked repeatedly on his heels.

Deputy Leslie said, "Joe, you know I'm gonna be with ya in spirit down there, buddy. You have any trouble, don't hesitate to radio me and I'll be sure to call search and rescue tomorrow."

Phewell replied, "Yeah, kiss my ass too Leslie," as he handed over his hat to his fellow deputy. Phewell cinched the straps of his bulging backpack of equipment and supplies and sighed.

Leslie roared in laughter and then remarked, "Now professor that's not very Christian of ya, I must say."

Phewell answered again, "I won't even be very Muslim by the time I get down this crap-hole."

The rising sun shone through the clouds as the

snows abated. Phewell smiled a grim smile and scissored his long legs cautiously over the remains of torn, bent, and razor-sharp guard-rail metal. He was grateful for the protection lent by his expensive Kevlar gloves. He immediately slipped on an icy rock and crashed upon his buttocks while sliding against rock, dirt, and muddy snow. "Dadgummit!" he muttered, as he righted himself and began to descend a rough trail. Deputy Leslie became silent and reserved. Phewell could see him grow smaller as his travel eased downward. The flashing lights of the two parked patrol cars were eerie in the morning light.

Thirty-six hundred thirty feet below where Phewell strode, he could see the wreckage of the morning's incident. He figured the accident to be another drunk driver plunging to his death. Or another over-tired Central Washington University student falling asleep at the wheel on the way home. Regardless, he was the trained accident investigation specialist for the county, and the man for the job. But, as he hiked and pondered, he was the trained investigator of most *everything* in this county, and always got the call. He never knew if he should be flattered to be chosen by the Sheriff to investigate any serious incident, or offended that he was merely the man whom would not complain about such assignment. Regardless, he was here on this cold morning, slipping and sliding on the trail at an un-Godly hour, before he'd had the benefit of his first cup of coffee.

Some could view the basalt cliff ridge and desert trails of the area as bleak and uninteresting. But Joe Phewell, having lived here all his life, saw otherwise. Even in late winter he could see emerging blossoms of golden currant that would adorn the area in beautiful yellow blooms atop the ever-present sage-brush. Below, he could see service berry and wild Oregon grape vines in abundance, ready to supply their wares in future months. He paused to view the light of late sunrise upon Mount Rainer, towering above the Nelson Mountain Ridge, some 90 miles away, yet seemingly touchable with a reach. A small frozen creek below shimmered like a Christmas scene. Phewell knew he could well be accompanied by thriving herds of bighorn sheep. He did not waste the time to scan the topography for such, as they blended in effectively.

A skilled hiker in the area, Joe Phewell made rapid progress toward the crash site. He was over half-way to the floor of the canyon when he stopped to sip from a bottle of Gatorade. He had to wipe perspiration from his forehead, despite the 20 degree temperatures. For a moment he felt the presence of animal life staring at him. He looked around for a mountain lion or coyote. But he saw none, and pressed on downward with a shrug.

Above, and deeper west of the deputy, crouched two men atop a rocky canyon butte. They were dressed in camouflage gear. One held a pair of binoculars trained upon a man far below. The other held a high-powered rifle. In his sights lay deputy Phewell. The man with the binoculars spoke hurriedly into a cell phone, "We couldn't get there first… these hayseeds must have had a slow donut day and were there immediately."

The sniper could hear the other end of the phone line and angry words being uttered in rapid succession. His partner asked on the phone, "Do you want him taken out or not?"

The sniper released the safety from his .223 assault rifle and readied for the kill. He felt no emotion toward the law enforcement officer at all. He was nothing more than a paper target at a training range, moving very slowly. It would be an easy shot.

The man with the binoculars patted the other on the shoulder and said, "King's ex, man. It's a no-go. We don't need the locals looking into a dead cop. Besides, there's nothing left of that below." The two figures disappeared into the scenery.

Deputy Phewell's weary legs burned as he reached the bottom of the canyon floor and approached the crash site. His once neatly pressed uniform was muddy and wet. He was relieved to finally reach his destination and exhaled slowly. He remembered his many hikes in the canyon as a youth. He recalled the occasional finds of arrowheads that he still maintained meticulously in hardened containers beside his home office shelf. As he approached the crash site he slipped on an icy loose rock and again tumbled to his backside. The backpack served to cushion his fall only slightly.

"Dad Gummmm…" said the deputy.

He then became intrigued with the wreckage. In front of him lay a perfectly intact body of a uniformed United States Airman. The stripes on the body's sleeves were immediately noted. There was scant blood, nor apparent trauma to the body, as he lay peacefully upon his back. The eyes were wide open, seemingly staring at the deputy — an effect that never failed to give Phewell the chills.

Deputy Phewell quickly dismissed his aversion to the eerie sight and set about to his work. He noted to himself that his preconceived notions of a drunk or young irresponsible driver had been wrong. He knew with certainty from where the victim had come. The deputy quickly amassed a miniature crime scene investigation station from the meager belongings that filled his backpack. He elongated aluminum tripods in a triangular pattern around the site. He was careful to allow considerable space for the countless miniature fragments of the vehicle in question. Broken glass adorned the rocks and ice like expensive diamonds that shimmered in the morning sun. The scent of gasoline and burned debris was pungent. A sophisticated laser measurement tool was mounted atop one of the tripods. Within half an hour a meticulous "total station" workplace structure was erected. He placed hundreds of plastic "mini-kiosk" evidence markers next to alternately minute and more obvious evidentiary items.

Deputy Phewell retrieved an expensive digital camera from a carrying case. The camera bore his engraved department badge number. As usual, he had purchased the camera with his own money. He began to document the condition of the deceased. The seemingly peaceful state of the body was betrayed as he rolled the uniformed cadaver onto its face. The rear of the head was badly damaged. The telltale signs of severe brain trauma were clearly evident in the ear canals. Law enforcement always referred to the substance as "cottage cheese" due to the similarity of appearance.

Deputy Phewell made mental notes in a hand-held tape recorder, also purchased by him.

He noted, "White male, maybe thirty, athletically built....apparent cause of death massive head trauma.

Body ejected a considerable distance from the vehicle. Probable ejection from extreme initial impact. No signs of a seatbelt having been worn. Subject wears a wedding band." He thought to himself how ironic it was that the body was so intact. The Honda product had become a heap of melted rubble upon impact and the resultant explosive fire. His laser measurements from the guardrail far above indicated that the vehicle had travelled far outward from the roadway. He also noted the crushed driver's side of the chassis. The vehicle had not rolled. It lay impaled in the snow-covered clay and rocks on the passenger side. Phewell knew immediately that the vehicle had had "help" propelling itself laterally — "considerable dadgummed help," he thought.

Over three hundred fifty quality digital photographs were taken of the suspected crime scene from every imaginable angle. Phewell utilized color code swaths for later clarity comparisons. He placed a ruler methodically next to each photographed evidentiary item to provide depth perceptions. Phewell then drew extraordinary crime scene sketches, the quality of which would put many artists or architects to shame.

The deputy then began a search of the body, almost as if searching a live suspect. He placed blue rubber gloves over his hands. He then parted the legs of the body and began a top to bottom search. He found a U.S. Air Force identification card in the left breast pocket. The card identified the man as "John Smith," having worked in the "telephonic technician" section of the U.S. Air Force. "Yeah, sure," thought the deputy, "where's the dadgummed air force base around these parts?" The search continued down the body, from left to right, top to bottom in a highly organized manner. A photograph of a man, woman, and two young boys with the backdrop of a Christmas tree was located in the right breast uniform pocket. A crucifix was obtained from around the neck. He used an elongated cotton swab to obtain a sample of the victim's blood. All items were placed into separate Ziploc baggies or small paper bags and marked with the deputy's badge number, using a black sharpie. He placed the baggies in a row upon the frozen ground.

Deputy Phewell continued his search until he found a hard item tucked into the black sock of the body's right leg. He reached his hand into the sock cautiously, ever fearful of syringes prevalent on suspects. Phewell was surprised to find an over-sized computer thumb- drive secreted deep within the sock. The drive was platinum in consistency and elongated strangely. It was made of an alloy he had never before seen for such a product. The deputy peered through his circular spectacles at engraving upon the item. In small bold print could be seen, "Government property. Top Secret."

After a detailed search for additional evidence at the site, the deputy gathered all the baggies of his discoveries and placed them within a large paper bag. Included were the personal effects of the airman, glass fragments from the wreckage, burned contents of a glove-box, and samples of the nearby affected soil. He meticulously secured them within the backpack for the long journey upward from the canyon's floor. He placed the thumb drive in question in another Ziploc baggy and then within another. The deputy placed the double baggy in an inside jacket pocket and zipped the pocket shut.

The mysteries of government activities in the mountains outside of the Manastash ridge had fascinated Joe Phewell since he was a child. Hundreds of square miles of barb-wired properties with conspicuous "U.S. Government — No trespassing" signs dominated the area. Constant dronings of helicopters overhead could be heard. Dusty rumblings of endless convoys of Humvees always dotted the landscape. And massive power lines had always led across the lands toward distant "phone company" facilities. Joe Phewell had always had his theories about the compounds in the mountains. They were located in an area renowned for the prevalence of radio wave "skips" from around the world. These skips had often allowed him to listen to New York Yankees radio broadcasts from across a continent. He had once flown his Cessna airplane over the area, and viewed a massive parabola dish carved into the shadow of a mountainside. He had been immediately escorted away by darkened helicopters that emerged from out of nowhere. Phewell had never forgotten the caustic greeting by M-16 laden sentries when he once chose to take his county jeep into the back country to 'take an excursion.' His office and uniform meant nothing to them.

The deputy patted his pocket and stated to himself, "Maybe I just found my favorite arrowhead." He retrieved his equipment and folded the items within his now very bulging backpack. He was surprised that his police portable radio functioned properly in the canyon and reached Deputy Leslie. He stated, "Tell the Coroner he has a helluva hike. One body to go. And tell Night and Day towing they'll need a substantial cable to bring this thing up.

Chapter 4

Three men in expensive suits sat gathered in a vast and ornate living room of a stately Virginia mansion. All were seated in a semi-circle, on decadent leather chairs. A fire crackled in a huge river rock fireplace. One of the men seemed to be doing the majority of the speaking. He was a very tall man in his mid- seventies. But he looked fifty. His only slightly graying black hair was perfectly coiffed and meticulously parted down the left side. He sipped from a glass of fresh squeezed orange juice and his free hand waved animatedly as he sought to make a point. The tall man was named David Rosenweiler. A second seated man was of Greek ancestry, and appeared to be of similar age. His remaining long black hair was combed backward to cover his sweaty and balding pate. He was sixty pounds overweight, drinking uzo from a small crystal glass, and drawing from a very large Cuban cigar. His name was Giorgio Soudas. A younger bespectacled additional American fidgeted in his seat and could not resist dividing his attention between the two colleagues and his ever-present laptop computer. The others called him Joseph Yeats. The room was warm and inviting, despite the bitter cold snow-scape seen outside the huge picture windows. Men in dark outfits prowled the expansive grounds like panthers in a zoo.

A fourth man entered the room and was invited to sit upon an uncomfortable looking stool, across from the other three. He was much younger and less expensively dressed. He appeared to be considerably less at ease than the gathering of friends. He was known as Michael Portworth, the Director of the N.S.A.

Rosenweiler leaned back in his leather chair and crossed his legs casually. His dark Italian shoes were huge, which matched his six foot five height. He commanded the attention of his peers as he inhaled deeply and smiled.

He said, "So, Mr. Portworth, it would appear we have a problem, do we not?" The other two men leaned forward in their seats. The Greek hurriedly stubbed out his cigar and lay down his glass, while Yeats shut down his computer. Their eyes bore into Michael Portworth, intensely awaiting his response.

Portworth responded, "Sirs, we really don't know *wha*t we have at this time."

Before the last syllable of the words was uttered Rosenweiler cut in. "We pay you a shit-load of money for you to NOT know!" He followed more calmly, "What is it that you DO know?"

Portworth inhaled slowly and answered almost sheepishly, "We now know that it works. Against all predictions to the contrary about this science fiction, the damned system works. To what extent we are not exactly sure at this point. I had it shut down immediately and tried to contain the damage. But there were witnesses to what it can do. There is no way I can make this disappear."

Soudas cut in, "Can't you make *them* disappear? A similar fate to that airman would seem to make sense."

Portworth replied, "I was not party to the senseless killing. That was never our agreement. I was merely paid to keep you apprised of imminent issues. I have done that and will continue to do so. I had matters well under control. Sir, you are talking about eliminating some of the most powerful men in U.S. Intelligence, as well as Senators and Congressmen. They don't just *disappear* without notice. And at this point, all but one has little knowledge of what was presented." Portworth righted himself upon the stool and seemed to gain a sense of confidence.

Soudas countered, spittle flying from his mouth as he spoke loudly, "Well then maybe we should make *you* disappear!"

Portworth grew red and began to respond.

Rosenweiler cut him off with a wave. "Gentlemen, let's be rational. This is a major issue that will require a great deal of tact and planning. Mr. Portworth, we are grateful for your measures taken to apprise us of this looming issue. We never really thought this day would come. But we didn't make our billions without preparations for any contingency. A rainy day has arrived, and we will tap into our rainy day funds. This will all go away one way or another. The sun will rise again, and when it does we will own three quarters of that as well." With that, the two colleagues nodded and laughed.

Rosenweiler suddenly displayed a more gracious side. He asked the NSA Director, "Mr. Portworth, is there anything you would like to eat or drink?"

Portworth answered," No, thank you sir, I have a country to cross and a job to return to before suspicious minds wonder where I have gone at such a time." Two unfriendly men in dark attire soon entered the room and grabbed Portworth by the arms. He shrugged away their grasps angrily and turned to the seated three billionaires. He stated, "I have only one question for you sirs… when is enough money enough?" The three men looked at Portworth as if he were a rodent. Soudas answered bemusedly, his faint Greek accent becoming more pronounced, "Commoners don't even think properly. Little boy, it was never about the money. It was about the power. Something the foolish classes will never comprehend." Michael Portworth was escorted abruptly from the premises.

Joseph Yeats excused himself from his peers and joined Portworth outside the home. He slipped a metallic key card in the N.S.A. Director's jacket pocket and patted the pocket, smiling weakly. He said, "Next time you use your supposed system, slip this instead into the key slot. Let me know what happens. We call it the torpedo."

Yeats hurried back to his colleagues like a child late for class.

Rosenweiler turned his scornful attention to the taciturn Joe Yeats. "You've been awfully quiet throughout all this, what say you?"

Yeats righted his glasses upon his large nose and brushed back sandy blonde hair from his squinting hazel eyes. "First of all, I still find it extremely difficult to believe that such technologies have evolved within the parameters of government employees and a few professors and IBM employees. I employ the greatest technical minds in the world and they advise me this technology is at least a century away, if *ever* developed. It is my belief that the venerable Mr. Michael Portworth is profiting greatly by some contrived notion that causes alarm in ourselves. Just in case, I have provided him with a virus option. But fellows, I have made my fortune with the acquisition and distribution of knowledge. And that is the very item we lack in our current arsenal."

The two peers nodded in agreement. Rosenweiler said, "We approach this methodically. We groom, acquire, and utilize additional resources. We will find out if the 'little boy' and others we have hired have conspired to make a fortune off of our unduly paranoid souls".

With that Yeats chuckled, "How ironic that would be…we are fearful of a conspiracy that may expose our conspiracy."

Rosenweiler responded, only half- jokingly, "Mr. Yeats, the world is a complicated place, and I think you were the one to make it thus."

The meeting broke up. Promises were made to communicate extensively. Soudas promised to sleep like a baby, as well as Mr. Yeats. Rosenweiler remained quiet on the subject. His brilliant mind was already collating scenarios and options. He planned to remain the most prepared of the three men, as well as the wealthiest.

Chapter 5

Professor Huard rang the doorbell at the ornate porch of a beautiful Tudor home, located in a lovely tree-lined Palo Alto neighborhood. The home was 15 minutes away from campus by bicycle, and the athletic Professor had yet to break a sweat. It was the home of his fellow professor, Leah Steinberg. He could hear the tintinnabulation of the beautiful doorbell tones echoing within the home of his creative and brilliant peer. Huard's intent was not to pry into the details of her personal involvement in the government project. The NSA had made quite certain that all segments of involvement had been strictly sequestered. But his curiosity drove him to inquire as to possible clues regarding the success or failure of the project, for which they had worked so tirelessly, without the promised rewards. It was, after-all, his baby as well.

Professor Huard rang the doorbell a second time, and then a third. There was no answer. He noted that Leah Steinberg's Volvo was parked in the driveway. He knew he had felt the engine heat when he squeezed by upon his approach. He surmised that his attractive computer genius friend was engrossed in yet another piece of endless research. She was a kindred academic spirit. Huard retrieved a house key from the mouth of a nearby sculpture and let himself in.

Huard called out, "Leah, you're not much of a bloody host. I'm thirsty for some good wine." He removed his riding shoes and walked across the maple floors in almost a shuffle. He saw the back of his friend, seated in her favorite Victorian wing-backed chair. She was clearly ignoring him, as usual--glued to the computer screen. Huard approached his friend from the right side and lightly touched her elbow as he circled to the front. The elbow felt icy cold. He froze in shock at a macabre sight. Leah Steinberg sat in a darkened pool of blood, contained by the upturned contours of the chair. Her throat was sliced from ear to ear. Her eyes remained open in a fixed state of obvious terror. Her body was clearly posed for effect. Her hands were crossed neatly on her lap. In her hands lay her tongue, cut jaggedly from her mouth. And the bloody mouth was accented by the painted trails of blood, extended from the corners. She looked like the Joker character in the movies. Clearly, a message had been sent.

Professor Huard turned away in horror. Tears of anger filled his eyes as he bent over and vomited upon the floor. He reached for a phone to summon aid, and then replaced the device. His hand was trembling. He had an uncontrollable feeling that he was not alone in the house. He ran to the door and grabbed his bicycle. He rode away hurriedly, leaving his shoes on the front step. Six blocks away, he was nearly struck by a rapidly approaching black Audi. He steered his bicycle up and over a curb and nearly fell. He looked back at the vehicle as it passed. The driver wore a dark baseball cap and looked very familiar.

Huard covered the three miles to his home rapidly. His shoeless feet throbbed from the pressure upon the hard pedals. He swung his right leg over the bicycle frame and coasted the last downhill half-block deftly, in a one-footed stance. He felt relieved to be nearly home. From a place of safety and comfort he could gather his thoughts and begin to make decisions regarding developing circumstances. He would call the police and fire departments. But then he would have to go.

Looking ahead, he noted the same black Audi parked in front of his home. A shadowy silhouette could be seen moving stealthily past the living room window. Huard swung his leg back over the bicycle and accelerated downhill frenetically. He was grateful that his expensive Italian racing bike emitted virtually no detectable sound. He rapidly rode beyond his home and down a steep decline. His heart and mind raced. He knew that he was prey for entities not entirely known. The link between he and Steinberg was obvious. The bloody project! He and his peers had always held grave reservations about collaborating with ultra-secretive persons employed by the federal government. But, in the end, the intriguing possibilities of the project were just too awesome to ignore. They unanimously agreed that they could change the world forever by finding the ultimate truths generated from a technological marvel that they had helped to create.

Now, that quest for knowledge could cost him his life. Huard thought momentarily of riding toward the home of the third piece of the project — Professor Jeffrey Bontrager. But he dared not risk detection. He pedaled another mile and pulled into a Starbucks establishment--one of his favorite hangouts when he had rare free time. The crowded environs would be a perfect place in which to blend. His brightly colored bicycling outfit would be one of many at the off-campus site. Huard ordered a cup of mocha and seated himself in a corner chair. His hands shook almost uncontrollably. It took three tries to dial upon his cell phone, but he reached the number of Jeff Bontrager. He reached only a voicemail response. An immediate sense of dread enveloped the Professor.

Huard then thought about whom he could call. He had very little contact with his family. The family was somewhat estranged, living on the east coast. He almost laughed when he searched his memory for a friend to call. Outside of the other two professors, he had had little time to nurture friendships beyond academia and the project. He saw the phone number of one of his teaching assistants on his call list. He therefore dialed his favorite aide — Greg Southard. The 23-year-old sandy blonde genius looked more like a surfer than a gifted aspiring physicist. But Huard treasured him as a tireless and competent future peer.

Southard was driving home from school when he saw Professor Huard's face on his cell phone as it rang. He turned down the droning rap music that was playing in his car stereo and cleared his throat. He clearly idolized his mentor and was thrilled to receive the call.

Huard said abruptly, "Greg, this is a very serious call. I want you to listen very carefully to my instructions. Something terrible has happened and is happening. Send the police and the fire departments to the home of Professor Steinberg at the end of this call."

A hushed Greg Southard replied, "Of course, professor, are you OK?"

Huard said, "Not at all, buddy. But I can't explain what I don't understand. No time. Next, I want you to drive over to Professor Bontrager's house. Don't go to the door. Just park down the block and call me immediately. Do you feel me, homie?" Greg Southard almost laughed at the professor's eternal quest for hipness, but he sensed the gravity of the situation.

Huard momentarily savored the tall mocha from which he sipped. His favorite beverage brought him comfort. The familiarity of the Starbucks provided slight solace as well. He began to formulate a mental plan of escape. He knew that he could not return home. He did not know even if his cell phone was being traced. He wished that he could turn the cell phone off for such a possibility, but he awaited the call of Greg Southard. He knew he must ultimately leave the area in order to find safety and time to think.

Huard's consciousness was startled as the phone rang. He did not even speak before Southard began to stammer, "Professor, I'm here. The cops keep trying to call me back. I did all that you asked of me."

Huard interrupted, "Greg, tell me all that you can see at Professor Bontrager's house."

Southard answered, "The curtains are shut. He *never* closes his curtains. You know when he got in trouble for that. Anyway, there are two cars parked in front and it looks like somebody's inside."

Huard curtly interjected, "What do the cars look like Greg?"

Greg answered, "There is a silver Jeep Cherokee and a black Audi."

Huard abruptly said, "Greg, leave the area immediately. When you are a safe distance away call the cops and tell them there is a burglary in-progress at the residence. But leave now!"

Greg remained on the line as he started his 90's

Toyota and drove hurriedly away from the home of Professor Bontrager. When he was nearly a mile east of the location, Professor Huard spoke again, "Meet me at the Hoover Tower." The phone was disconnected. Greg placed a burglary call to 9-1-1 and quickly hung up on the operator. He lay his cell phone upon the passenger seat. Three minutes later the phone began to ring. He picked up the phone and read the number — Palo Alto Police Department. He let the phone continue to ring, his downloaded Star Trek theme now suddenly annoying.

Professor Huard stood atop the observation deck of the scenic Hoover tower, 285 feet above the base. From his perch he could see most of the beautiful campus of Stanford University. He could see the San Francisco bay in the distance. It was a perfect vantage point from which to view all activities approaching him. Huard knew the tower like an old friend. He had run the 300 stair steps of the structure innumerable times during afternoon breaks, in training for his many triathlon events. He looked away from his persistent scanning of the area below for a moment. He noticed one of the 48 bells that comprised the cacophonous carillon that ringed the upper reaches of the historic structure. Inscribed upon the bell was the phrase, "For Peace Alone Do I Ring." Huard could not ignore the irony of the phrase, in light of the abhorrent situation he had observed and sought to evade.

Huard returned his gaze to the periphery of the tower and noted the arrival of Greg Southard in the parking lot. His prized assistant ascended the steps rapidly. This came as no surprise to Huard, since Mr. Southard had joined in the triathlon addiction. Southard balled a fist and gave the professor his usual hug greeting.

Greg Southard said, "Professor, you look like you've seen a ghost. What the hell is going on?"

Professor Huard replied, "Greg, you know you are my treasured aid and favorite student. I am going to ask a series of profound favors of you, for which I will provide scant explanation."

Southard answered, "Professor, after all these years, if you told me up was down and down was up I'd follow your directions empirically. But you have me worried."

Huard stated, "Greg, there is too much that I know today, and too little that I'll know tomorrow. But I do know that the world is changing fast and could so change exponentially soon." Huard asked Greg Southard for his cell phone and a note pad. Ever the engineering mind, the Professor diagramed and designed an extensive written plan for what he expected of the student. He explained what he could of the situation, but speed was of the essence. In the end, arrangements were made to obtain thousands of dollars in cash from the Professor's savings from an off-campus bank. The funds would then be wired on a pre- determined day and precise time to an east coast account. Greg Southard was told to first rush back to the University to the Professor's office. He was to obtain stored data from the Professor's research. Forty-nine falsified copies of the discs were then to be made — each mailed to remote sites around the world. One disc containing the actual data would be mailed to another pre-designated site. If similar efforts could be made with the research of the other two professors, both now presumed murdered, all the better. But Greg was advised to be wary.

Professor Huard concluded his detailed instructions and grabbed his prized student by the neck. He said, "My dear friend, it has been a privilege. My last lesson for you is one I have only recently learned myself — that with the acquisition of knowledge comes cost. I suspect I will pay dearly for the remainder of my life. Follow our research and be extremely careful in whom you trust your findings. I suspect you will never see me again. Thank you and goodbye."

A stunned Greg Southard soon departed.

Chapter 6

NSA Director Michael Portworth seated himself at the center of a sterile black conference table, deep beneath the super-secret agency facility. He was encircled by six invited guests. In actuality, they were guests to whom he had loathed extending the invite. Yet, the ranking Senate chair of U.S. Intelligence had insisted on such a gathering. Therefore, Portworth had cleverly portrayed himself as an enthusiastic catalyst for such a decision. He had even positioned himself to chair the meeting. His scheme would ensure that no suspicion would be directed toward him. His intense hatred for the United States government remained a highly guarded secret. He could simultaneously posture with the powerful Senator and his invited dignitaries and see that they never obtained the vital information that he was paid to conceal. All bets were hedged. Just as he always arranged.

Seated closely to Director Portworth's right was positioned White House Chief of Staff Amanda Neal. She was a highly attractive blonde woman of 36 years of age. Ms. Neal had been receiving limited updates on the project's status for months, with the dire understanding that the information could not be shared. To Ms. Neal's right sat the corporate vice president of IBM, Jason Marks. Marks looked every bit the part of a computer super-genius, as he seemed to lack knowledge of the location of a good barber or even a dry cleaner. Directly to Portworth's left was Cardinal Antonin Napolitano, replete with the full raiment of his high level

Vatican office. The Cardinal was flanked by Imam Zaid Abdul-Rahman, whose bearded appearance reminded Portworth of Bin-Laden. Across the table, at two o'clock sat renowned Harvard Professor Michael Bridgemann. Bridgemann sported a tan from a recent trip to Hawaii and looked more like a professional golfer than a historian of great repute.

Finally, the venerable Senator Trent McLean positioned himself directly across from the NSA Director. The Senator had been intensely involved in the project since the inception. He had obtained the needed massive funding for the project via undetectable means and joined the agency Director in choosing and recruiting the talent to build the system. The immaculately dressed politician from Florida appeared much taller than his five foot eight frame. McLean leaned forward, his arms crossed upon the table, in almost a challenging pose. It was clear that his ego would jump to the fore in the event Portworth stammered.

Director Portworth leaned back in his padded leather chair, an agency pen clutched in his right hand, and spoke, "My esteemed colleagues. I thank you for accepting my hasty invitation and taking your rightful place at this table. What we have invited you to witness is historic. We shall partake in an endeavor that is the modern counterpart to the Manhattan Project. Our weapon, whether productive or destructive, shall be that of knowledge. All that innumerable generations have sought to discover is now at our fingertips. What we shall discover together will demand a reasoned, cautious, and ultra-confidential approach. The knowledge gained will either heal this fractured world of ours, or tear it apart at its very seams."

Michael Portworth's audience moved to the front of their seats, highly engaged with their orator.

Portworth continued, "If you will follow me, I will present to you Project HYDRA. It would seem that human technology has taken a quantum leap forward on possibilities."

Senator McLean was the first to pass through the three smoked-glass sets of double doors that led to the super-secret listening room. His confident stride commanded immediate respect. He passed through a massive magnetometer weapons detector. An armed sentry smiled at the Senator and said, "Welcome back, sir." The Senator extended his arms outward, Christ-like, as a second armed sentry waved a hand-held sensor over his body. He looked backward at the first sentry and replied, "Good to be back, Marine, I *think*."

The next to make an entrance was Amanda Neal. She strutted through the magnetometer hurriedly, her high heels clicking. The second sentry could not help but notice her perfect breasts seemingly promising to escape from her provocatively unbuttoned blouse. Her $500 per ounce perfume emanated deliciously from her person. The sentry hesitated only slightly during his search duties. Yet, Neal turned to him and snarled, "Why don't you take a frigging picture, you pervert." She flung her shoulder-length blonde hair over her shoulder and strode unchallenged past the sentry and into the room. She shot a menacing sneer at Portworth as she entered. Portworth returned the same vitriolic glance and disappeared into a back room. The hatred between the two was palpable.

The assembly finally convened in the rear of a dimly lit room. Their attention was immediately drawn forward, toward an enormous set of computer consoles and massive screens populated with scrawling words, symbols, and numbers. IBM's Jason Marks smiled as he stared mesmerized at the console and stated, "Hello, Watson." A lone individual was seated at the fore of the consoles, typing intently, and staring at the screens. He was a non-descript, very tanned male of 35 years of age, with a nearly shaved head. He spoke only rarely, but appeared to have a Texas drawl.

Director Portworth approached the group from out of the shadows and nearly startled them. He looked briefly at Amanda Neal with a faint sneer. He then turned to the gathering and smiled broadly, "Lady and gentlemen, welcome to all the answers. Please come forward and be seated." Portworth escorted the group to a collection of uncomfortable rolling plastic chairs circled behind the seated male.

The man at the console again turned around to face the group. He removed an over-sized headset with a large microphone and hung it from his neck. He wore a grayish jump suit lacking any insignias designating rank or responsibilities. The man also lacked a conspicuous name tag that was ever present within the government facility. It appeared that he was relegated to anonymity.

The smiling man said to the dignitaries, "Welcome to the U.S. Government's version of the Matrix. I will assume y'all have taken the red pill."

The Director interrupted, "Enough. Get on point, technician."

The members of the group were all handed headsets to be worn. The technician affixed microphones over the lips of each individual. They heard his voice over the headsets as if over a radio. The group felt as if they had entered a cockpit.

Portworth stood to the side of the Cardinal, wearing his own headset. He spoke through his microphone, "Sir, with all due respect to all factions of our distinguished group, someone must be chosen to be the first in history to officially begin this process. Since your church was historically the first at the table, we think it is only prudent that you begin. What is it that you would most wish to learn of the history of man — first- hand!"

With a few voiced words by the technician and some typing, the extraordinary journey began.

Chapter 7

Greg Southard drove into the carport of his tiny off-campus graduate student housing unit and was met with an official greeting party. Two white male San Francisco Police Homicide Detectives and a Native American Palo Alto Police patrol Sergeant confronted him the moment he closed his car door. The dark suited detectives flashed their credentials, while the uniformed Sergeant needed no identification.

Southard smiled at the officers and said, "Folks, what took you so long?"

The female Palo Alto Sergeant said, "You were hard to locate. You find this funny?"

"Not in the slightest," answered Greg Southard.

Southard politely invited the Sergeant and Detectives into his apartment. As expected, his living space was extremely cluttered and untidy. He cleared the surface of a rickety dining room table. One of the detectives began to move a stack of papers from the other side of the table.

"Whoa, whoa, please. That's two years of my life sitting there, sir," exclaimed Southard.

The detective did not seem impressed. Southard offered the officers each a glass of water. It was all he had. They quickly declined.

The older of the two detectives spoke. He said, "I'm Detective Allen and he's Detective Stewart. He gestured toward the attractive but plump officer and said, "This here is Sergeant Mahala Thompson." The detectives did not bother to offer a handshake. Sgt. Thompson extended a hand, smiled, and simply said, "Hi." Southard immediately thought inwardly that Thompson could easily fill the role of "good cop."

Detective Allen said, "Mr. Southard, before we ask you any questions we want to advise you of your rights."

Southard responded, "Skip it, man. I know my rights. I have nothing to hide. Let's get to the point."

Detective Stewart leaned toward Southard and said, "Alright, that works for us. You obviously know why we're here. It is protocol for San Francisco P.D. to assist Palo Alto on major incidents. Well, we have two major incidents."

"For sure," said Southard.

Allen said, "We find it curious that you would call 9-1-1 about a set of burglaries that were actually homicides, and then disconnect. Multiple return calls were made without an answer. Why might that be?"

"I was a little busy."

Stewart said, "Can you give a little more detail on what you mean by *busy*?"

"I was busy trying to avoid becoming the next victim. When I arrived at Professor Bontrager's house I saw at least one car that I believe belonged to the killer. There might have been two. But I know that the black Audi parked in front belonged to the killer."

Allen asked, "How did you know that the Audi belonged to a killer."

Southard was hesitant.

Sergeant Thompson spoke, "Greg, we have your cell phone records. You need to be truthful with us."

The two San Francisco detectives seemed annoyed that the lowly, small-town Sergeant had interrupted.

Southard said, "Then you know who called me."

Allen sighed, "Professor Gordon Huard called you at 4:21 P.M. Do we need to play this game?"

Southard answered, "Alright, alright. The Professor called me and told me that he had just found Professor Steinberg murdered. He thought the killer or killers were after him, too. He asked me to check on Professor Bontrager. I did just that. When I arrived I saw the curtains closed on Bontrager's house. That was very unusual. And the same black Audi that had been stalking Professor Huard was parked in front of the house. I told Professor Huard that, and he advised me to avoid the area at all costs. I therefore called in the burglary. I didn't know *what* you would find inside there. I was busy trying to stay alive myself."

Stewart leaned over and said, "Did you know that the offices for all three of those professors were ransacked?"

"No, but that doesn't surprise me."

"Why not?"

"I'd rather not say."

Detective Allen pulled a series of 8 X 10 photographs from a file and tossed them upon the table. The photos fanned outward as they landed. Greg Southard had to stifle vomiting as he stared at macabre crime scene photos of a decapitated Professor Geoffrey Bontrager. The man's body had been propped in a living room chair. The head had been placed in his hands as if he were cradling a baby. A corner of the photo of Leah Steinberg could also be seen.

Southard grabbed a nearby trash can and spewed bile into the receptacle. He wiped his mouth with his shirt sleeve.

Sergeant Thompson scowled and turned to the detectives. She simply said, "Nice." She did not wait for the detectives to speak. She deliberately took over the conversation. She stared intently into Southard's eyes and said, "Greg, at this point we are very interested in Gordon Huard's involvement in this. He seemingly had all the knowledge about these murders long before anyone else. And, as you might be aware, he seems to have left the area. We want to know what he told you previously about his situation with the other professors, and where he might have run." She collected the photographs, gave the detectives a glare, and handed them back.

Southard regained his composure. He said, "Look, if you think Gordon Huard had anything to do with this, you're completely off-base. Do you think an award winning Stanford Physicist is practiced at strangling and beheading people? Folks, I'm just a grad student, but you and I know that took a very strong and skilled killer. Gordon catches flies in his hand and puts them outside-- gimme a break."

Detective Allen spoke gently, "You are probably right, Greg. We are not insisting your friend did this. But you and I both know that Mr. Huard knows more about this than he is divulging. We're no physicists, but if he is completely innocent, why did he choose to run? Why did he not come to us and tell us what he knows?"

"Because he's *running from them*." Look, I don't

know who they are. He doesn't either. But somebody is hell-bent on exterminating Stanford Professors!"

Sergeant Thompson spoke again, "Greg, what is the connection between these professors? We know they are associates and all that. But other than that, what do they have in common. Is there a possibility of a lover's trial of any sort? We are just looking into possibilities. Were they involved in any joint financial activities? Help us understand this thing."

Southard answered, "I probably shouldn't say this."

"Say it," said Thompson quickly.

"All I know is they were once involved in some sort of secret government project. They never let me in on their work. But it was obvious to me that they were involved in something outside of Stanford. I thought it was in the past. Professor Huard often told stories about working for the N.S.A. a long time ago. Now, I don't think that was the case."

Thompson asked, "What type of work at the school or elsewhere did they do that would involve all three of them?"

Southard answered, "I'm not sure about the else-where part. But Professor Huard is a rising mega-star in the field of astro-physics, with a focus upon the dynamics of sound. Professor Bontrager is... er was both a physicist and computer scientist with a specialty in sound decryption. He won his Nobel on work to decipher ancient native languages and his progress toward understanding whale songs. And Professor Steinberg was another Laureate winner in the field of artificial intelligence. These are/were brilliant people."

Sergeant Thompson asked, "And what do *you* do?"

Southard answered, "I have been studying under the great Gordon Huard, but my hope is to become an amalgamation of all three disciplines in which these professors excel."

Thompson said, "Sounds like you're no dummy in your own right."

Southard said, "Thank you. I'd like to think so. But I have now lost my mentors."

Thompson said, "I am very sorry for that. But we are here because we care and want to help you. Can you give us any information on the whereabouts of Professor Huard so that we might offer the man protection? You know that the sooner we apprehend these killers, the sooner he gets his life back?"

"I have no idea where Gordon Huard is," Southard lied. He avoided eye contact for a moment and then raised his head, " I wish I knew. I would tell you. But I am sure he's running from our very own government. I believe you all work for the government as well."

Stewart said, "We'll find these killers. Rest assured. We're good at what we do. And you might pass that message on to your friend."

"You have no idea who did this, do you?" said Southard. He received no answer.

Detective Allen tossed his business card upon the table, and said, "We'll be in touch."

Southard answered, "I'm sure you will." The grisly homicide scene photos were already emblazoned in his memory.

The three officers exited the apartment.

Once outside, the detectives and sergeant conferred briefly in the carport.

Detective Allen commented, "He's hiding something. I know it."

Sergeant Thompson said, "But most of what he told us is true. He's scared. That's understandable. Did you guys get that? Computers and unraveling sound? National Security Agency? That sounds like some freaky shit to me, boys. It's your case, but I'd be calling the Feebies if I were you."

Detective Stewart said, "Never been overly fond of the F.B.I., but you might be right on this one. Those were professional *and* sick hits. It's obvious they don't want certain people to talk."

Detective Allen handed another of his business cards to Sergeant Thompson. He said, "Mahala, if you ever want to come work with us, I will gladly put in a good word for you with the high-ups. We'd find you a spot."

Thompson merely smiled and nodded.

Chapter 8

Falling Waters, West Virginia

Professor Gordon Huard sat in a crowded living room of an austere three-bedroom rambler, on 9 acres of scenic rolling hillside. He was seated in an aged and comfortable leather recliner with a cup of his beloved coffee in his right hand. He was surprised how much he had missed his mother's coffee — and, more importantly, his mother. He was surrounded by family members. Three brothers, two sisters, numerous cousins, nieces and nephews were scattered in a disorganized din. Small children bounded down a nearby hallway and babies demanded feeding and changing. The Professor's father, Ben, stood to his right, acting as a traffic cop at the entrance to the hallway. He was wearing his red flannel shirt. Some things never change.

His mother, Patrice, leaned against the arm of his chair, patting her wayward son on the back in gentle circular motions. She was a petite and wiry woman who had yet to see her first grey hair. She was fastidiously dressed, as always, and her hair was pulled back in a neat bun.

Patrice Huard said to her son, "Good Lord, Gordie, but it is good to have you home."

Gordon realized that it had been six years since he had been home. No one had called him "Gordie" in a long while. He knew that he had deeply hurt his mother and the rest of the family with his distance and silence. The guilt and regret hit him in the stomach like a body blow. He recalled that he had last spoken with his father on the telephone several years previously. The conversation had ended badly. During the conversation his father had alleged that he had become a changed man, with his education and time away from home. He had told Gordon, "You forgot where you had came from." Gordon had corrected his father's grammar and hung up the phone. It was an act that he had immediately regretted. But he had been too proud to re-dial and apologize. Time passed rapidly without ever making that effort.

Sitting in the family home again, Gordon knew that he had not deliberately disowned his family. They were fine people. He had merely become too engrossed in academia and the "project" to right past wrongs. Further, he knew that he could not share any aspects of his government work with anyone outside the cloistered circle of those involved. But he knew that he wielded a sad excuse for ignoring family. The pain caused by that choice, it would seem, cut both ways indeed.

The Professor wanted to chide his mother for morphing what was meant to be a private meeting into a cacophonous gathering of the entire extended family. But he knew better, and couldn't help but draw delight from the hastily summoned reunion. From a nearby kitchen emanated delicious aromas of crock-pots and baked items. Several aunts tended to the pending feast. There was never a hint of any resentment levied toward him by the members of the family. His father had briefly attempted to distance himself with a cold handshake when he first arrived at the doorstep that morning. But the gesture was quickly followed by a powerful hug, as his bear of a father had warmed to him.

The Professor found that he treasured every moment of the Sunday afternoon and early evening with the family. He bounced brand new baby nephews off of his knee and spun the kindergarteners around from his shoulders like a county carousel ride. Deep conversation was impossible, as each member wanted a piece of their "Gordito" — the baby of the family.

At one point his mother pointed to Gordon's left hand and said, "No wife yet Gordie?" Gordon answered that he had rarely had time for any relationships, much less a wife. His mother asked, "How bout a girlfriend at least?" Gordon's oldest brother, Pete stood across from his little brother, holding a baby. Pete said, "Gordie, what Mom is saying is that you need to help with making grand babies. We're not fast enough." The entire family laughed. Gordon's head lowered for a moment. He said, "There was a wonderful woman I was growing close to. She recently passed away." The family offered condolences, and the conversation returned to happier subjects. With pledges to re-acquaint, each eventually drifted out the front doorway tearfully, in order to soon begin their respective weeks. Their hugs and kisses were powerful and welcome. He knew painfully what he had missed during those years. He felt unbridled joy with the re-connection with the family. Yet his joy was tempered by powerful dread. He knew that the contact would be ephemeral.

As Gordon's mother completed the last of clean-up duties, she returned to Gordon's side. She hooked her right arm through his left and clasped her youngest son like a prom date.

Patrice Huard said, "Gordie, you know I don't pry, but I see you don't even have a suitcase. Are you goin' somewhere, son?"

Gordon inhaled deeply and exhaled slowly. He answered, "Mom, Dad, I am going to be taking a trip far away for a long, long time."

Ben Huard stared at him and said, "Gordie, you in some kinda trouble?"

Gordon poised himself and stood. He transitioned into a professorial mode — something that came much more naturally to him than speaking with his parents. "Dad, Mom, you know that you could always trust me my entire upbringing. I don't get in trouble." His parents nodded.

Gordon continued, "I am eternally sorry for the hurt that I brought you. It was not my intention to do so, but I did so just the same. For the record, you are wonderful parents and I'm honored to be your baby boy. But I fear, with my answer to your question, that I will bring you even more hurt. I assure you this was not by my doing. Due to my well-intended choices, I find myself an unwitting pawn in a chess game that I do not fully understand. But it is a very deadly game nonetheless."

The parents seated themselves together on the couch. The senior Huard wrapped his arm around his wife protectively. Their faces were furrowed with concern.

The Professor said, "There are many things that I cannot tell you. That is for your own protection. I can tell you only that I let my greed for knowledge influence my judgment. I agreed to involve myself with our government in a super-secret project. I was not alone in that greed. Our intentions were noble, but something is horribly wrong. As a probable result of matters beyond my control or knowledge, people are dying. This is occurring at the hands of dark and stealth people who give me the creeps. I fear I've told you too much already. But I will tell you this — that I am one of their targets. I probably have endangered you by my mere presence in our home."

Patrice Huard gazed at her son with an impassioned stare. She drew closer to her protective husband.

Gordon continued his impromptu lecture, "I came here because I knew not where to run. I could only think of home--a place far from these dark and dangerous people. I know that they would find me here eventually, and I will be leaving momentarily. I just wanted to see you one more time and leave you with the knowledge that you are loved. That I am not running from you. I would *never* do that again. If I can someday contact you I will. But I cannot further endanger you. Know that I will be thinking of you always."

Ben smiled at his son and said, "I have no doubt, son, you have a plan. You always have. Make sure it's a damned good one. And if you want to involve me in it, I'm all for it."

The son brushed back tears and merely stepped forward to hug his dad yet again. He felt five years old again in his father's arms. His father stepped away tearfully and excused himself down the hallway. The door of the master bedroom could be heard opening. His mother took her opportunity to hold her baby boy once more. She said, "You be careful, Gordie. This is crazy."

The father returned immediately and handed Gordon's high tech winter jacket to him. He stared passionately into his son's eyes and merely said, "Win!" Gordon immediately recalled the incantations of such advice many times during his younger years of swimming competitions. It was that swimming prowess which had enabled him a free education at his beloved Stanford University. The word uttered yet again from his father gave him an immediate flood of confidence and sense of purpose as he put on his coat. Yet, Gordon thought to himself, this was a contest more complicated than any race. He didn't even truly know who comprised his competition.

Gordon walked down the steps of the old house, careful not to slip on the icy rock- salted surface. He hesitated to pet the family Airedale "Duke" one more time at the foot of the steps. He scratched around the dog's ears and noted the existence of graying fur. Duke whimpered as Gordon walked away. The 25-degree air felt refreshing after sitting in the stuffy living room for hours. He could see his breath — a rare experience in central California. He glanced sideways and around the grounds. The snow-covered acreage was beautiful. The wood shed and barn in the distance evoked many fond memories, as did the tractor beneath the snow-laden tarps. He treasured the location for a second, tactical reason. There was only one narrow country road leading in, and one leading outward. Unwanted guests would be immediately evident in the rolling farmlands.

Huard entered his rented "Hummer" SUV and started the engine without looking at his parents. They were standing on the porch and clutching one another. He drew a deep breath and placed the vehicle in drive. He drove away gradually down the driveway.

He simultaneously desired to savor the last moments of home, yet he also wished to hit the nearby highway in a hurry. Finally, he stopped the vehicle and rolled down his window. He held out his hand with a thumbs-up gesture, honked, and waved at his saddened parents. Moments later he was gone for what could be forever.

The heated seats of the vehicle and the defroster soon began to take effect. "Bless that Greg Southard for making the arrangements," Huard thought. There was virtually no traffic on the early Sunday evening. He quickly reached the northbound State 95 Highway and accelerated. As the car warmed, he removed his expensive winter coat. He tossed the coat upon the passenger seat. A vast roll of hundred dollar bills spilled from the pocket. Huard thumbed clumsily through the bills, as he maintained his hurried speed, in efforts to leave the area. It appeared that his father had stashed some ten thousand dollars in cash in his pocket. Tears filled his eyes, and he wiped them away and focused. He could not turn back.

Huard began to re-familiarize himself with his hastily-conceived plan. His ever-loyal aide had completed all requests with distinction. Huard had in his possession airline tickets for Santiago Chile. Vast amounts of research material, both real and falsified, that he and his two murdered peers had compiled had been mailed to the far stretches of the planet. Only Huard and Southard knew which of the fifty designated mail stops would experience his eventual presence.

An hour and a half later, Huard pulled his vehicle into a Safeway, outside of Gettysburg Pennsylvania. He fed quarters into a phone booth in the parking lot and dialed Greg Southard. Greg answered the phone on the first ring. Huard again thought, ("Bless that kid.") Huard spoke for mere seconds. "I cannot thank you enough for what you've done for me, Greg. God bless, and I hope we meet again. Watch yourself and know that the answers indeed *are* out there. I guarantee it."

Huard hesitated only momentarily and then told Southard, "Make it so, number one." Southard laughed at the common joke between the Professor and assistant and replied, "I'm beaming it over, Kepteen. All the best, Gordon. I will miss you very much."

Huard hung up the phone abruptly. He looked at his wristwatch. The conversation had spanned less than two minutes. Exactly as he had planned. He entered the store and quickly retrieved a money order for fifty thousand dollars — every dime from his savings. Huard knew that the withdrawal of monies would draw attention to both the amount and location to which it was sent. He had no intention of cashing the order at his current location. He tucked the order in his jacket pocket and walked brusquely to his vehicle.

An hour and three quarters passed uneventfully. The blurring lights of passing vehicles across the median put the Professor in a peaceful state of mind. He let his thoughts drift back to the gathering of his family. He had seen new baby nieces and nephews for the first time. Others had grown extraordinarily. His father had grown more grey, and his oldest brother "Pete" had grown more balding, replete with "love handles." He tried to think of anything other than his treacherous predicament.

Huard turned northwesterly onto the Pennsylvania

Route 65 beltway. In less than an hour he was in the outskirts of Pittsburg. He stopped at a smallish hillside Chase Manhattan Bank. The bank was known to stay open until midnight, even on weekends. He put on his coat again, with the collar raised, and walked the twenty steps across the parking lot. He could see the Allegheny River shimmering far below the hill. He affixed a pair of sunglasses and pulled down a baseball cap over his face. He felt ridiculously conspicuous in his efforts to conceal himself. But the cameras within the bank were ever-present. He was greeted at the door by a young branch manager who was cordial and meticulous in his suit and tie. Huard learned that Greg Southard had contacted the bank an hour before his arrival so that they could ready for the cashing of such a large money order. The process of identification and waiver-signing was therefore performed without delay or complications.

Huard emerged from the bank into the late evening cold air. There was no snow on the ground, as there had been in West Virginia. The winter night was not as painfully cold as traditionally saddled the area in late February. He entered his vehicle and started the engine. His was the only vehicle in the lot, save for employee parking. He scanned his environs as he drove away. He noted a city park of several hundred acres spanning below him. The lights of emptied Pittsburg office buildings glowed across the river in the distance. There was scant little traffic in the area. No vehicles lined the street, save for one darkened and seemingly empty Dodge Ram pickup. He let out a deep breath, relieved to be leaving a place of obvious detection to relative "safety" along the roadways.

Huard approached the on-ramp to re-join the state highway. In the rear-view mirror he could see the lights of the pickup truck coming on. The pickup approached him rapidly. Huard had little doubt as to the occupant of the approaching vehicle. He had a decision to make. He could turn onto the freeway and try to speed away from the looming threat, or he could somehow attempt to elude the potential assassin. He gunned his engine and hurriedly approached the freeway onramp. His pursuer followed commensurately. Huard began his uphill merge onto the freeway ramp. The pickup rapidly gained ground.

Huard caught a glimpse in his mirror of a darkened figured reaching out of a rolled-down window. The figure held a gleaming object in his left hand. Huard knew that shots were coming, and his belief was soon confirmed. Glass fragments flew ballistically throughout the Hummer. Huard was now one hundred feet from the freeway. He feigned acceleration only momentarily and sensed the pursuer near contact with his rear bumper. At the last possible moment he braked abruptly and veered to his left. His vehicle skidded laterally and the tires screamed in pain. He could feel his seatbelt bite angrily into his side. The Hummer tilted heavily toward the passenger side. Huard dreaded that he was about to roll.

Huard realized that the vehicle had righted itself, and he completed his 180 degree maneuver. His driving prowess was surprisingly exceptional, for a bicycle riding professor, he thought for a second. He did not hesitate to accelerate forward. The oncoming Dodge pickup sped past him and onto the freeway. Huard thought he could see hatred in the passing driver's face. His assaulter could not stop in time to avoid joining the flow of light freeway traffic.

Huard drove the Hummer in the opposite direction, past the bank in question. He parked for a moment, some 100 yards beyond the bank, at the end of a dead-end street. Again he could see the skyline of Pittsburg, shimmering across the vast river. Virtually no people were walking within the lovely grassy grounds of the city park, stretched below him. Huard attempted to let his breathing slow and his pounding heart gain a reprieve. He felt blood trickling down the back of his neck, but did not devote the time to check his wound. He decided to turn around at the end of the street and return to the freeway onramp. He had a long-distance flight to gain at the nearby airport, after all.

As the Professor took his foot off the brake and began to drive, he saw a set of headlights approaching rapidly from behind. The lights came from where he had just driven. There was no escape route. Huard cursed himself for overlooking such a possibility. He turned his vehicle abruptly to the left and over a steep curb. He was grateful that the SUV maneuvered deftly into the terrain. The undercarriage scraped only slightly. He drove rapidly downhill, through the vast park, with his headlights turned off. At one point the Hummer glanced off a rockery that he could not see. But the vehicle continued accelerating forward. Huard could see the huge river to his right and turned away from the impending shoreline. In his mirrors he could see the lights of the pursuer's vehicle, far uphill, nearly a half mile to his east. It appeared that the driver was waving a flashlight, in search of his prey.

Huard stifled a triumphant chuckle, as he drove the Hummer rapidly uphill. He soon exited the park and was amused to discover that he had returned to his original starting point. The Chase Bank was just closing, as the yawning manager was securing the doors of the dimmed building. The manager stared intently at Huard as he drove past in the parking lot. The Hummer was a damaged and muddy spectacle.

Huard drove onto the freeway onramp at the speed limit, seeking to blend in, and saw no dreaded headlights. He therefore began his drive toward the city. He noted the freeway signs denoting the approaching "Historic Fort Duquesne Bridge." Occasional headlights of oncoming traffic came and went harmlessly from across the concrete freeway barrier. No traffic could be seen behind him for the moment. He reached his hand behind his neck and felt a sticky mess of blood. He felt reassured that the bleeding had at least ceased. But the myriad of glass fragments within his neck now felt like a hive of angry hornets exacting revenge upon him.

Huard's thoughts again drifted to his family. He missed them already. But he shook his head to re-focus himself. He thought through the inherent risks to arise upon presenting his identification at the airport. But he believed that Southard had made clever preparations for the issue. He was further aware that his copious amounts of cash would draw more attention. But the attention was inevitable. He could explain the monies as needed for charities, in which he and Greg Southard had a reputation for involvement. He patted the dash of his rented vehicle and was eternally grateful for his trusted ally's choice of transportation. The Hummer had proven to be an invaluable means of escape. He almost felt guilty in knowing that he would abandon his four-wheeled savior on the side of an airport road.

Huard approached the looming bridge. It was a beautiful double-decker steel tied arch, some 279 feet in length. He knew that the locals referred to the bridge as "The Bridge to Nowhere." The irony did not escape the humor-laden Professor, even under the dire circumstances. He recalled that a drunken college student had once driven a '64 Chrysler station wagon over the beginning edge of the bridge — only to suffer nary a scratch some 50 feet below. The expansive and dark Allegheny River shimmered below in the moonlight, and the adjoining Ohio River curved nearby. Reflections of the city skyline completed the scenic image.

Huard's vision was impeded by exceptionally bright lights from an approaching oncoming vehicle, across the barrier. Huard shielded his eyes and cursed the high beams of the opposing driver. As the vehicle drew nearer, Huard realized that the vehicle was actually coming from the direction of his own lanes of travel. He braked abruptly, as he approached the lights, and came to a stop. He was located in the center of the bridge. He realized that there were, in actuality, two vehicles blocking the eastbound lanes of the bridge. Huard sought to reverse, but immediately noticed two oncoming sets of headlights rapidly approaching behind him. He saw darkly clothed human predators begin to exit vehicles and approach on foot from both directions, some 100 feet away. They did not look like government men to Huard. They looked more like thugs — like something from the cover of Soldier of Fortune Magazine.

Gordon Huard stepped out of his vehicle and faced a group of his approaching pursuers. He noted a widened smile upon the tallest of the men. He was a muscular man with short-cropped hair. He again looked familiar. Huard placed his hands behind his neck in a stance of surrender. He could hear the animated voices of the menacing men. He wondered momentarily if he would merely become a captive. But the grisly sight of Leah Steinberg immediately jumped to his recollection.

Huard hesitated only momentarily to make his decision. He sprinted to his right toward the guardrail. He climbed through the support cables of the bridge deftly. Out of his periphery to his left he managed to see a figure draw a firearm. He looked downward at the dark and rapidly flowing river far below and jumped. Huard's right hand caught a cable as he soared outward from the bridge. A gunshot rang-out and the hiss of a bullet flew past Huard's right ear. The guy wire interference propelled him off-balance in flight. He waved his hands frantically in an effort to right himself for the plunge into the river.

Huard was able to breach the water feet first. But his body was at a decided slant to his right. The 60-foot descent made the water feel almost like solid ground. The surface battered his feet upon impact and the water slammed at his right temple. All was suddenly dark and silent. Time slowed to suspended animation. Strangely, the sensation of penetrating the river surface immediately created a flashback to a childhood memory. He recalled the feeling of playing paratrooper from the roof of his family rambler--how the ground collided with his feet. He was helpless for a moment.

Huard was then shocked into reality by the frigid Allegheny. The water felt like thousands of needles piercing his skin. The sheer darkness of the river was disorienting. He could barely determine which direction was upward. His lungs begged for oxygen.

Thankfully, human buoyancy finally prevailed. Huard rose to the surface with a startled gasp, facing into the raging current. The elation at filling his lungs with air was immeasurable. He felt nearly helpless to the forces of the powerful river. He knew that he could not prevail over the current to reach the immediate safety of the banks. The shoreline was some 180 feet to his west, as illuminated by the scant few midnight lights. The Professor put his venerable swimming skills and knowledge to use. He righted himself in the water down- current. Rather than fight the current, he embraced the forces with his swim strokes. He simply tried to take a slight angle to the deep rumbling waters. He passed beneath the shadows of the huge bridge, as the shoreline grew slowly nearer.

Huard turned his attention to the lights above the shores. He could see the darkened restaurants and walkways in the distance. He was desperate to feel the safety of solid ground. He swam harder, taxing his strength, despite his better judgment. His body suddenly slammed against a hardened surface. He thought he had struck a boulder. His right shoulder gave him moderate pain, despite the numbness of his limbs. He looked upward in the darkness. He could see that the surface he had struck spanned upward for several feet, and for considerable distance laterally. He felt flat fiberglass against him and could make out the lettering upon the structure-- "Allegheny Gateway Clipper." The Professor braced himself against the bow of the boat gratefully. He knew that a dock would be nearby. He looked upward at the towering bridge to his immediate west. He could see powerful search lights scanning the river below. The lights drew nearer.

Huard removed his jeans and zip-up sweatshirt. He placed his winter coat back on his torso. He allowed the clothing to fill with air. He tied them together meticulously, despite numbed fingers. His lifeguard training so many years ago was proving useful. As the searchlight again neared his position, he tossed the makeshift scarecrow into the beam and beyond the bow of the boat. The clothing floated rapidly down the river and was illuminated for several seconds by the spotlight. The spotlight eventually went dark. Huard could hear vehicles above driving away hurriedly, engines roaring. He was safe for the moment and he felt gratitude for the boat.

Huard side-stroked toward the dock in question and quickly reached his destination. He propped his aching arms over the side of the dock and seal-kicked in the water. He vaulted onto the surface with a dull thud that seemed incredibly loud to him. He crawled across the creosote-laden boards and braced himself against the boat. His shivering was nearly uncontrollable. He could see his labored breath. He was grateful for freedom from the dark river and the slow return of feeling to his extremities. His body ached in totality. He reached into his deep jacket pockets. He was enormously relieved to find that his rolls of cash were still intact within those pockets. "Thank you God," he whispered. His mind was already formulating his next steps.

Minutes earlier, on the bridge deck above, the captors had stood together. The new morning traffic occasionally passed the re-positioned pursuit vehicles. It appeared that at least one passing driver had been speaking on a cell phone and staring at the scene. It was obvious that police would be summoned to a purported accident or suicide scene. Several of the men leaned against the rail of the bridge. A darkened figure stood separately from his peers. He seemed disappointed in his failure to shoot the fleeing academic before he jumped to his death.

The assassin ultimately turned toward the other men and turned off his powerful spotlight. He called out, "Ah, he's toast. Let the fish take care of his remains. Make the call."

Chapter 9

Cardinal Antonin Napolitano sat at the console of the HYDRA system with his hands clasped over his headset. He was transfixed. Over his headset came three words from a trembling voice, "It is finished." Over the headphones a man could be heard breathing laboriously. More words followed, "Father, into thy hands I commend my spirit."

The Cardinal turned toward Director Portworth and spoke angrily into his microphone, "Why do you insult me with this well-planned hoax?"

Senator McLean rolled his chair toward the Cardinal and placed a hand gently upon the holy man's shoulder. He seemed to be measuring the Cardinal's anxiety level. He said in a hushed tone, "Cardinal, what you are hearing is real...the voice and words we are *all* hearing were generated over 2000 years ago in a city known as Jerusalem. I believe you know who the speaker is."

With the exception of the IBM executive, who smiled and nodded, the invited gathering sat stunned. The Cardinal nearly collapsed in his seat. He was braced gently by the Senator and the Imam. Portworth brought the Cardinal a glass of cold water.

When the Cardinal re-gained his poise Portworth turned to him, "Shall we continue? Is everyone in agreement?"

The dignitaries all nodded animatedly, and finally verbalized their desires.

Portworth addressed the group and stated, "As you all can clearly see, the use of this complex system is fairly straightforward-- you choose a series of words and the HYDRA will scan history for the use of that series of uttered sounds. Choose any point in world history and, hopefully, in minutes we will find the page number and quotes."

Professor Bridgemann thought out loud to himself, "Jesus!"

Portworth responded, "Exactly, Professor, that is the page we are currently on."

Cardinal Napolitano whispered to himself several prayers and then muttered, "The Sudarium of Oviedo." Portworth asked him, "Sir, what are you saying?" The Cardinal only repeated, "Sudarium of Oviedo." Portworth began to speak again. He was interrupted by the technician, who said, "Got it, got it. Stand-by." As further spoken words of enormous biblical significance began to pour forth, Senator McLean interjected.

"Stop!" McLean stated. And the process was halted.

McLean was focused upon a highly agitated Cardinal. He interceded by saying, "I believe now is an excellent time to step away from this for the day. Cardinal, I wish to assure you that we had little idea what we could witness today. I want you all to return to your quarters for the evening to digest this. This is powerful and emotional, and I want you to ponder whether each of you wishes to continue in this groundbreaking effort. In a way, you are all being asked to become de-facto modern day apostles. That is something you all must consider. For now, you will all be escorted from this room and driven back. Those whom wish to re-convene will be brought back in three days. In the meantime I thank you and wish you a good night's sleep — if that is now humanly possible."

Portworth did not bother to escort the dignitaries out of the room. He remained behind at the console of the elaborate N.S.A. brain-child. He blended into the low-light environment. He always drew comfort from darkness. The NSA Director was clearly dismayed that the Senator had chosen to steal his limelight. His hatred for American politicians was again reinforced.

Portworth dismissed the lowly technician from the room. He took the technician's comfortable leather seat and clasped his hands behind his head. He leaned backward and crossed his ankle across his other leg. He smirked, and surveyed the mass of computers and screens. The Director was alone with his thoughts. He relished the delicious irony of his position. He was a very powerful director of a United States government agency. He had the ultimate control over the most significant secrets in world history. Yet, little did his government know, he was destined to become a very wealthy man by concealing those secrets.

In a twisted sense of irony, Michael Portworth was actually a legacy government agent. His father had been an agent for the CIA during the Vietnam War. His father ultimately disappeared. The government would tell the family nothing of what had become of his father. But, from what the family could glean, agent Justin Portworth had been inserted into Hanoi during the height of the war in 1969. His qualifications were in high demand. Justin Portworth had been the son of a Vietnamese mother whom had emigrated to the U.S. following marriage to his merchant marine father. He was fluent in Vietnamese and did not bear the physical traits of his

Caucasian father. He was able to insert himself into the high levels of the North Vietnamese army. A highly intelligent man, Agent Justin Portworth had been trained by the CIA in Mandarin Chinese. He thereby proved to be invaluable to the North Vietnamese command during high level meetings with the Chinese forces.

Somehow, during the fall of Saigon in April of 1975 the American government blundered, and revealed the identity of their mole. It was believed that, in the haste to depart, no one had taken efforts to destroy sensitive documents. Agent Justin Portworth was captured by the Vietnamese government and imprisoned. Endless torture surely followed. The U.S. government merely advised the wife by terse telephone communication that her husband was missing in action. All contact was forever severed. Phone calls to local congressmen were dismissed with demands to "call my aides."

Over subsequent years information would filter to the family via a myriad of strange contacts — usually anonymous sources who claimed to have worked with Agent Justin Portworth, as well as former Vietnamese nationals whom spoke admiringly of the man. Over the years there had been numerous unconfirmed sightings of the agent, purportedly moved constantly throughout the Vietnamese countryside. He was an abused slave without a country. Solid information was sometimes leaked to the family that the U.S. government had reliable evidence of Agent Justin Portworth' whereabouts. But no efforts to extricate he, nor thousands of peers, was ever made. Similarly, no efforts were ever made by the U.S. government to provide assistance, whether financial or otherwise, to the wife and three children of a devoted agent. "Uncle" was merely a former employer.

Michael Portworth's hatred for the U.S. festered over his youth, as he saw his mother labor at an all-hours janitorial job to support her two sons and daughter. She had been left inexplicably penniless, as her husband's paycheck merely ceased to arrive. Additional phone calls to the employer merely led to bureaucratic run- around. The message was clear — you're on your own. The mother's tireless sacrifices enabled Mike and a younger brother and sister to attend fine private schools outside of Baltimore. Michael appreciated those efforts enormously. But he often resented the ridicule from wealthy schoolmates who knew of his situation. He could still hear them calling across the gym floor, "Hey Portworth, your mom can come over to our house and scrub the toilet." The teachers often did nothing. Michael internalized the resentment and often thought to himself, "The government will scrub MY toilet some-day."

Michael Portworth was able to attend Johns Hopkins University on a partial scholarship. Loans and unwanted gifts from his mother had covered the remaining costs. He excelled in foreign languages and international studies and was an exceptional student. He breezed through subsequent law school at Georgetown, almost bored at the lack of a challenge.

Post- graduation, the exceptionally bright young man found that no law firms were hiring in the area, despite his exceptional academics. He found himself in need of a job of any sort. He wanted desperately to take care of his amazing mother. He often thought of her, succumbing to back pain, when she thought her kids were out of sight.

Michael found it comical that, on one fateful day, the N.S.A. came recruiting at his college campus. He did not even know the agency sought college students. He met with a recruiter nearly as a joke. He wondered to himself why he had even entertained thoughts of such an option. An impressively immaculate woman merely a few years his senior garnered his attention. Strangely, Michael Portworth became intrigued with the profession, both for the high pay and the innumerable applications for his talents. His desire to work for the U.S. government began, at least initially, with good intentions. But his deep-seated hatred eventually pervaded his character. As he rose up the ranks, his authority became considerable. Power and hatred would someday morph into betrayal of the government that had betrayed his family.

Director Portworth regained a consciousness in the present. He turned toward the massive computer system and affixed a headset. He began to type a series of codes into the HYDRA system. He knew how to re-boot the console with the two key cards remaining inserted. The seemingly eager system sprang to life. "Good morning Hal," Portworth said bemusedly. He half expected a response from the extraordinary system. In his wallet he held another key card for the system. He examined the card once given to him by Joseph Yeats. It was Yeats' continued belief that the card could disable the HYDRA system, even erase every byte. Portworth pulled the strange metallic feeling card from his wallet and held it to the dim lighting. The card was designed to resemble the actual agency key cards for the console. But the card was in actuality more alloyed and shiny. He smiled at his "torpedo" and pondered instant destruction of the source of such paranoia. But he had another idea.

Portworth began to type a series of words into the system. Those words began with "Justin Portworth." He added key words, inclusive of "Agent, Hanoi, Capture, and Conceal." He followed with four numbers, "1975."

HYDRA began collating frenetically, like a search engine system on steroids. To be sure, the NSA Director could not begin to navigate the system as could the technician. It seemed the Texan and HYDRA had a symbiotic relationship. Nonetheless, a mere three minutes later, the system asked Portworth if he wished to listen. The process was astonishingly simple. He stated, "Yes" into his microphone. Almost instantly he heard the voice of his father, as clearly as if he were seated next to him. His heart pounded so rapidly he could only hear his heartbeat in the headphones. Portworth knew that he was not imagining the experience. He ordered HYDRA to "Stop!" for just a moment.

Portworth took a deep breath and let his lungs empty slowly through pursed lips. He wiped his perspiring hands on the legs of his slacks as he sat hunched over the console.

He spoke into his microphone, "Repeat!" He almost shouted the word, although knowing that the system did not recognize the inflection of his orders. But there was great emotion in the uttered word nonetheless.

"You must protect my family at all costs," said the voice of Justin Portworth.

A pleasant and calm sounding southern male voice followed and said, "Justin, you are my friend and colleague. You have made a huge sacrifice for your country. I fear we have asked too much of you. And you are now making a huge sacrifice for your family."

Justin Portworth responded, "Mr. President, I knew what I was getting myself into. None of us had any idea the nature of the forces we are actually opposing. Sir, they have already killed one President. We have to close the lid on this. What I learned had to be learned. I know now that gaining knowledge has its costs. I alone must pay those costs. And there must be no way a connection is drawn to my family."

Director Portworth sat at the console, stunned. He knew that his deeply personal revelations were similar in impact to those which the Cardinal had earlier experienced. He now understood fully. Portworth sat transfixed for hours, as the sorted spoken words spilled into his headset. Above all, he sought to find the location of his father, if he still lived. But even HYDRA struggled to find that particular needle in a haystack. His father had changed names and lives and therefore would be difficult to track. Portworth's only hope was that his father had errantly uttered key words regarding his past life that would be captured by the system.

Portworth was startled as his console phone rang loudly at 0400 hours. The technician merely asked about his well-being. Portworth dismissed the call and continued listening for another hour and a half. Nearly exhausted, he wandered out of the room in a quasi-daze. The truths he had gained would forever change his world.

Chapter 10

Off-duty Deputy Joe Phewell was at home, sipping from an ice cold bottle of Corona beer, resplendent with a slice of fresh lime. He looked at the bottle in his hand with admiration and released an emphatic, "Ahhhhh." He was seated in an over-flowing but very orderly study within his beautiful log home. The home was located on fifteen scenic acres overlooking the spectacular Ellensburg Canyon. Far below, a world class- rated trout habitat wound steadily through the serpentine 18 miles of deep cathedral gorges. The chasm had once been forged by massive volcanic action. The canyon was home to innumerable archaeological finds, inclusive of intact mastodons and petrified forests. Shell Oil coveted the billions of gallons of oil suspected to be beneath the floor of the protected national lands.

Joe Phewell cherished a front row view of the gorge and river out of massive picture windows throughout his home. His favorite view was out of his study, or "war room" as he referred to the expansive office. Massive tamarack logs spanned across his ceiling and outside to a vast and comfortable deck. The huge room held tremendous caches of books and magazines, from floor to ceiling, in perfectly organized rows. The library filled three full walls. A rolling ladder was tucked into a corner of the room. A librarian would have been proud of the order and symmetry. The home had won several awards for design and innovation. Joe Phewell was, in fact, the designer of the home.

Phewell thought of the conversation he had held the previous day with the elected Sheriff of Kittitas

County. The conversation had become heated. Phewell had attempted to convince the Sheriff that the incident at the ridge was a homicide. He had repeatedly attempted to present his case to the Sheriff. With each attempt the pompous bureaucrat had shrugged off his claims. Ultimately, the Sheriff called in the deputy's Sergeant to resolve the dispute. He asked the Sergeant what he thought of the situation. The Sergeant merely responded, "Sheriff, it's just another drunk over a guardrail. We don't need another Phewell-injected case." With that, the debate was essentially over. The Sheriff patted his talented but eccentric deputy on the back patronizingly, and expressed feigned appreciation for his talents. The Sheriff tried to explain to Phewell the expense of detailed investigations on "every little piddly-assed thing" in an atmosphere of diminishing budgets. Phewell had ultimately excused himself in anger. He had no way of knowing that the Sheriff's inane choice might well have saved his life.

Phewell turned to the heavily windowed fourth wall of his beloved war room. The windowed side was lined with ornate hand crafted desks that spanned nearly fifteen feet. Numerous encased arrowheads and other artifacts were contained in a glass rotating case in the corner. The desktops were laden with extensive computer systems with over-sized monitors. The powerful computers were only occasionally utilized by Phewell. He did so only when he could not readily summon information he desired from his treasure of leather-bound books, or other publications. While highly educated and adept at the technologies at hand, Phewell neither trusted nor relied upon computers. He preferred the human mind. However, he knew that this day was such a day to embrace the necessary evil.

Phewell unzipped two plastic baggies containing a shimmering platinum-like thumb drive device. He gently grasped the device and held it high above him. He examined the item in the sunlight pouring inward from his windows. The thumb drive was much heavier than conventional devices and wielded a true metallic composition. Phewell smiled and spoke at the device in an altered voice, "My precioussssssss." He placed the drive into the port of his newest computer. He was pleased to see that the device did fit into a conventional computer. The computer system in question was stand-alone for a reason. No outsiders could gain access to Phewell's investigations and personal research. He attempted to format the compatibility of the drive to the computer. Within moments the computer screen came alive. The wording, "Top Secret" scrolled across his enlarged monitor. He turned to his beer and drew more cold refreshing courage. He crossed his arms across his chest and stared again at the written admonishment. He pondered whether to continue or not.

Phewell spoke again to himself, "Ah, dadgummit, you coward, let's do this." Information unfolded in front of him in an organized but frenetic fashion. He noted that the drive held dates and times, and then attached recordings. Brief footnotes seemed to have been hurriedly attached to numerous events, as typos abounded. The name Jacob Knapse was scribed conspicuously within the contents.

Phewell knew that the fingerprints from the body had come back via the AFIS identification system to Jacob Knapse. The original prints had been taken years previously when Knapse was a young man from Wisconsin seeking to obtain a firearms permit. Phewell thought, "Well hello Mr. Smith." His innate investigatory juices were already flowing. He had never doubted that the young man had been murdered. His Sheriff had been a fool, as always. And the newly promoted subservient Sergeant had stupidly ordered the case be closed, categorized as an accident. The Sergeant had uttered terse admonishments to "move on to the next case, deputy." Deputy Phewell had chosen, very privately, to ignore those orders.

Ever logical, Phewell decided to begin at the beginning of the listed archived information. The first date displayed was that of November 22, 1963. The time was 1230 P.M. The place listed was Dallas Texas. Phewell 's pupils flared. He spoke out loud, "My God!," and gulped heartily from his nearby beer. He leapt to an adjoining office chair and gave life to yet another computer and screen. In front of him stood a detailed computer matrix of details of the mysterious death at Umtanum Ridge. Hundreds of crime scene photos contained detailed evidentiary notations and measurements. Information on the body and involved vehicle were included. All was drawn together in detailed link- charts and graphs. Phewell had re-programmed an existing law enforcement "Penlink" system to improve the capability of linking and sorting enormous caches of case information. His personal system far exceeded the capabilities of that developed by the FBI to handle the Columbine shooting investigations. His work was paying off.

Phewell excitedly typed additional linkage information into his system. He suspected he would be in-putting a great deal more this day. He turned to his bank of books and repositioned the ladder. He climbed to a top row and retrieved three leather-bound publications. He searched each book rapidly and bookmarked several sections. Phewell was grateful to be "furloughed" from his work week for the next three days. He was further grateful to be a single man and devoid of distractions. He knew he would not sleep this night. He would prob-ably forget to even eat.

Through the following days Joe Phewell would no-tate and categorize a myriad of spoken information via the recovered drive. The information was powerful and stunning. If the information were to be true, the pro-verbial "lid" would be blown off of many government and corporate institutions. Phewell had initially thought the drive wielded a cache of recorded conversations of historical significance for only the past fifty years or so. That would explain the killing of this airman. It appeared he had stolen recordings of a very high sig-nificance. But the information gleaned in subsequent days was to prove even more perplexing and bizarre. The conversations were noted to have transpired during times of the civil war. Others seemed to hold biblical implications. Most "recordings" were incomplete and hastily compiled. He was obsessed with the puzzle and missing pieces.

Deputy Phewell was confident that he had access to information of enormous scope and importance. He had pre-conclusions and doubts. As with any case in-vestigation, he would have to weigh facts and beliefs for veracity and verifiability. He knew one thing to be certain — that he was privy to something both extraordinarily secretive and dangerous. There were affected parties of great power and influence beyond his comprehension, at this point. They were clearly willing to kill to contain such knowledge. Phewell had no intention of attracting their attentions. He patted his wall of printed material behind himself and smiled, "My un-hackable friends come to my aid yet again."

Deputy Phewell knew he would make no further mention of the Knapse homicide to peers or superiors. His future questioning of a trusted professor friend at Central Washington University would be guarded. He suspected that this investigation would span many years and take many turns. He remained forever thankful for his extremely private home where he could develop his plan. It was a beautiful sanctuary above the flowing river. Within Joe Phewell the traits of a genius engineer, coupled with the wariness of a seasoned cop, would serve him very well. "Phewell injected my ass," he said aloud.

Chapter 11

White House Chief of Staff Amanda Neal arose from her ornate bed in an equally ornate Washington D.C. townhouse to use the bathroom. She draped a black silk kimono over her nude and perfect body. Her petite bare feet, complete with painted toenails in the color pink, made pattering sounds upon the polished hard wood floors of her bedroom. She hesitated at her dresser to take a sip from a half-consumed glass of vodka. She admired herself for a moment in the mirror and brushed her hair over the kimono. The contrast of her shoulder length strawberry blonde hair to the black silk made the beauty of such even more distinct. She corrected her smudged glossy pink lipstick with a pinky finger.

A man's right hand slipped into the front of her top and cupped her left breast. The man said, "Why don't you come back to bed. I miss you already."

Neal answered, "Haven't you had enough?" But her answer had already presented itself. She felt his hardness behind her, through his boxer shorts. Her lover wrapped his left arm around her and embraced her closely. He smelled her intoxicating perfume behind her neck. He moved her body with him in a gentle dance-like move. Neal wanted to be rid of the man, but in spite of herself, her body indicated otherwise. Her lover's hand gently stroked her breast and aroused her own response. His kisses upon her neck were warm and moist. She hated herself for her desires. She hated him even more for placing her in the moment.

The lovemaking was slow and gentle the second time. Her partner was aware of her every need, and none were ignored. Not like the first occurrence of frenetic sex — her lover tearing her clothing off of her like an escaped convict. They lay together in the huge bed in a lengthy embrace. The embrace was actually far too long for Neal's liking. Her lover was the female of the couple — always needing lengthy time and cuddling. (An intimacy freak.) Neal, conversely, could have discarded her lover seconds after his moaning climax. The deed was done and she was a busy and powerful woman.

Neal was prepared to dismiss her company when he began to speak passionately. He said, "Amanda, I know the truth about my father. Nothing I was led to believe was remotely true. I believe he is probably alive and well. But I don't know where he is."

Neal remained only mildly interested in the words of her partner. She was about to rise when he stated, "I know more of the truths about the gulf wars. I already knew a lot, but the details are dramatic. There are people I know who have even greater knowledge of the truths. He stopped himself from relating more. He only added, I am even hearing truths about the Kennedy's. This is enormous." Amanda caressed her lover and gently kissed him. She said, "I'm listening, babe."

Michael Portworth continued relating to his lover the complexity of what he had previously learned, while devoting an overnight to the HYDRA system. The cache of knowledge he had obtained, albeit fragmented, was of nonpareil impact. He even let slip some of his interactions with a group of corrupt billionaires. Neal devoted the entirety of the winter's night and early morning to the role of supportive pillow-talk listener.

Portworth eventually let himself out of the town-house with an apology for his droning. Neal was supportive and understanding as she kissed him goodbye. She said to Portworth, "When is it MY turn to listen in again." Michael frowned and merely stated, "I don't know. So much has changed for me in a week that I don't know what to think. I was wrong about so much. I'll call you." Neal thought to herself, "Sure you will."

At 1:30 P.M Zurich time the secure phone of David Rosenweiler's Execu-Jet rang with a text message. Rosenweiler typed, "Yes?"

The caller said, "We need to meet."

Rosenweiler countered, "Well I am rather busy right now, some four thousand miles away."

The caller countered, "It cannot wait."

"My phone line is secure, as you well know. Get on with it."

"No. This will be in person."

Chapter 12

Santiago, Chile.

Professor Gordon Huard was tremendously relieved to be greeted at the gates of Santiago Internal Airport by a dear friend. A short and balding fifty year-old man wearing a trench coat and sunglasses linked his arm in his and continued walking with him. Gordon immediately engaged the man in very fluent Castilian.

Huard said, "You look like a secret agent."

His friend responded, "Your friend, Mr. Southard, said to take any measures necessary to remain incognito. I am, therefore, doing so."

Huard refrained from commenting on how ridiculous his friend looked. He was tremendously grateful to actually have a friend, so far away from home. The colleague was legendary University of Chile Physics Professor Juan-Enrique Perales. Once again, Greg Southard had done a tremendous job of arranging for all logistical needs for Huard.

Perales was not inclined to engage his friend in conversation at the airport. He learned that his friend lacked any luggage other than a small satchel. He quickly ushered Huard to his car that was parked nearby. He drove away quickly, and onto a nearby freeway. Finally, Perales let his guard down. He removed his sunglasses to reveal his beautifully huge brown eyes that friends always referred to as "Saint Bernard Eyes." Huard patted his friend warmly on the shoulder and an awkward hug was attempted while the man drove.

Huard said, "Juan, I cannot express how pleased

I am to see you today. You are a blessed sight indeed. How is Donna?"

Perales smiled and replied, "She is still far too beautiful for the likes of me. I *still* owe you, Gordon."

Huard answered, "Not after today, my friend. I do not know how much you know of my situation."

The conversation first drifted toward the occasion when Gordon had introduced the taciturn Chilean professor to a beautiful anthropology professor at Stanford University nearly a decade ago. Huard had even done most of the talking for his brilliant and treasured visiting friend.

Huard said, "You know, Juan. I think that I did *both* of you a favor that week."

"Bless you, Gordon," said Perales.

Huard eventually asked Perales what he actually knew of his situation.

Perales said, "I know that when Mr. Southard will only give me the essential details of your plight, that his silence speaks volumes. I am very concerned for you." He spoke disconsolately regarding reading about the murders of the two Stanford Professors. They were also Perales' friends.

Huard said, "Juan, I implore you not to take me to your home. When I tell you my circumstances you will understand. I cannot bring more danger to you and Donna than I am already doing."

Perales answered, "That is what I expected you to say. I have prepared for that contingency. We will go to Viña. I have always pontificated to you about us someday visiting there. It is very private, and very beautiful."

Huard said, "Perfect."

Two hours later, Perales' vehicle turned left upon a serpentine one lane roadway and down a steep hillside. Hundreds of acres of immaculate vineyards passed. While he could not yet see the ocean, Huard could smell it. He commented to Perales about how the unique downhill roadway reminded him of Lombard Street in San Francisco. Perales offered that he fondly remembered being driven down Lombard by Huard on one of his trips to the U.S. Finally, the Pacific Ocean could be seen in the distance. The foamy crest of endless late afternoon waves seemed to align themselves in patient approaching rows. Huard had his window rolled down and savored the warm tropical beach air.

Perales parked his Cadillac in the carport of a lovely fifty year-old stucco "ranchero" style bungalow. He offered to carry Huard's small bag.

Huard displayed a sheepish grin and commented, "This is all I have to show for my life at present. Pretty sad, no?"

Perales countered, "You have your life."

The two men spent three days together at the house on the beach of Viña Del Mar. There was a great deal of catching up to do. Much of the conversations were jovial, often reflective of past times together during numerous seminars in the U.S. Perales did not initially press his friend for details on his situation. He allowed the man to rest, eat, and savor the seclusion so far from his troubles. Huard asked about borrowing a spare vehicle and disappearing into the fabric of South America. He gave scant explanation for his plans.

Finally, one night, after a third bottle of Pisco was consumed on the scenic balcony, the conversation became heated. Midnight waves pounded the beach as the tide came in. Sand pipers provided a delightful chorus beneath the deck. Perales pushed his friend to share all that he knew of matters to the north.

Huard said, "I have to go this alone, Juan. It is far too dangerous to involve you."

Perales pounded the glass dining table and the crystal- ware reverberated. He said, "Damnit, Huard. I have survived a Russian and Cuban invasion, two hundred thousand countrymen stacked dead in Estadio de Chile, a volcano, and two massive earthquakes. Danger is part of Chilean life. It is my right, as a friend, to know."

Finally, Huard relented, and the conversation spanned well into the morning. He seemed to be relieved, at last, to unburden himself of his secrets. He told his story of involvement in "the project" from the inception to present time. He treasured the perspectives and insights of his brilliant peer. It was the mutual conclusion of the two esteemed physicists that Professor Huard was facing extraordinarily powerful forces at work. He could not trust his own government. And he had stumbled upon knowledge that could threaten the status quo for the most powerful people on the planet. Many entities could conceivably be at work in order to ensure that the past and present remained securely cloistered in the chambers of the elite.

The two colleagues opined that U.S. intelligence forces might be involved. Corporate power brokers seemed highly culpable. Law enforcement could have been corrupted or deceived. It was suspected that even religious factions could have a stake in a global level cover-up. The greatest danger lay in the lack of knowledge from where a given threat was being launched. But they concurred that the scope of worldwide power, knowledge, and greed could have far reaching tentacles. They agreed also that Huard must hide himself in the far reaches of South American terrain. They began to formulate a plan.

The following day Gordon Huard alone strode toward the "Apartado Postal" in the central core of Chile's largest city and capital. He still marveled at the beauty of a country he had heard much about, but had failed to visit. The towering Andes Mountains lay to his east, some fifty miles distant, seemingly spanning endlessly. Innumerable spires of 400 year-old Catholic churches loomed above him. He admired the overt sense of pride displayed by the residents. The Chileans strode down sidewalks and plazas with their shoulders thrown back, smiling, and courteous, in massive on-foot crowds. The fragrance of curry-laden deep-fried seafood wraps known as "empanadas" emanated invitingly from nearby marketerias.

Huard had planned on blending into the bustling city of four million residents. He was pleased to see that Santiago was experiencing a plenitude of Anglo tourists, both from North America and Europe. They all swarmed to the warm February temperatures of the southern hemisphere. The tourists flocked to the nearby beaches that spanned the entire 1600 mile coastline, from Antarctica in the south, to Peru in the north. He felt silly wearing the ridiculous ballooned white shorts and flowery shirt, complete with a camera. But he was undistinguishable from countless others.

Huard could not help but marvel at his current situation, upon reflection. He was amazed that he remained alive. So much could have, and often did, go wrong in his escape from unknown assassins. That he would find himself 16,000 miles from his home without weeks of pre-planning was unfathomable. He knew that he had chosen a haven as remotely located as any possible, outside of the South Pole. He was highly conversant in Spanish, and therefore functioned easily. He was grateful that his thousands of dollars in cash translated into a small fortune in Chile's post- earthquake economy. He was further grateful that he was allowed to leave the American airport with so much cash in-hand. Customs had removed him from the passenger line and grilled him for over an hour. The fact that the agents released him to travel reinforced his suspicions that his pursuers were in fact, not government. But he still had no idea which entity desired his eradication. He shivered at the thought and entered the post office.

Huard approached the uniformed postal clerk and glanced laterally. The clerk's nametag read "Osvaldo." The clerk smiled warmly at the Professor and said, "Do I have something for you sir?" Huard was still surprised at how many Chileans spoke fluent English. He responded to the clerk in fluent Spanish and requested a mailed package. The irony of the two parties fluently speaking concomitant dialects of the other struck each as comical. Huard was therefore able to relax, just slightly, during a time of possible detection.

The clerk soon returned with a sealed package large enough to contain an inflated beach ball. He smiled at

Huard and said, "Oh, I see, cooking from home. I love your chocolate chip cookies and coffee." Huard relaxed a bit more and said, "Osvaldo, if I were ever to receive those, you will have a dozen of them and Starbuck's best." He bade the clerk farewell and quickly exited the post office.

Rush-hour traffic crawled peacefully past the city's central core. Huard was able to summon a cab almost immediately. This was not difficult, considering that Santiago wielded three times more taxis than New York City. But the Chilean cabbies still drove in a distinctly New York manner. The cab was quickly enveloped in a sea of similar vehicles and became indistinct. This was just as the Professor and Perales had planned. Huard allowed a deep breath to escape, as the cab flowed with the traffic, slowly heading toward the freeway out of town.

Huard patted the box with a smile. He knew that 49 other decoy boxes had arrived at points all over the world. He thought to himself, "Let those piles of dung chase down all *those* leads." He could not resist opening the large box to examine the contents. He was thrilled to find that the box was filled to the brim with computer discs and notebooks. The penmanship atop two of the notebooks was clearly that of his two murdered professor friends. A deep sadness pervaded his psyche. He could not help but wonder if he would be next.

Placed atop the voluminous cache of information were several newspaper clippings and a note. The articles pertained to the murders of the two professors. Police were said to have few leads on the grisly homicides. But mention was made of Professor Gordon Huard being a "person of interest" whom had mysteriously fled the country. The note was from Greg Southard that read, "Professor, I was able to recover a great deal of materials from you and your friends' offices before anyone arrived. I gave my side of what I know to the cops and was let go. I told them they're crazy to even suspect you. I hope I get an A on all my arrangements I made for you. God speed, boss. I hope to see you again soon." Huard's pride and appreciation toward his prized student was enormous. He knew that he would not be alive this day were it not for the loyal support of Greg Southard. The brilliant kid was like a son to him.

After an hour of driving, the cab finally escaped the clutches of downtown Santiago traffic. Huard directed the taxi driver to deliver him to a side street, just outside the city. He overpaid the cabbie and heard him say, "Mucho gusto," as he drove away with a smile. The 60 year-old driver had clearly known to ask no questions or interrupt the Professor's thoughts. He left Huard standing alone in the middle of a remote street, clutching a box.

Huard wanted to pore more thoroughly through the box and examine the contents, even while standing in the roadway. But he knew his curiosity would have to wait. He walked nonchalantly down the street and around a corner. There were no witnesses to his walk, as he was located in an abandoned development. The development had come to a halt due to economic factors. Mere occasional house foundations stood beyond the curbside like the footings of Arizona ghost towns. In the middle of the subsequent block a white 2003 Citroen Neo sat abandoned in a driveway. The car reminded

Huard of a recumbent bicycle with metal panels around it. But the vehicle was a very welcome sight. Huard located the key to the car atop the passenger rear tire — just as promised.

Huard unlocked and entered the car. He placed his prized package in the front seat next to him. There were no back seats. He placed a seatbelt over his inanimate passenger with great care. Atop his steering column sat a note. The note was drafted in immaculate penmanship and stated in articulate Castilian, "My dear friend, I regret that this vehicle is all that I may provide you in your day of turmoil. I remain at the ready for any and all that I might do to further your journey. I look forward to our reunion. My regards. Juan-Enrique."

Huard started the vehicle and heard the tiny motor engage. The seat was Spartan and uncomfortable. Leg room was lacking for the six foot three man. He could not help but think of how much he missed his utilitarian rented Hummer that he had abandoned in a crumpled mess outside of Pittsburg. He noted that the gas tank was filled completely and knew that the tiny car could travel several hundred miles on one tank. He backed the car out of the driveway and exited the neighborhood. As always, he was wary of being watched. But he was completely alone.

Within 20 minutes, Huard was northbound on the major north to south highway of Chile. Ironically, the highway was Ruta 5, or Route 5. He found it curious that he was driving the same highway number he had travelled thousands of times in and out of the bay area. The speed limit sign indicated 100 km per hour. He doubted that his vehicle would challenge that limit. The two lane highway was not crowded, and he could blend into the fabric of other drivers — ever polite and smiling as they passed.

It was almost unimaginable that Huard could find himself driving northbound in the center of Chile, seeking remote refuge, while justifiably paranoid every mile of the way. He knew that Perales had pledged to re-connect with him at the Peruvian border, armed with whatever information he could gain. Perales had powerful government and academic friends with whom he had pledged to consult. But Huard also knew that he would break the agreement with his friend and disappear. He could not allow another brutal murder to weigh on his conscience, especially with himself as the intended target.

Huard had a very good idea where he was to hide. He deliberately omitted mention of the actual destination to Perales. His knowledge of South American geography and culture was extensive. He merely wondered how he was to get there. He would be completely relegated to his own devices. He was grateful that his knowledge of languages could enable future interactions. He was extremely fluent in most Castilian dialects and could even fumble through Portuguese if need be. If his plan were to come to fruition, he would need that knowledge. He felt the immediate dread of being completely alone.

Chapter 13

Patrice Huard had just completed vacuuming the living room of the family home at just past noon when she heard Duke bark outside. She was alone during the mid-day, as always. Husband Ben still managed the local lumber mill. Her attention was drawn to the view from the large picture window. A black SUV came rolling slowly down the long driveway of the acreage. She could hear the icy surface crunch beneath the tires of the car. The vehicle stopped fifty yards short of the end of the driveway and parked beside a clump of pine trees. A very muscular man in a dark jump suit exited the vehicle. His shaved head moved from side to side robotically. Only then did the man approach the house.

The man breached the steps of the porch adroitly. Duke growled from his position upon the porch, but did not approach, as the man shot a glare at the family dog. The man succeeded with one knock upon the door before Patrice Huard answered. She opened the oaken door, and then the screen door. She smiled at the large man in the strange outfit and said, "Can I help you?"

The man smiled, albeit coldly, and answered, "Yes ma'am. Is this the Huard residence?"

Patrice Huard answered, "Why yes, it surely is."

The man said, "Wonderful, ma'am. I am a friend of your son Gordon. Ma'am, I'm worried about him. May I come in and explain?"

Patrice Huard said, "Oh my goodness. Why, of course. Do come in."

Duke growled yet again from the porch, and Patrice Huard called out, "Oh, shush, you."

She seated the visitor upon the family couch and asked him if he would like coffee. The man politely acknowledged a desire for coffee — black, no sugar. Patrice asked him, "I'm sorry, I did not catch your name."

The man answered, "Brown. Robb Brown."

Patrice excused herself toward the kitchen and commented as she walked, "I sure don't remember my son ever mentioning a friend named Robb Brown." She then asked over her shoulder, "How does my son know you?"

The man called out, "We work together at the university." Patrice Huard immediately thought to herself that she had never seen a college professor dressed as was this man.

Mrs. Huard returned momentarily with a steaming cup of coffee, complete with a saucer and napkin. Mr. Brown thanked her. He was a very polite man. She seated herself at the recliner, at the entrance to the kitchen and hallway.

Mr. Brown explained to her that he had read in papers that Gordon's clothing had washed up on the shores of a Pittsburgh river, as reported to police. But that the clothing had been tied together. Nobody had ever been located. Mrs. Huard clasped her hand over her face in deep concern.

Patrice Huard asked, "Oh, so you are with the police?"

The man smiled and said, "Something like that."

The man then stopped smiling and leaned forward. He said, "So, ma'am, when is the last time you saw your son?"

Patrice Huard answered, "It has been years, young man."

The man countered, "I doubt that."

Patrice Huard responded, "I'd like to see your badge, sir."

The man rose and smiled, placing Gortex gloves upon his hands, and said, "Then you won't mind if I search your house, will you?"

Patrice Huard answered, "I surely will."

The man smiled at her and wrapped a half bicycle chain into his fists. He then said to Patrice, "I'll try not to make too big of a bloody mess in your lovely little house, ma'am." He took one step toward his prey. Patrice Huard remained seated in her reclining chair, frozen. Her attacker paused momentarily and smiled wickedly. He stated, "This will be too easy."

A half second later, Mrs. Huard reached quickly beyond the hallway wall. She deftly retrieved a shotgun. Her movement was rapid and fluid, and caught her attacker by momentary surprise. The barrel of the shotgun arose toward the eyes of the man. He hesitated as she chambered a round into the magazine in one smooth motion, with a loud metallic clang.

Patrice Huard remained seated in her recliner. The barrel of her shotgun followed every slight movement of the standing man's head. It was she that then smiled widely, as she said "Mister, do you take me for a fool? Nobody comes down a West Virginia back woods driveway without being seen." The assassin pondered an attack, but the bore of the shotgun looked like a cannon from his angle. And the woman holding the shotgun clearly had knowledge in the use of it.

Patrice Huard said to the man in a determined voice, only slightly above a growl, "The only thing saving your life is one thing — you are looking for my boy. So you haven't hurt him. But you would like to." She lowered the barrel of the shotgun to the groin of the standing man. She said, "Mister, if I weren't a Christian woman I would be changin' you from a rooster to a hen with one pull of my finger." She rose smoothly from her recliner, almost levitating. Adrenaline was serving her well. She returned the shotgun barrel sights to the head of "Mr. Brown."

Patrice Huard backed the intruder out of the living room door, down the porch steps, and into the driveway. Her aim never wavered. The man jogged toward his waiting vehicle, almost too cocky to run. As he neared his car, Duke approached from the side. The dog tore into the intruder's left Achilles with a ferocious growl. The man began to retrieve a firearm from a side jumpsuit pocket. A shotgun blast immediately followed. The intruder could hear the passing pellets like the buzz of bees, and saw the windshield of his vehicle explode into shards. He shook the large snarling dog from his leg and entered his vehicle. Blood drops could be seen upon the ice.

The intruder drove away rapidly, the SUV sliding laterally upon the ice.

Patrice Huard shouted out at the fleeing vehicle, "You're lucky my husband wasn't home!"

The vehicle was immediately out of sight. She summoned the dog, and petted him vigorously, and said, "I'm so glad you didn't shush." She began to tremble uncontrollably, and retreated within her home.

Chapter 14

Two weeks had passed since the initial gathering of dignitaries within NSA confines. Senator McLean and Director Portworth had conferred repeatedly during such time, both by phone and in person. They wrestled with how to proceed in deciphering the limitless wealth of information that appeared to be wielded by the HYDRA system. The system had been sealed to all personnel during the two weeks, exclusive of the agency director himself. The Senator was unaware that the Director had availed himself the system to a certain extent during such time. But the savvy politician immediately noted a change in the man with whom he had chosen to collaborate. The NSA Director was more patient and pensive.

The Senator and Director cancelled earlier plans to expand access to the system by more invitees. Instead, it was decided that they should minimize further access indefinitely. The impact and ramifications of what they were learning was proving to be shockingly explosive. They concluded that only those with a specific knowledge base and vested interest in a given "chapter" of information would sit in on future HYDRA sessions. Ultimately, truncated and limited outlines of the depth of available information had been gleaned jointly by Portworth and McLean in an exhaustive 20 hour segment with the system. They did not know the extent or means of the information available, but they were confident that it was nearly infinite.

The first two parties invited back to the table were the Imam Zaid Abdul-Rahman and Cardinal Antonin Napolitano. At this gathering, Director Portworth deferred the role of moderator to Senator McLean. McLean, ever coiffed in an expensive suit, loosened his blue silk tie only slightly. McLean bowed to the two holy men and said, "To you two great men I bid welcome. It is my regret that we have made you wait so long for our invitation to return. Yet, we had much to ponder. We are venturing into uncharted territory. In our date with destiny, we hope to advance carefully and with reverence."

McLean extended his hands outward before the two men and said, "Gentlemen would you please put on your headsets. I believe we are in for an adventure." Director Portworth whispered into the ear of the silent attending console technician, and a nonpareil journey soon began.

Within a minute, a date appeared upon a computer screen. The date read March 11, 638 A.D. The purported site of the spoken words to follow was listed as the Cave of Herra. The location was a mountain retreat of profound solitude, within walking distance of Mecca. HYDRA, it would seem, could also narrate the information it spilled forth. A conversation between two men flowed into the headsets, almost melodious in nature, yet foreign in dialect. Nonetheless, the words spilled forth from each respective conversant eloquently and passionately.

The Cardinal appeared to be perplexed at first. He was almost disoriented as he searched his memory for recognition of what he beheld. Three feet to his left Imam Rahman prostrated himself upon the carpeted floor. The Imam began impassioned prayers. He began bowing animatedly. Tears ran freely down his face. It quickly became apparent to the Cardinal upon whom the two holy men were retroactively eavesdropping.

Portworth turned to the Imam and asked, "Can you explain what exactly it is that we are witnessing?" The Imam finished a prayer and turned to his hosts. He answered somberly, "Abu al-Quasim Muhammad Ibn Abd Allah Ibn Abd al.Mutallib Ibn Hashim." Portworth and the Senator looked more confused. McLean began to speak. He was interrupted by the Cardinal. The Cardinal said gently, "Gentlemen, we are privy to a very secret meeting between the Prophet Muhammad and Pope Honorius I, the Monotheist." The two holy men looked at one another and shook their heads with incredulity. They joined trembling hands for reassurance. Even the two weeks' distancing from the experience did not diminish their senses of awe with additional revelations.

The Imam offered to provide translation for the Senator and Director. He knew that his friend, Cardinal Napolitano, spoke fluent Arabic. The technician interrupted, "Sir, that is not necessary, the HYDRA can translate many languages into captioning or vocalized versions." The witnessing of history thereby continued…

The aging Pope had travelled a great distance in secret. He endeavored to meet with the leader of a newer emerging religion. In the Pope's final months of life he desperately sought to unify the world's three existing theist beliefs into one diverse, but unified faith. The conflicting natures of Judaism, Christianity, and the newer Islam, created an immeasurable sense of dread for the Pope. He was convinced that factionalized religions would lead to endless strife. He was certain that centuries of war and hatred would follow. He felt that the depth of hatred could someday end mankind.

Similarly, Muhammad had sent word that he passionately desired a meeting with the Pope. It was clear that he held great respect for the peaceful leader of the Catholic Church. He related to the Pope that he was aware that his guest lacked a plenitude of remaining life to live. Muhammad felt it was vital and prudent to relate a story to the Pope. The story had been passed down from his grandfather's grandfather's grandfather. It was only now that he felt a leader of the Christian church would accept his truths devoid of the need for instant retaliation.

Muhammad began a lengthy oration, "I am the descendent of many, many generations of caretakers of man. For centuries we Hashimites have been honored to provide life- saving food, water, and other necessities to peoples from across the world. They were outsiders who dared to cross this unforgiving desert, in search of spiritual enlightenment. We opened our arms to all of them. It was right."

The Imam and Cardinal continued to clasp hands, transfixed with what they were hearing.

The ancient voice continued, "Even during the time of your enemies, the Romans, we were largely free to traverse the landscape in loving support of all whom arrived. It was thus that a great young man by the name of Haashim found himself to be present at a place and time of great importance to your church, and forever affect your destiny…"

The genius that was programmed into the HYDRA system immediately re-calibrated. The system was actually *listening* to the spoken words. The technician typed words of guidance for the extraordinary artificial intelligence. The system turned the historic pages to the beginning of yet another "chapter," almost as if a time machine. The noted time frame dated another 600 years back in world history. Yet, contents of the previous conversation in the cave were displayed in captions upon one of the many computer monitors. HYDRA was somehow explaining what was being related. It was as if the time travelers in the room were witnessing two times simultaneously.

Suddenly, the words that spilled forth again nearly overwhelmed the Cardinal. A story of actual events began to unfold. Soon the Cardinal felt he was truly present at the events in question. The experience was shared by his attendant peers. The trip was in time was extraordinarily visceral…

It was nine o'clock in the morning. The day of the week was Friday. Upon a cross outside of the Mount of Olives Israel hung a condemned man. It was intended that the man would suffer for days. He was not alone upon a cross, as others whom had been labeled criminals accompanied him. By early afternoon, Roman soldiers approached. As was customary, the soldiers had been directed to break the legs of the occupants of the crosses. The soldiers wielded large wooden mallets. They broke the legs of a purported thief into mere shards. The man cried out in pain and collapsed from the agony. Yet, the man lived, as was intended. But when the soldiers soon approached the man doomed by Pilate, they found him to be already dead. They had little knowledge why this man had attracted such rejection and hatred. They cared even less. They had earlier smiled to one another as the dying man displayed profound sorrow at the advent of his death. They had paid no attention to his labored final words. He was now only a body to be dealt with.

When word travelled to Pilate that the man had prematurely died, he was incensed. He had ordered the crucifixion of the defiant man in order to appease the crowds of bickering Jews. It was intended that the man would die a slow and painful death over several days. He would then hang upon the cross beyond his death, as a symbol of appeasement to the crowds, and testament to Pilate's breadth of power. Now, Pilate would have to make arrangements for the treatment of the body. The body could not hang upon the cross into the following day. The following day, a Saturday, would be the beginning of Sabbath. Pilate did not desire the wrath of the Jews for offending them with such a decaying public distraction during Sabbath. The disciples had fled the site of the crucifixion. Three poor women from Galilee, all bearing the name of Mary, lacked the means to bury the man known as Christ. They withdrew to the background.

A wealthy man by the name of Joseph emerged in the square. The traveler from Arimathea displayed profound grief at the crucifixion of the Christ. He hurried to the location of Pilate and begged for authority over the body. He and the women were desperate to bury the man. They openly quoted gospel about their holy obligations.

Joseph was allowed by Pilate to attend to the body. But Pilate was angry and menacing. Joseph feared for his own life. He was soon joined by a teacher from Israel by the name of Nicodemus, and the two carried away the Christ. They anointed the body with a heavy amount of spices in order to cover the stench of death. The women assisted. They wrapped each limb of Christ, and then his entire body, in quality linens. A special linen cloth known as the Sudarium was donned about the head.

While others who had been crucified were to be buried in cheap graves, Pilate afforded Christ a burial of the wealthy. A modicum of respect was clearly evident. The body was thereby taken to the Garden Tomb in a nearby hillside. A massive stone at the door of a vast cave was rolled away, and the body was placed with reverence within the chamber. The mother of Christ wept openly as she departed the cave.

Over the span of three days, several mourners arrived at the mouth of the cave. Yet, none entered the tomb. Two centurions stood guard on the hillside across from the site, awaiting further orders from Pilate. They had heard that mass disturbances within the nearby city had resulted from the crucifixion of the man whose body they now guarded. The resultant earth tremors had brought greater unease to the Romans. Pilate, it was known, was growing restless. Rumor travelled rapidly throughout the region that Pilate was re-considering the honorable burial of Christ. Some claimed that he would soon order the removal of the body. Further, that he would order the desecration of the body by having it dragged behind a donkey throughout the city streets. He would prove Christ to be merely human, and nothing more. An imminent rebellion could thereby be quickly stymied, without the need for further violence.

A young man by the name of Haashim was present in town when he heard widespread talk of the purported planned atrocities. He was obtaining food, water, and silks in the markets. He was loading the goods into a mule-drawn cart. Haashim and his family were well known visitors to the townspeople. They were admired for their humanitarian efforts to provide food, water, or whatever sustenance the needy required. Often the family's efforts focused upon desperate pilgrims, seeking to cross the brutal desert sands that the family called home. They were held in equally high regard by Roman soldiers, whom also often benefited from the kindness and generosity of the family. Haashim drew little notice from the Centurians. He was twenty years of age, smallish, thin, and agile. He quickly finished acquiring his goods and exited the town.

Within an hour, Haashim met with his family at a tented home-site at the desert's edge. He excitedly decried the travesty of the impending treatment of the crucified Christ. His family held great respect for the man known as the teacher. While they had never been in his audience, they knew of him from others. It was believed that the Christ was a great prophet, and worthy of profound reverence. They could not bear the thought of demeaning the prophet in the dirty streets of the township. They developed a hastily conceived plan to thwart the cruel plans of the powerful Pontius Pilate. Young Haashim was dispatched immediately toward the mount, with the donkey and cluttered cart. His task would entail risking the deadly ire of Pilate, were their plan to be uncovered.

By nightfall, Haashim arrived at the foot of the Garden Tomb. He feigned profound grieving at the entrance to the cave. He was watched by four centurions upon the nearby hillside. The number of guards had doubled from that previously reported. It appeared that Pilate had plans for them. The courageous young man continued walking around the grounds of the holy site, seemingly deep in prayer. All the while he was evaluating all aspects of approach and escape from the cave in question. Haashim bade thanks to his God for the extensive knowledge that he possessed of the hillsides. He knew what he must do. He would rest for part of the night.

In the very early morning, as the darkness began to abate slightly, Haashim arose from a hidden position against a fig tree at a proximate hillside. He had dozed occasionally. He concealed a cart and mule nearby, as best he could. He pulled out and examined six small candles that he had protected in a large carrying pouch. Haashim sprinted to a nearby boulder and braced himself against a rocky wall. With great difficulty he used his legs to slowly move a large boulder a mere seven inches. He struck a flint and alighted one of his candles. A minute opening into a dark tunnel then revealed itself. He glanced behind himself and saw no one. The young man deftly contorted his head into the opening. The rest of his body followed easily, almost reptilian. He was extraordinarily flexible. He managed to move the boulder nearly back to the original position to conceal his entry.

Haashim entered a portal into a vast series of fissures in the mountainside. He had explored the cavernous labyrinth since he was a young child. He had always hidden the entrance. His secret caves of adventure had always appeared to go undiscovered by others. In reality, only a smallish adult of profound dexterity and strength could hope to maneuver within the caverns. Only a wise such adult would not become forever lost.

The young man's candle provided scant illumination within the crawl spaces. Yet he required little lighting to find his way. His extraordinary memory served him well. The crawling upon stone made his knees ache, but he was accustomed to such sensation. Whereas he would usually explore the caverns cautiously and slowly, he dared not hesitate this night. His left hand and arm thrust out in front of himself for propulsion, and his pumping legs followed loyally. At times he doused his candle and plowed forward with two arms through the darkness.

The air within the cave was exceptionally stifling. The heat was nearly as foreboding as the desert at midday. Yet there was even less breathable air. The dust and heat made his lungs burn, longing desperately for better sustenance. But the young man forged onward without hesitation. He had a great distance to travel for the next day.

Haashim had no idea how long he had been navigating the caverns when he finally reached his destination. Time always stood still in the caves. He moved a series of boulders in specific directions to enhance the approach to his goal. The task required considerable strength. He was then able to remarkably contort his body and gain access to another channel within the mountainside. He lit one candle off of the remainder of another and peered into a tiny opening. The extra brightness at first offended his eyes. They had long become accustomed to the darkness. As his pupils regained their functions, he saw a spacious enclosure. It was just as he had remembered. He peered through the opening to his left and saw nothing. He re-positioned, and turned his attention to the right side of the vault. There, lying peacefully upon the stone lay the enshrouded body of Jesus Christ of Nazareth.

Haashim sat his candles upon the inner ledge of the opening. He began to claw at the edges of the portal. He soon grabbed a large stone and began to break the shale barrier that he remembered he had long ago placed at the opening. Finally, with one last crash of the stone upon the surface, a large portion of rock crumbled before him. He crawled into the cave. One candle flickered and ended. He lighted yet another from the remaining candle. He had two remaining candles. He dusted himself off to the best of his ability and stood. He then bowed before the man who lay before him. He knew he was in the presence of greatness.

Haashim set about un-wrapping the bloodied body. He felt his heart race. A sense of panic befell him. He felt that he would soon be discovered were he not to hurriedly escape. Yet he managed to calm himself and un-wrapped the body gently, almost as if the man before him still lived. He neatly rolled the bloody cloth shrouds that enclosed the body of Christ and placed them upon the stone hearth, at the feet of the body. He then removed the woven Sudarium that embraced the face and placed it similarly. He was reverent of the holy wraps. But he had to seal the Christ in wraps of great utility for his journey.

The young man stared at the face of Christ in the candle light. He bowed and kissed the forehead of the great prophet and teacher. The face showed evidence of great pain and suffering. Yet the prophet appeared to possess a smile upon his lips at the time of death. Haashim knew he must make a hasty retreat from the room. Yet, he could not refrain from removing a large thorn from the brow of the prophet's face.

Haashim spread a colorful silk blanket beneath the body and gently lifted the man upon it with great effort. He hurriedly sewed the blanket about the body, from the feet upward. When he came to the face, he glanced one more time at the prophet. The face of the man was beautiful. He finished sewing the fine silk together. He then sought to sew the body with yet another, much less ornate blanket. The second sewn blanket was much stronger and more durable. Haashim was immensely grateful that the prophet's body was not overly heavy. While the prophet had once stood some six feet two inches in height, the effects of considerable fasting were evident. The young man had many narrow channels to navigate with the body.

The courageous young man removed the body from the cave, sliding the package through the opening. He carefully replaced rocky rubble within the entry portal and the cave was again sealed. He thought he heard excited voices coming from within the cave, but could not be sure. He could hear his own heartbeat and rapid breathing, as he contorted his body yet again through a channel and pulled his companion behind him.

The journey back through the labyrinth was exponentially more difficult than the previous efforts. Haashim lacked any lighting, as he needed the use of both hands. Only rarely did he use a candle to re-acquire his sense of direction. He perspired enormously from the heat and exertion. He dreamt of cool water. Once again the endless dust violated his lungs. But he pushed onward with immense purpose. His only regret was the irreverence he had to show toward the body that he dragged. Sometimes the body collided solidly against the floors of the caves. Haashim would mutter, "Forgive me, my lord."

Over an entire day had passed when Haashim finally reached the merciful end of his travails. He thankfully arrived at the boulder that concealed the entrance to the labyrinth. Breathing heavily, he sought to again move the barrier with his feet. He found that he was unable to move the boulder at all. He made a second attempt and was unsuccessful. He began to weep. He lay upon the body of Christ, completely exhausted and dejected. He knew then that he would fail in his efforts.

Summoning what little energy he still possessed, Haashim re-gathered his composure and made one last effort to free the entrance of the boulder. He was startled to feel the boulder move easily out of the entrance. He could not believe his newfound strength. He peered beyond the entrance and saw the early evening starry sky. He then saw the smiling face of his older brother Ahmad, peering into the cave and dusting off his hands. The largest and strongest of his many brothers, Ahmad was a blessed vision.

Ahmad quickly lifted his youngest brother from the cave. Together, the two brothers gently removed the

dusty blanketed body from the opening. Ahmad directed Haashim to place the body into Haashim's mule cart.
There, the blankets were cut apart with a knife. Ahmad
gasped at the spectacle of the great prophet before him.
He bowed quickly and then returned to the task at hand.

The two brothers completely treated the body with
an anointment of myrrh and aloe powder. The sub-
stances would serve to conceal the odors again beginning to pervade the body. As they did so, Ahmad said
to the brother, "My brave brother, much has happened
while you were on your journey. There is great anger
and turmoil in the towns. Word has travelled regarding
the disappearance of the great prophet. The Christians
are celebrating a miracle. And the Romans are seeking
to spill more blood at the hands of the thief of this body."

The two gingerly rolled the body of Christ within
a purple silk carpet of high quality — an adornment for
a king. They then rolled the body yet again into a large
Persian rug. The brothers lowered the concealed body
of Christ into the back of a second, larger cart, belonging to Ahmad. The cart was filled with spices, rolled
carpets, and barrels of water.

Ahmad provided his brother with a welcome blad-
der of water. He allowed the brother to empty half of
the container. He surveyed his brother's dusty, battered,
and bloodied appearance. Ahmad poured the remaining water upon a cloth and hurriedly cleaned his brother.
His appearance would otherwise attract attention too
soon. He tossed the former wrappings of Christ onto
Haashim's cart. He then retrieved a newly slaughtered
lamb from the bushes and tossed the carcass upon the
wrappings within the cart. Haashim did not question

his brother's intentions.

The cart belonging to Ahmad provided perfect concealment for the body of Christ within his cluttered and colorful cargo. The rolled and covered body would blend easily into the reams of carpets. And the many spices, purposely spilled within the cart, would further serve to conceal the odor of decaying flesh. Ahmad kissed his brother three times. He walked hurriedly from the cave with the cart that contained an extraordinary package. He looked backward at his brother and stated, "God be with you." He was then gone into the growing darkness.

Haashim gathered his cart and ventured toward the town. The water had brought him a resurgence in strength and spirits. The sight of his beloved brother had further proven inspirational. Above all, the knowledge that he was honoring a great holy man brought him strength and a sense of purpose.

Within two hours, Haashim was back in the middle of the town. A great tumultuous sight was evident, just as his brother had reported. There were jubilant celebrations in the streets. There were reverent prayer gatherings within nearby halls. And everywhere he could see there was the presence of the Roman soldiers. Just as his family had surmised, the Romans initially sought to apprehend the grave-robbers throughout the inner city. Soldiers could be seen turning over produce tables, confronting all passersby, and interrupting the prayer sessions within structures.

Haashim made no efforts to evade the soldiers, as he continued forward into the center of the city. He was soon confronted by two angry centurions. They demanded to search his cart. The young man readily agreed to the search and acted ignorant of the causes of local turmoil. Food stuffs and water were thrown about in the cart without concern for damage. The first of the soldiers was prepared to end the search when another spoke. The soldier raised a finger into the air and displayed the dried blood upon such. He spoke, "What have we here, young traveler?"

Haashim replied, "The site of a messy slaughter my lord." He grabbed a lamb carcass from within the cart and held it in his arms. Blood dripped from the carcass. Haashim said to the inquiring soldier, "Now that you have trashed my goods, would you kindly make a meal of this for you and your friends?" Haasshim thought to himself how grateful he was for the clever placement of the lamb by his brother.

The soldier turned away from the young man and waved his hand. He muttered, "I do not prefer lamb." The soldiers walked away.

Haashim continued throughout the town through the night, cleverly enticing the attention of the Roman soldiers. Even those soldiers who knew him had their orders. All the while, he was hopeful that his brother was making a hasty escape in the countryside, gaining distance from the angry city…

Chapter 15

The Cardinal Napolitano and Imam Rahman continued to witness the biblical revelations of epic proportion wordlessly. They were stunned, yet intrigued. Senator McLean and Director Portworth were only slightly less astounded. Time seemed to stand still as the stories unfolded about them. They continued to listen…

Ahmad continued his escape southward and away from the city throughout the night. He was surprised and grateful to have evaded detection. He saw no other persons along a remote countryside trail. His thoughts turned to his young brother. Amazed at the courage that the young man had always displayed, he was nonetheless worried about him. He knew that Haashim would deliberately invite confrontation from the Romans as a diversion. Ahmad knew that, while *he* was considered the strongest of the family, it was Haashim whom possessed unrivaled outer and inner power. He was very proud of his brother.

Ahmad travelled freely until sunrise. He quickly lost the benefit of concealment with the arrival of daylight. Soon, the countryside was filled with human activity. Traders passed by with horse and mule-drawn carts. They strode toward the city to make their regular Wednesday morning exchanges. Horses carrying harried soldiers pounded past him, the hooves echoing eerily into the hills. He bowed reverently toward each passing soldier and prayed they did not stop. None did stop, save for one familiar Centurian. The soldier leaned downward toward Ahmad and smiled. He then said,

"My friend, this is not a time to be travelling. There will be blood spilled at the close of this day. Ensure that it is not yours." Ahmad bowed and nodded.

Ahmad soon deviated from the commonly travelled routes southward for another hour, uncontested. He was alone in the sands. Vast empty stretches of level land spanned behind him. He felt a sense of reassurance knowing that he would see any approaching party far in advance. There would be no reason for others to join him in the area. He was truly nowhere. The nearby Nahr al-Urdun river could be heard in the distance. The powerful waters were at high levels during this time of the year.

Within the hour, Ahmad suddenly heard the ominous pounding sounds of horses, several miles behind him. He had little doubt as to the source of such sounds. He knew there could be only one reason for the soldiers to follow his tracks. He turned toward the cloaked body in his cart and stated, "If you are the God, as many have prophesized, you will not sleep in Roman hands this day."

Ahmad sprinted with his mule and cart toward the sounds of the river. The mule balked, but trotted onward. The sounds of the pounding horses drew louder. Within minutes he reached the shores of the river. He was completely isolated. The river waters were far too high to cross and there was no bridge to enable escape. He was trapped. He guided his mule downstream and around a slight curve. The river widened and flowed more slowly. Ahmad breathed laboriously. The horsebeats grew seemingly deafening upstream. He had lost all hope.

"Brother, I am here." Ahmad was startled by the familiar voice. He thought for a moment that he was hearing a verbal mirage. But he saw his brother Haashim below him, upon a small barge that was concealed in the reeds. It was as pre-planned. Haashim was gesturing to him to hurry down to the water. Ahmad lifted the sacred body easily from his cart and cradled it, as he ran to the river's edge. He placed the body of the prophet upon the barge gently.

The sounds of screaming soldiers could be heard nearby. There was no time for contact between the two brothers. Using a long pole, Haashim merely guided his barge into the river's current and stared hopefully toward his brother. Ahmad called out in a muted voice toward the body of Christ, "The very river in which you were once baptized will now take you to your resting place." Haashim and his precious passenger quickly drifted out of sight.

Within moments, a team of soldiers arrived to confront Ahmad. He was found kneeling at the waters with a barrel as they approached. He was jerked from the riverside by the leader of the soldiers. They inquired as to his activities. Ahmad politely pointed-out that he was doing as his family had done for generations. He was filling water casks in order to supply pilgrims, and even soldiers, with the cold refreshing waters of the River Jordan.

The technician typed into HYDRA and returned the listeners to the conversation between Honorius and Muhammad. Muhammad's oration continued…

113

"It is thus that your people and ours are forever inter-woven. We have kept the story secret for generations. The body of Christ has been concealed in a place of honor for six centuries. He lies next to the great man who rescued his body. I will take you to Jerusalem to show you the beautiful location of my family's resting place. It is where I shall be placed when my time comes."

The conversation between the two holy men ended with Honorius expressing his shock at the revelations bestowed upon him. He was deeply honored to have been entrusted with a secret of such enormity. He promised the huge resources at his disposal to one day build an extraordinary shrine to the resting place of noble people. He knew he would not live to see the day. But the Pope foretold of a massive marble dome that would one day celebrate the two holiest men in human history. One of the men had long ago taken a seat beside the father. The other was seated in front of him.

Director Portworth ordered the technician to end the HYDRA section. He and Senator McLean turned toward the Cardinal and Imam. McLean began to speak, but was interrupted by the Cardinal. The Cardinal's face was contorted in fury. He screamed, "This must stop. This must stop!" The Imam was equally furious and growled at the two men. He said, "You have no right to these conversations. No one does. Destroy this evil or it shall destroy us all!" The Imam and Cardinal stormed out of the room. The Senator followed, seeking the role of peace-keeper, to no avail whatsoever.

Within minutes the Senator returned to the room. He pointed at Portworth and merely said, "This must *not* stop. Knowing what extraordinary tales this is capable of relating, there are certain truths that I wish to hear above all. They are of a much more immediate nature. We have some phone calls to make. Sleep well tonight. We will spend a long day here tomorrow with invited guests."

Chapter 16

Portworth was exhausted. He ignored the advice of Senator McLean to enjoy a good night of sleep. It was nearly midnight when he arrived at his next meeting. A hasty two and a half hour drive brought him to Seattle. Another twenty minutes passed as a luxury boat carried Portworth across beautiful Lake Washington, to his destination at exclusive Mercer Island. The lake was calm, and a near full moon shone across the face of Mount Rainier to the south. Portworth was too tired to be impressed with the scenery.

Director Portworth regained some sense of energy as he witnessed a very unique means of entrance into a private residence. He had only once previously been afforded such entry. An advanced system of locks lowered the boat some twenty-five feet below the actual surface of Yarrow Point Bay. It was as if his host's ubiquitous power encompassed draining a huge lake. Portworth thought to himself, "Maybe he walks across the water to me next." He was too tired to chuckle. Within moments the boat was moored in a highly secure underground marina. Portworth felt as if he were a participant in a James Bond film.

As always occurred at such meetings, the NSA Director was greeted by highly armed and even more highly unfriendly sentries. The hosts of his meeting never lowered themselves to approach him in welcome. One of the two darkly clad men searched him and affixed a GPS locator with a micro camera to his lapel. He walked several hundred yards through intricate and lengthy corridors. The compound was believed to span some 45,000 square feet. He noted the obvious artwork of Leonardo DaVinci adorning the hallway walls. The Dead Sea Scrolls were illuminated conspicuously in a glass enclosure in a vestibule.

Portworth walked past another opening into additional ornate catacombs of obscene wealth. He saw a stone wheel on display in the middle of the room. A babbling stone brook, complete with salmon, curled around the display and drifted downhill gracefully. Engraved bronze captions indicated that the stone had origins in ancient Mesopotamia. The largest caption for the stone merely stated, "The beginning of technology."

Portworth thought to himself, "This guy has one hell of a home field advantage."

Minutes later Portworth was seated in front of the usual semi-circle of the world's elite. Unlike the home of Rosenweiler, no overt appearances of prowling armed guards could be seen outside enormous windows. Only an intricate computer board displayed on a back wall mirror gave indications of the extent of security. Former Secret Service Agents, lured away by quadrupled paychecks, were much more discrete.

Director Portworth was pleased to be seated in a much more luxurious chair on this occasion. Apparently, he thought, the owner of this home did not require an outward display of the caste system of which the group always reminded him.

"Mr. Portworth, it is so good of you to join us," said Joe Yeats. It was readily apparent that Yeats felt a greater sense of comfort in his own extraordinary home. Yeats ignored protocols that usually entailed Rosenweiler taking a leadership role.

Portworth responded, "Sirs, this could not wait."

Yeats spoke yet again, "Apparently not. We are very busy men and had to hurriedly travel a great distance for this meeting. Mr. Portworth, we are quite tired tonight. I hope you have not wasted our time."

Portworth immediately thought to himself, "You selfish bastards. I'm sure you've slept much better than I have this week." But he smiled at his hosts demurely.

Portworth said, "I have no doubt you want to hear what I have to say. I have had occasion to spend countless hours with the system. By powers above my pay grade, I was not alone. As I previously related to you sirs, the system is highly functional. In fact, the massive project has exceeded our wildest expectations, both in applicability and simplicity of use."

The three men of the triad threw concerned stares at one another and continued to follow Portworth's words.

The Director continued, "Gentlemen, in short, it's all there. All of it. The world may soon hold no secrets."

Soudas stood from his chair and scratched his ample belly. Surprisingly, he did not speak in anger toward Portworth. He put his hands in the pockets of his white slacks, rocked on his heels, and thought for a moment. He then said to Portworth, "Mr. Portworth, please reassure us that you have a plan for keeping these secrets in their rightful places."

Portworth answered,"Mr. Soudas, I believe I do. It is my regret that I have not already destroyed the project. Yet I have not had a moment alone at the system to date to launch the torpedo. The Senator has restricted entry into the vault. (Portworth did not make eye contact while uttering his lies.) I am very confident that I will soon gain access under a ruse and render the system worthless. But the current timing brings another obstacle. Tomorrow, I fear the journey will be guided to chapters that involve you sirs."

Rosenweiler interjected, "And might I remind *you*, sir, that you are very much involved."

Portworth responded, "Not a day passes that I am not keenly aware of that fact, Mr. Rosenweiler. It is just that fact that should prove reassuring to you gentlemen. Very soon this multi-billion dollar project will go down in history as an elaborate fraud. The damage will be contained and no more lives need be lost." The triad again exchanged glances.

Soudas re-seated himself and smiled. The triad jointly clanked the crystal glasses of their respective drinks. Soudas said to Portworth and his peers, "And we all will become exponentially wealthier — even you, little man."

Chapter 17

A revised group of dignitaries was summoned for the next cloistered morning session of quasi time-travel, compliments of the NSA. Senator McLean was clearly taking the lead role in directing the current operations. It appeared to the Senator that Director Portworth had become increasingly taciturn since the first gathering of invitees. While Michael Portworth had proven to be respectful and indispensable for the Senator during the same time frame, his heart did not appear to be in his work. At one point during the week, McLean had even asked Portworth about his health. The Director looked haggard. Portworth stated that he was merely tired from losing sleep. Being privileged to information of epic proportions had taken a toll upon him. The Senator, on the other hand, appeared indefatigable. His energies, as always, were boundless. The two powerful men had conferred regularly regarding which individuals should next be invited to attend a session. They also debated what information was next to be examined.

Ultimately, there were four people seated at the HYDRA console for the next session. Harvard Professor Michael Bridgemann had been invited back. It had been determined that the famous historian should no longer be omitted from any further HYDRA events. His historical perspective and insight could prove invaluable. And someone needed to be entrusted with annotating human history in a learned manner. White House Chief of Staff Amanda Neal was similarly deemed a valuable participant. McLean and Portworth felt they were not prepared to involve the President to date. Neal would suffice for executive branch involvement until more was learned. She had proven that she could keep her mouth shut.

Senator McLean got directly to the point. He said, "Good morning and thank you for joining us. You are now somewhat familiar with what this incredible system may do for us. The Director and I have become additionally familiar with the capabilities of HYDRA. What we have been witness to is extraordinary. It is almost overwhelming to get your head around it. But the system is proving to be incredibly accurate and reliable. Today we have chosen a certain chapter in American history for a specific reason. I believe that reason will soon become plainly evident. No one here can possibly know what we will learn for certain. But we have little doubt, if previous experience is any indicator, that we will be gaining stunning clarity on what has actually transpired. What more can anyone ask for?" He then asked if there were any questions.

Amanda Neal asked, "What were we deprived of learning in the last session?" Despite her usual scowl, Neal looked attractive and sensual, as always, in an expensive maroon pant suit, complete with heels.

Portworth answered, "Ma'am, much of what we are beginning to focus upon is classified. Classified means just that. On a need-to-know basis. Let us just leave it at that. When the time is appropriate, all information will be shared."

Neal glared at Portworth and he stared back at her. Senator McLean caught something beyond contempt in their mutual stares. The politician's personal radar caught a conspicuous blip. Portworth turned to the technician and began to speak to him. He hesitated and placed his hand on the left shoulder of his silent subordinate. The Director smiled and said to the technician, "You know, I don't even know your name." It was the first outward display of humanity he had ever directed toward the technician.

The technician answered, "Really, sir, it doesn't matter. I'm nobody. Just your cable man." Portworth and McLean laughed heartily. The Director patted the technician on the back and sat down. Amanda Neal rolled her eyes and crossed her arms. Portworth and the still nameless technician entered their console key cards simultaneously. As always, the system sprang to life instantly. It was as if the HYDRA was awaiting human companionship eagerly.

Once again the technician entered a series of preplanned words and numbers into the system. And, once again, conversations and captioned information poured onto screens and into headphones in an extraordinarily real nature. The witnesses were transported in time…

Zurich, Switzerland. February 20, 1999

Four men were gathered in a living room of a very private presidential penthouse of the prestigious classic 1844 hotel known as the Baur al-Lac. The men were dining from an exquisite array of catered fares. They were enjoying a spectacular marina view out of expansive bullet-proof, sound-proof, and one-way windows. Hundreds of ultra-expensive yachts were coming and going in the distance. The area was alive with activities of the very wealthy. Each of the men was savoring glasses of $2500 per bottle champagne, inclusive of a man whom rarely drank alcohol. The conversation was jovial and amicable. It was almost as if the four men comprised a fraternity reunion.

But the four men had come from very diverse corners of the earth. An unidentified European shipping tycoon was one of the members. He had made billions of dollars by gaining a monopoly on virtually all Asian port markets. He had made profound inroads with politicians and the royalty in the region, whether legally or otherwise. But shipping took voluminous time and energies. He was in search of a better way. A second and oldest member of the group was a nameless American. He came from old money. The family had gained their mega-fortunes via earthly resources — namely iron, oil, and timber. His empire spanned some 127 subcompanies. He was very adept at avoiding taxes. But capitalizing upon American resources was beginning to prove a finite venture. He obsessed upon expanding his empire. The third of the friends came from the nouveau riche. Rising technology had afforded him membership into the world's elite. But even he knew that there were only so many cell phones and pieces of electronics one could sell. Three of the men were dressed in impeccable Italian suits that heralded their wealth and good taste.

A fourth man shared the champagne and fine foods with equal zeal. But he was attired much differently from his peers. He wore flowing white robes and a commensurate headdress. He sported a well-groomed beard that revealed a hint of grey. He was a Saudi national who now called Afghanistan home. He spoke perfect English that revealed his Oxford education. Unlike his ultra-wealthy peers, the Arab was barely a millionaire.

The conversation turned from friendly banter to very serious business.

The oldest of the four spoke to the Saudi. He said, "If you would like to elevate your status from a paltry few million to billionaire status we have a proposition for you."

The Arab sipped from his champagne and said, "You have my attention."

The oldest continued, "We need your power and influence in this region to light the fuse of a bomb. Not the kind of bomb you are accustomed to, but a series of events that make us all very, very wealthy men."

The Arab smirked and responded, "I thought you gentlemen already were very wealthy."

The youngest of the four interjected, "Enough is never enough. And you, above all, will see your fortunes grow."

The oldest leaned toward the Arab and said," My country abandoned you. They do the same with anyone, once their usefulness is exhausted. We believe that is very wrong. What we are offering you is a means of revenge. Revenge beyond your wildest imaginings. And we are willing to pay you for your pleasures."

The shipping magnate snapped his fingers at the youngest and drew an unappreciative glare from him. The youngest then carried a laptop computer across the lavish carpet. He placed the device on a coffee table in front of the Saudi and opened the screen. He typed a few characters into the laptop and the Arab stared at the display.

The European said to the Arab, "That is a one, followed by nine zeroes. One billion dollars, sir."

The youngest spoke to the Arab, "That has been placed in an off-shore account in the Cayman Islands. Totally undetectable to U.S. Intelligence forces. A touch of a keystroke at the conclusion of your modest efforts will ensure your name upon that account."

The Arab asked the group, "So let me be clear on this, gentlemen. You want me to orchestrate an attack upon your troops in the region for a billion dollars?"

The oldest spoke up, "Mr. Bin Laden, this shall not occur upon your soil."

Bin Laden looked into the eyes of each respected peer and answered, "My esteemed colleagues, you are cunning and ruthless. Those are traits that I greatly admire. I find your invitation as delicious as this caviar and champagne. I am listening."

The conversation spanned in great detail regarding the schemes of the three men. Bin Laden would recruit, train, and motivate a team of martyrs to do the unthinkable. The World Trade Center would crumble from his efforts — something many had failed to do. The singular symbol of world capitalism and American greed would be forever excoriated. Bin-Laden could not resist laughingly pointing out the irony of the proposal with the group — world greed would be attacked, while their personal greed would be rewarded. The group laughed and toasted themselves.

Bin-Laden said, "I will do as you ask on two conditions."

The oldest leaned forward and his smile disappeared. He said, "Name them."

Bin-Laden countered, "There will be four additional locations of my choice to strike. I think your Disneyland would prove a tantalizing target. And my fee shall be *two* billion dollars."

A deal was soon brokered. The agreement put into motion a catastrophic series of world events. The acts of terrorism, coupled with manipulative intelligence provided by well-placed informants to U.S. agencies, could create the pandemonium the three men desired. The conversation, albeit incomplete, seemed to indicate that war in the gulf could enable an incursion of invisible forces with greed, rather than national security, the prime motivation. But the documentable identity of the leaders of those forces, and the full extent of their plans, remained uncertain to the HYDRA listeners…

The technician froze the HYDRA system, at the demand of the Senator. McLean leaned upon the console. His face had lost all color. He appeared prepared to vomit. The Senator shook his head slowly and said, "All those lives." He finally righted himself and regained his composure. He then said, "I want to be in denial, but I know that what we are hearing and seeing is the truth." Even the usually callous Amanda Neal seemed to be moved. The Professor sat transfixed. Michael Portworth placed his hand on the Senator's shoulder in a comforting gesture. He said to the Senator, "Trent, I strongly recommend that we close this session for the day." Portworth flashed a glance at Amanda Neal. Again, the politician noted the glance.

McLean spoke loudly, "Not a damned chance. Let's

go."

The technician gave the system specific prompts and another meeting could be heard. The cited date was June 30, 1999. The meeting occurred outside of Hamburg Germany, in a nondescript hotel. Nineteen individuals packed two conjoined rooms at the invitation of Usama Bin-Laden. HYDRA translated the transcript instantaneously. Bin-Laden bid welcome to four great friends. An Egyptian national by the name of Mohamed Atta was singled out for recognition. Similarly, a Saudi National by the name of Marwan Al-Shehhi was greeted warmly. Ultimately, they were joined by Ramzi bin-al Shibh and Ziad Jarah, two Afghani al-Qaida leaders.

Bin-Laden summoned the four friends forward upon an improvised stage. He heralded them to the others as emblematic of the type of soldiers needed for his crusade against the west. He lauded the sacrifices made by two of the men. He explained that Al-Shehhi possessed a personal pilot's license and had once sought to become a personal pilot for oil sheiks. But he could no longer stomach his complicity with American greed. He had joined the cause and helped orchestrate the attack upon the U.S.S. Cole.

Bin-Laden turned to Al-Shehhi and asked if he had any words to the gathering about his successful attack. Al Shehhi responded, "It was not a success. The ship did not sink."

Part of the audience laughed nervously. Bin-Laden quieted them with a stare. He then spoke of how Mohammed Atta had devoted himself to gaining a pilot's license. He boasted of how the two pilots would experience incomparable success in the future. He spoke of how their training would prove invaluable in the crusade against the infidels. He then bowed to Ramzi bin-al Shibh and Ziad Jarah and smiled grandly, acknowledging their efforts in Afghanistan to fight the Russians. They, too, Bin-Laden explained, had made efforts to become future pilots, for a greater cause against a new enemy.

After great polished orations about sacrifice for the cause of Islam, Bin-Laden bowed again to his four co-conspirators and announced, "My four friends will make the ultimate sacrifice for our God. They and others will guide the missiles of our fury into the bellies of the disbelievers. Are there any among you who wish to join their cause?" The fifteen members of the audience all raised hands and shouted in unison. Their intentions to partake in the next step of a holy war reached a frenetic pitch. They sang praises to their God and treasured the moment.

Bin-Laden smiled inwardly as he announced to the group, "It is my great regret that God does not allow me to yet join you in this quest. I have more justice to inflict upon the infidels before I may see you in heaven." He neglected to make mention of two billion dollars lying on a Cayman Islands table for himself.

HYDRA displayed innumerable probable related conversations to be heard, spanning two plus subsequent years. The amount of topical information was seemingly insurmountable in scope. Senator McLean turned to his colleagues and asked, "Lady and gentlemen, where do we even begin to sort this?"

Professor Bridgemann interjected, "Might I suggest

we use the system to collate what we already know of the following events from what we clearly don't know? In other words, let us brush over the very obvious and follow these still unidentified individuals throughout subsequent dates and times, to the extent that the system may show linkage?"

The technician nodded and said, "Yeah. I get where you're going, Professor. HYDRA can annotate and link information beyond what the folks at the Library of Congress can ever dream of doing." He looked toward the Director and Senator sheepishly after speaking up.

The Director spoke up, "That is exactly what we will do. Let us hit the highlights today, and then move onward to a conclusion. We will fill in the gaps in subsequent days, weeks, or months in order to grasp the complexity of this conspiracy."

The group remained transfixed with the system for another ten hours, with only minimal breaks.

It was clear to the group that Bin-Laden was receiving ample funding from his corporate "sponsors" for orchestrating a concerted attack upon American icons. He searched for and obtained the assistance of Kuwaiti born Khalid Sheikh Mohammed, and paid him well. Mohammed possessed advance knowledge of the World Trade Center, after orchestrating an earlier nearly catastrophic bomb attack upon the buildings, using Ramzi Yousef. Mohammed was armed with an obsession with finishing the job, using more powerful explosives. Further, Mohammed was passionately seeking a way to destroy the CIA headquarters and other buildings via airliner attacks. Mohammed proved to be an invaluable asset to Bin-Laden.

Mohamed Atta and Marwan al-Shehhi were dispatched to the U.S. in June of 2000. They jointly entered accelerated pilot programs at Huffman Aviation in south Florida. Two additional pilots in training, named Ziad Jarrah and Hani Hanjour, were summoned soon thereafter from Mujahideen efforts in Afghanistan and Sudan. They enthusiastically accepted deployment to flight schools outside of San Diego. Shortly thereafter, a secret U.S. military intelligence operation, code named "Able Danger" reported to top military commanders that four al-Qaida pilots- in -training posed a threat to national security. But the message was quickly and inexplicably silenced.

Planning continued with the deployment of the remaining "warriors," secreted in the Maryland countryside. The additional members of the team were to be trained in forceful and effective physical skills, for use in subduing flight crews and passengers. And the funding continued to arrive, unchallenged, from an unknown location in Sudan…

HYDRA opted to focus upon a seemingly unrelated conversation between Oklahoma City F.B.I. agents and a former Iranian "Savak" Intelligence official whom had defected. But the technician trusted the artificial intelligence to find a link. It became apparent that the paid informant was highly valued for the time- proven quality and veracity of his information. He was known only as "the asset." The conversation was being held between the informant and F.BI. Special Agent Behraz Shareff and another agent identified by HYDRA only as "Tony." The captions indicated the date of the conversation to be

May 10, 2001.

The informant was heard to say, "Listen, I was recently contacted by two extremely credible sources. One of them is from Pakistan. The other, Afghanistan. They have often provided me vital inside information from formidable secretive terrorist cells. My sources were able to penetrate these cells. They have forwarded information to me that a leading member of a mujahideen group led by Usama Bin-Laden has ordered an imminent major attack upon certain targets in the U.S."

Agent "Tony" interrupted, "When and where?"

The asset answered, "Exact dates are unknown. But my sources believed the attack would occur very soon — probably in the next ninety days. As for where, my sources indicate major cities — believed to be one or more, including New York, Chicago, Washington D.C., and somewhere on the west coast — possibly Los Angeles, San Francisco, or Las Vegas."

Agent Shareff barked at the informant, "How?"

"Airplanes. Commercial airplanes."

The two agents could be heard sighing heavily.

The asset continued, "I can only offer a guess as to what that means. But I would expect their plans to include mass quantities of explosives hidden in the cargo holds. And that the planes would be set to explode over the populated cities. I would take these kamikaze plans very seriously, gentlemen." One of the agents whistled…

HYDRA again moved forward to another conversation, just as directed by the technician. Senator McLean nodded his approval. He seemed to be following each uttered word with a high level of comprehension. The dialogue was between the same three parties again, three months distant from the previous meeting.

The asset asked of the two agents, "What actions did you take with the intelligence I provided you three months ago? Did you relay it to your command?"

Agent "Tony" replied, "Affirmative. We sent it up the chain, all the way to the top."

The asset's anxiety could be heard in his voice. He asked, "What the hell is your agency doing about this? Because two days ago I again heard from those sources in Pakistan. He insisted that the attack was to be implemented soon. No more than two months, at the most!"

Agent Tony could be heard to say, "I hear ya, man. But this is way above our pay grade now. Plus, we can't personally deal with five cities and airplanes. In order to get more personnel on this, our high ups say we need a lot more specific information to go on than Bin Laden and a bunch of planes. We need a date to work with"

The asset screamed, "Specific information! You and I know that intelligence does not get any more specific than this!"

The agents countered in unison, "We know." They could be heard to sigh again.

The asset followed, "I have been seeking more specifics. My sources made vague references to tall buildings. Maybe the planes will explode over tall buildings. That is my educated guess. I pray to God your people are not ignoring this. I am forever amazed that your last administration refused to answer the Sudanese calls to turn over Bin-Laden. I heard that your President was too busy chasing skirts at the Master's Golf Tournament."

There was an awkward pause.

The asset continued, "I have done your job for a long time now. And I could always sense when blood was to be spilled. This is such a time."

The two agents became frustrated and dismissive. The conversation was ended shortly thereafter.

After the informant left the room the conversation between the two agents was brief.

Tony said to Shareff, "We're screwed."

Senator McLean directed the technician to navigate HYDRA rapidly past events of September 11, 2001. The awkward sounds of the system scanning through vast occurrences sounded like an old radio dial rapidly rolling through stations. Screams of terror emanating from the Trade Center was inadvertently broadcast and the four listeners were sickened from the sound. The technician said, "Sorry, folks. We're learning every day on this machine." The four fatigued attendants agreed to a half hour break in order to regain their composure.

An animated argument between Director Portworth and Senator McLean occurred in the shadows of the room. With superior authority, the Senator clearly won.

Chapter 18

Professor Gordon Huard was finally nearing the border of Chile and Peru. He knew that passage across South American borders was laughingly easy. There would be no scrutiny of his credentials in the name of Greg Southard, as had occurred with U.S. Customs. He opined that the Peruvians were not inordinately fearful of an influx of illegal immigrant Americans. His back ached mightily after driving the 2700 miles of winding highway in only four days. The tiny Citroen car was a loyal, but Spartan servant.

He stopped at a local filling station. Huard took eternal joy in watching the waiting attendants sprint to the car to take care of pumping and vehicle maintenance. He harbored only faint memories of real "service stations" in America during his childhood in West Virginia. He tipped each of the two young attendants 10 Chilean pesos each--nothing to him, but considerable for the locals. The young men bounded away with a "gracias" and raced one another to engage an arriving young woman motorist.

Huard exited his vehicle in order to stretch and use the facilities. He entered the adjoining marketeria and was again amazed at the beauty and cleanliness of a full-sized market with an adjoining lovely hotel. It was a far cry from seedy gas marts in the states. His needs fulfilled, Huard approached a pleasant young woman at the front counter and made efforts to purchase three more seafood empenadas. He was addicted to them. He made jovial small talk with the cashier while receiving his change. He looked down at the national newspaper,"El

Mercurio," on the counter. He was instantly devastated. The bold print headline decried the brutal torture and murder of Chile's most famous physics professor.

Professor Huard gathered his belongings and ran to his vehicle. He felt a strong desire to, literally, run away. He started his car and drove toward the highway yet again. He could barely see the roadway due to the flood of tears in his eyes. He tasted the salt.

Huard said to himself as he drove, "I am poison. I am a doomed man."

As he re-entered the highway, he attempted to gain some degree of composure. He now knew that his trail had been followed to the extent of another hemisphere. And that trail had led to the death of a dear friend. He could no longer dare contact anyone close to him. He could be their death chime. He also knew that his only hope of life was to find a sanctuary of extreme remoteness. He believed his original plan had entailed just the place.

Another three hours of driving brought the Professor to the Chile-Peru border. Unlike pleasant Chilean officials, the Peruvians were all business. Not a smile was cast his way, as the youngest of several border agents examined his vehicle and identification. Also unlike the Chileans, the Peruvian officials did not even offer to converse in English. Their Spanish was more staccato and less melodic than that of their neighbors to the south. But Huard had little trouble understanding them. Within mere minutes, the young agent waved the Professor across the border and into Peru. The young man was less than competent. He addressed Huard as Senor Luis-Perales, from the vehicle registration. This was despite Huard's obvious Anglo appearance and false identification in the name of Greg Southard. The Professor felt no impetus to correct the man.

Somehow, the mere fact that he had entered another country brought a modicum of relief to Huard. The beautiful and friendly country of Chile was now forever tainted. He had a choice of northward routes from his starting point. He could remain on Marginal de la Selva Norta (Highway 5, Jungle Road) or veer northwesterly on the Panamericana Norte. Each would take him toward his northern destination. His instincts told him to change course and drift toward the coast.

Before he placed his vehicle into gear, the Professor scanned the gathering of tourists and locals around him. None struck him as unduly menacing. He looked into his rear- view mirror. Behind him was a woman in a van with several children. She was trying to keep them contained and seat-belted for their continued trip. Huard was not concerned. The second vehicle to his rear was a black newer Audi product. The Audi contained a single adult male. He appeared to be European. Huard could not help but notice that the occupant of the vehicle did not take his eyes off of him for an instant. His chest suddenly felt as if he had been punched. He could taste his own bile.

Huard put his vehicle into gear and drove rapidly through the gravel parking area, causing dust to fly. The border officials took notice, but only watched him speed away onto the nearby highway. He entered moderate northbound traffic and hoped to disappear within the flow of vehicles. He checked his mirrors repeatedly for the first half hour and saw no glimpses of the Audi. He breathed a sigh of relief

The Professor only occasionally took notice of the spectacular beauty of southern coastal Peru during the next four hours of driving. There were rolling farm-lands and 400 year-old stone churches in profound abundance. Farmers were tending to crops. Some used expensive and modern equipment, while others still used Llamas to carry their wares. It was like a post card. Huard mostly noticed that the northern coastal air was much cooler than that of southern Chile. For a moment his renowned sense of humor returned. He thought to himself, "Now, their summer is our winter….do they invert their globes? Are we on top of the world or are they?" He finally seemed able to relax. He even enjoyed the cheerful local music on an A.M. station. He could not bring himself to listen to any news broadcasts.

Huard glanced into his rear-view mirror, as he had made a habit of doing for hours. He saw the black Audi approaching. He could see the driver pass numerous other vehicles until the Audi was positioned merely two cars behind him. He was certain that he was being fol-lowed. He saw an exit sign ahead indicating Supe Val-ley, Peru. He had not planned to deviate from his route. But he knew he must again flee.

Huard waited until the very last moment to veer abruptly to his right, and onto the Barranca Province exit. His tires squealed loudly in protest. His tiny ve-hicle leaned and slid out of control. He saw that he was about to roll off of a steep embankment and down into a ravine. He had no idea why he was compelled to gun the accelerator while in a full spin, but he made such a choice. It proved to be a propitious decision. As the passenger side tires lost traction on the gravel roadside, the driver's side rear tire took grip on remaining pavement. The tiny Citroen righted itself like a sailboat in a tempest. Huard began to speed eastward on a primitive roadway.

Huard heard vehicle horns blaring in the distance behind him, on the highway he had just abandoned. The sounds of squealing tires and chain-reaction collisions could be heard as well. Huard glanced over his left shoulder and could plainly see that his pursuer was hopelessly quagmired in a multi- car collision. He could see the fury in the face of his pursuer whom had lost his prey.

Huard's twisted sense of humor arose yet again. He spoke out-loud to himself, "Well, Gordito, maybe you can apply for a stunt driver job down here, with all of your newfound experience." The humor brought him mere moments of respite before a sense of dread returned. Ever the planner, his evasive actions had taken him out of his planned route. His recollection led him to believe that the roadway he now travelled had no outlets. He was driving 50 kilometers to a dead end.

Huard chose to continue driving the roadway nonetheless. He was at least creating distance between he and his pursuer. He was traveling steadily downward in elevation, as his popping ears revealed. Farmlands relented to a vast sandy desert. Forty-five minutes of driving passed. He was not at all alone upon the highway. In fact, the roadway wielded considerable traffic. Finally, the reason for the traffic was revealed. A sign indicated that in the distance lay "Chupacigarro Grande." Huard spoke aloud again, "Ah, yes, the ancient wonder of Caral."

Within twenty minutes Huard reached the end of the road. He entered a newly revitalized national park, celebrating the presence of a national treasure. An ancient 5,000 year-old city of Pyramids in the Peruvian desert stood before him like towering monoliths. The sight nearly took the breath away from the Professor. He remembered reading about the place in past studies. He had always wanted to visit the location. But he had never envisioned, in his wildest dreams, the current circumstances that brought him here. "Caral" was the most ancient city in all of the Americas. This was the site of the first Norte Chico civilization to have risen from the desert floor. Caral stood in eternal testament to the will and genius of the thousands of Incan former residents.

Huard shrugged his shoulders and stepped out of his dusty vehicle. He knew not what else he could do. In front of the Professor lay a vast maze of towering pyramids that would rival their Egyptian counterparts, at the very least. He stretched and looked at his surroundings. He was immersed in a crowd of tourists, all equally in awe of the spectacle before them. Cameras snapped all around him. They sounded like crickets on a warm Palo Alto evening. No one in the crowd even remotely evoked a feeling of dread.

Huard pondered his latest status. He was trapped in one of the most stunning sites in all of the world. And it was clear he had been detected. His carefully crafted plan had quickly been altered. He walked toward the pyramids, captured in his thoughts. There seemed few options. To drive back to the highway would bring him certain death. But would he remain at the park and await his persistent pursuers like captured sheep? He was tapped on the shoulder from behind and suddenly startled. He spun around, prepared to face his attacker. A pleasant looking local woman stood smiling before him. She was surrounded by children. The woman said in heavily accented English, "You are the man in front of me in line at the border. Señor, can you take a picture of me and my kids?" Huard gained sudden inspiration. He decided that he would spend the day in hiding with the cordial woman and her children, while wandering within the vast expanses of the ruins. At the end of the day, he would pay the woman to smuggle him out of the park within her van.

Huard smiled and turned to the woman. He said in perfect Castilian, "Mucho gusto señora." He interacted with the woman and her active children throughout the day. In fact, he served as a surrogate docent for the woman as they wound throughout the ancient metropolis. The children were fascinated by the information he orated. He in turn learned that the mother was a widow from Cuzco. Her name was Gabriella Ortiz. She was a very attractive, albeit plump woman of some forty-five years. Mrs. Ortiz had lost her husband to cancer some 10 months ago and was trying to enjoy the day of summer vacation with her children. By the end of the day, she was delighted to accept the Professor as a passenger. But she would not entertain notions of payment for her kindness. She even advised her guest about whom to call the following day to attend to his "disabled" vehicle. The children were delighted to retain their newfound playmate for a while longer.

Huard felt uneasy having to lie to the delightful woman. But he knew his truths had to be concealed for the good of all whom he might encounter. As the sun began to approach the horizon, beyond the shimmering pyramids, they all endeavored to return to the van. Huard felt almost a sense of belonging with the wonderful and open Ortiz family. He could not help but see the similarities to his own fine family, so many thousands of miles away.

The sense of belonging evaporated in a moment. Arriving rapidly in the parking lot was a damaged black Audi. The driver sprung from the vehicle and immediately began visually sorting exiting tourists. Huard quickly excused himself from the perplexed Mrs. Ortiz and began retreating slowly. Within moments his pursuer took notice of his target.

Huard broke into a sprint, away from the parking lot and into the desert. He had no other remaining options. His reaction was primal — fight or flight. He had never been a fighter, but he knew he could run with the best of humanity. He glanced behind himself and saw his pursuer give chase in a full and athletic sprint. Huard bounded beyond a park ranger who called out in Spanish, "The park is closing!" He did not slow his gate.

Huard covered a mile of dusty desert ground in a mere five minutes. He paused at the steps of a towering pyramid. He leaned against the stone edifice and gasped for air. He turned and looked to his flank. The pursuer was nowhere to be seen. In a panic, Huard looked beyond in the distance to other ruins. There was no sign of humanity sans himself. He clutched to the facade of the pyramid as he attempted to circumnavigate the mammoth structure. As he rounded a far corner of the pyramid, he regained a visual upon the other man. He was a mere 50 yards away and nearing rapidly.

While grasping the stone wall, Huard felt a loose rock of softball size. He pried the rock from the wall. He thought of throwing the rock at his approaching menace, but knew the man would be armed — and highly trained. Huard climbed the parapet of the pyramid and propelled himself upon the stony steps. His pursuer was not far behind and deftly clearing the same wall. The Professor began climbing the steps. He did so rhythmically and rapidly. The years of marathons in the Sierra Nevada Mountains had proven priceless. Hundreds of steps passed beneath his feet on his ascent. His pursuer grew more distant.

Two thousand two hundred steps later, the Professor stood at the pinnacle of Caral's most prominent pyramid. A scant ten square feet of stony space was afforded to those whom succeeded in the climb. Three minutes later, Huard could hear the pursuer approaching from below. The man was breathing laboriously and coughing. The sounds of the approaching man grew nearer. Huard's heart raced. He heard the obvious sounds of a bullet being chambered into a firearm. He knew that he would soon die.

For a moment, Huard pondered leaping outward from the top of the great pyramid. At least he would have chosen his means of death. Instead, he instinctively chose to sit in a crouch, much like a tiger. He saw the hand of his pursuer breech the crest of the steps. A dark semi-automatic Glock handgun was in his grasp. A smiling face of his would-be killer then began to crest above the steps.

Huard looked at his right hand. He had no idea why he had retained possession of the rock. Without even thinking, he slammed the rock into the face of his pursuer. The impact made a sickening crushing sound like ice beneath a tire. The armed assassin stared at Huard in shock for a nano-second, and then tumbled back and downward upon the many steps. Huard was shocked by his own actions. They were purely instinctive. He looked down the steps and could see the pursuer, lying sprawled across them in an unnaturally contorted position. Huard stared for a moment at his rock. It was covered in thick and sticky blood, which covered his fingers as well. He slithered cautiously down twenty five steps to the position of the motionless man. He found him to be lying in a puddle of blood that was dripping down the steps beneath his head. The gun was nowhere to be seen. The man's eyes moved and directed themselves toward Huard.

Huard stood over the man and almost growled as he shouted, "Who do you work for? Who do you work for?"

The man's dark brown eyes seemed to have no pupils. He bore those eyes into Huard's. He answered in an obviously Italian accent, "I work for God." He then smiled and took his last breath.

Huard stood atop the steps and witnessed the sun descending to the west. The desert floor was as if on fire. Huard threw away the rock and heard it bounce off of the ancient stone steps. He screamed with all his might, "Why! Why!" His voice echoed off of the ruins. But no answer ever came.

Chapter 19

The fatigued but determined four witnesses to history re-convened in front of the HYDRA console. The technician had been directed to move beyond the parameters of the 9-11 attacks and to seek the truths of the actual genesis of such events. Director Portworth quickly interjected. He demanded that the HYDRA be calibrated so that the NSA Director's involvement during the given time parameters would be removed from the scenarios. He explained that some of his personal classified information was highly sensitive and might exceed the scope of current operations. Surprisingly, the Senator readily agreed. Amanda Neal and Senator McLean agreed that the focus should narrow upon what detailed information was provided to the White House following the attacks. It was hoped, all agreed, that the vaunted system could create greater clarity on detailed and complicated information. HYDRA did not disappoint...

October 14, 2001

An Iraqi informant identified only by the code name "Red" was involved in a heated discussion within C.I.A. headquarters. He could confirm the fact that Usama Bin- Laden had indeed orchestrated the heinous attacks upon American soil. He was said to be planning additional attacks from his camps inside Afghanistan. Red's information corroborated that of numerous other imbedded sources. U.S. Intelligence officials were certain of their prime suspect.

But the informant passionately desired to change

the focus of the group from Bin-Laden. He wished to stress that even greater threats to American interests were imminent. The informant was an authenticated defector from Iraq's Department of Weapons. He insisted that Saddam Hussein possessed both the capability and the desire to exterminate the majority of American military and civilian personnel present in the gulf.

High-ranking members of the C.I.A. were grilling the man as to the validity of his claims. Fear and frustration could be heard in their voices. Each time the informant was challenged, he provided consistent and dogmatic insistence of the truth.

The informant offered that he had overseen the production of over three hundred tons of ricin, staphylococcal enterotoxin B, botulinim toxn, saxitoxin, and numerous mycotoxins. He provided that Hussein had ordered the manufacture of such a variance of toxins so that western forces could not possibly conceive of ample antidotes. The informant explained that the weapons could be delivered in a variety of means — by missile, by aircraft, or merely by strategically positioned series of packages. The favored chemical weapon in Hussein's chemical arsenal was said to be Bacillus anthracis. The particular type of chemical agent had been manufactured inexpensively and easily. If utilized, the weapon would emit durable spores that would invade a respiratory system of its victims. Symptoms would initially resemble a large-scale outbreak of the flu. But, by the time a population would notice the mutation, lethal hemorrhaging of the lungs would begin. In less than a week, over 90% of those affected could be expected to die a brutal death.

The informant was grilled as to the location of those vast caches of chemical weapons. His questioners berated him as a liar — growling that satellite photos and intelligence reports showed that no such weapons of mass destruction stockpiles were in existence.

The informant glibly responded, "You Americans take us for fools. That is a deadly arrogance for which you've already paid dearly. Do your adversaries know the location of *your* chemical weaponry?"

An unknown official interrogated the source continually and said, "And how is it that you come to believe your President wishes to use these weapons upon American targets?

The informant nearly growled his response, "You Americans are fond of monikers for your acts of war. Our hateful President has such a term for his plans. It is called Adala Mumit Ajl, or... Lethal Justice."

The final question was launched at the informant by the C.I.A. Director. He said, "And why would the director of the man's weapons program come to the enemy and share this information?"

The informant answered angrily again, "Because I do not desire the retaliation your country would unleash upon my people. We would be your next Hiroshima!"

The information gleaned was fast-tracked to the White House.

American Intelligence was thorough and diligent in subsequent weeks of information gathering. The quantity and quality of clearly knowledgeable informants continued to come forward, much to the surprise of U.S. Intelligence officials. It appeared that attacks that would dwarf those of September 11 were undeniably imminent.

January 21, 2002

Another interrogation of high level importance was transpiring within the walls of C.I.A. headquarters. An additional informant was providing powerful intelligence to his handlers. Rafid Ahmed Alwan was the right-hand man of Hussein Kamel, the son-in-law of Saddam Hussein. As such, he had jointly functioned with Kamel as the chief developer of Iraq's "special weapons program." When Kamel and his family were ordered killed by Saddam for perceived disloyalty, it was Alwan who took the point. He was code-named "Cobalt" by C.I.A. officials.

Cobalt was dismissive of intense questioning regarding the alleged biological weapons plans and capabilities of Saddam. He merely shrugged and told his handlers, "That is a fact. We have had them for years." He then further alarmed U.S. Intelligence officials when he forewarned, "That is not the beginning of what we now wield for weapons."

Cobalt was pressed for verification of his claims. He offered that he could summon a first-hand source of his information, "For the right price."

Once again the secure lines of the White House were busy.

Within ten days, "Cobalt" was again an invited guest of the United States Government. This time he was inside the secure facilities of the Pentagon. Two ranking members of the Joint Chiefs of Staff were in attendance. They were accompanied by the United States Secretary of State. A considerable gathering of officials and Pentagon weapons experts had convened for the meeting. Cobalt had brought a friend. Rafid Ahmad Alwan al-Janabi had been paid handily for his appearance. He was quickly code named, "Curveball" and had the undivided attention of the gathering of U.S. officials. Curveball was an Iraqi national whom had recently defected. He was the chief engineer of the super- secret Iraqi special weapons program, under the direction of Mr. Alwan. Yet again, the stockpiles of biological weapons were verified with a scoff of triviality.

Curveball focused upon the specifics of Saddam's nuclear program. He advised that his department had gained ample supplies of lithium-6 from French sources. He opined that the French would sell the Mona Lisa for the right asking price. He offered that it was child's play to convert the lithium materials into uranium-238. He and his fellow engineers had managed to split the atoms of his materials to a weight of 236, thus gaining the extra neutron necessary for fission. They were able to capture the 14 MeV neutrons within lead. They had thereby created nuclear material.

Curveball continued. He asked if he had overwhelmed his audience with technical data. The Secretary of State sat upon a desk and chewed on a cigar. He nodded, and gestured with his hands, as he said, simply, "Go on."

Curveball explained that his team had managed to trap the 14 MeV neutrons into the pre-existing uranium. The resultant fission hence created the release of 180MeV of high-grade fission energy. He said the difficult part of the program had been assembling a super critical mass of fissile uranium capable of creating a fission event on a large enough scale to create subsequent fission events. He was speaking of a chain reaction.

The Secretary of State and generals stared at one another in bewilderment for a moment. But the Secretary did not overlook the nuclear engineers and weapons experts assembled, nodding agreement with the man's explanations. The Secretary and Generals called a brief cessation of the questioning. They met separately with the technical experts in another office for a mere fifteen minutes.

The Secretary and his entourage then returned, shook the hands of his informants, and thanked them. He directed a Marine Sergeant to show them out of the building. He waited until the informants were far down the corridor. The Secretary looked his peers each in the eyes. He grabbed his briefcase and cigar and strode out of the conference room, flanked by the two generals. He turned and said to the group, "Gentlemen, I'll be at the White House. We shall advise the President to go to war."

Chapter 20

The assembled four at HYDRA would soon learn more about Afghanistan than they had ever previously cared to know. But the sometimes dry information was vital to gaining a full understanding of the insidious conspiracy...

Contrary to a commonly held belief, the topography of Afghanistan was not devoid of natural beauty and a barren worthless waste land. In fact, the towering 15,000 foot Spin Ghar mountain range, spanning some one hundred miles of boundary between Pakistan and Afghanistan, held stunning beauty at times. Lush and verdant green valleys that would comparatively diminish those of Scotland spanned in the shadows of the range. Farmers raised wheat and barley, using livestock for horsepower, as they had done for centuries. Beautiful Greek and Buddhist shrines, known as "stupas" were ever present in those valleys. One thousand year-old great arches and minarets in homage to Allah rose above the floor of the villages. Moisture was known to rise from the basin of the Kabul River and become captured amid the mountain peaks. The effect created stunning foggy sunsets on summer nights from heights as tall as 15,600 feet. The shimmering views from the mountain tops rivaled those of Everest. But what lay beneath the massive peaks held a unique beauty all its own.

Scant few entities in the world were aware that the Spin Ghar Mountain Range was home to an estimated five plus trillion dollars in mineral wealth. The pre-Cambrian era of volcanic activity in the area had forged a shelf of enormous riches. The highlands in the north and northwest alone wielded inestimable caches of gold, iron, cobalt, and copper. Above all, endless veins of lithium were enormously abundant. The soft, silverish-white metal is a member of the alkali group. The substance possesses tremendous values for usefulness. Lithium is used to construct batteries, inclusive of those used in the space shuttle. The substance is also widely used for pharmaceutical applications. But the penultimate value was by far the greatest. Lithium was highly sought for the creation of nuclear energy.

Ironically, Afghanistan could easily emerge as one of the wealthiest nations on earth. Yet the region was relegated to extreme poverty. Endless wars of occupying factions had occurred since invasions by the Khan, followed by the Greeks, and ultimately succeeded by the Uzbeks. In modern times the controlling hoards of marauders were clearly the Taliban. Development of resources had never been a goal of invading hoards.

The only current rivals to the Taliban lay in the opium smugglers. A tenuous peace had held for years between the two parties, as the heavily armed drug suppliers controlled the "golden route" of opiates. The drug travelled across the mountains to the Pakistani shipping port of Karachi on the Arabian Sea coast. Powerful and wealthy Imams ensured that 87 per cent of the world's heroin "needs" were supported by these groups.

It was obvious why mining had never transpired in Afghanistan. Gentle villagers in the valleys and plains were dominated by the Taliban and al-Qaida, while the mountain ranges were relegated to the drug lords. Only the farmers, in the rare regions capable of sustaining crops, seemed largely impervious to invasion. And they remained inexorably mired in the horse and buggy era…

However, the assembled four at HYDRA soon learned that change had indeed arrived in March of 2003. War had arrived on Afghani soil. Hundreds of thousands of American, British, Polish, and other nationality troops invaded the country. One thousand pound "bunker buster" bombs crashed into mountain passes, leaving expansive moonscapes upon the topography. Rebel forces attempted to fight back, supported by Iranian monies and munitions. Even drug runners were scattered. The region was in turmoil. What little political leadership that did seek to emerge in the country was in mere dormancy. War soon rocked neighboring Iraq as well, causing further confusion within the region. Allied forces completed strafing Afghanistan, and eventually departed in vast numbers in order to bolster other forces in their mission to conquer Iraq. The scenario was a perfectly orchestrated diversion. All while Bin-Laden sat in a Zurich suite watching on television.

An invasion of another sort poured into Afghanistan during the pandemonium, without notice. Highly advanced tunneling mechanisms began to appear out of nowhere in the isolated reaches of the mountains. They bore no specific markings, but were clearly western in nature.

A meeting of parties privy to the secret operations was occurring outside of Kabul. The voices were muted. A very diverse set of attendees was present. And HYDRA broadcast the meeting as if it were live…

A voice of leadership spoke, "Captain, if this is to work we must have a very clear demarcation of responsibilities here. We must have your assurance of safe passage into and from these mountains."

The apparent "Captain" responded, "You have our guarantee, sir. Your convoys will be secure. We have sufficient active U.S. personnel willing to maintain perimeter control as a side job, and your extra people will be used to supplement our troops."

The leader said, "And, Imam, I must have your word that we will not come under fire by your rivals in those mountain passes."

A voice answered, "I live without fear in the Mand of Afghanistan. You will go unchallenged."

A second leader spoke toward obvious political figures present and said, "Minister Jalal, I will need total access to your ports in Pakistan and unchallenged egress to the Arabian Sea."

And again a response was evoked, "All is in place for shipping to follow, sir."

Before the conversations could be completed and narrated by the HYDRA system, Senator McLean exclaimed, "I'll be damned. Those sons of bitches." Seemingly, he alone had a very good idea whom he had just heard. The Senator calmed himself and let the narration continue. It became abundantly clear that the meeting was being held amongst corrupted military officials, regional politicians, and powerful drug lords in the area. The gathered four at HYDRA gasped as the names of the hosts of the meeting soon became undeniable to everyone. They were David Rosenweiler, Giorgio Soudas, and Joseph Yeats — the wealthiest men on earth.

Within moments, the stunned group was witness to a massive conspiratorial industrial enterprise. The four group members forged onward with their unique investigation. Their "time travel" took them to a juncture a mere month backward from the present date. It would seem the triad and their corporate lieutenants were very busy…

Rosenweiler, Soudas, and Yeats had been transported via military convoy far up into the base of the Spin Ghar Mountain range of Afghanistan. They arrived at a remote secret location a half hour thereafter, compliments of an U.S. Army Blackhawk helicopter ride. It would seem that the triad and their management teams could travel nearly unchallenged within the region. Military leaders had long ago become convinced by the previous Vice President's office, and by their own peers, of the legitimacy of the three men's efforts in the war zone. It was said that they were invaluable contributors to efforts by the Texelrod Company to maintain uninterrupted extraction of gulf oil, despite current hostilities. This was a national security priority.

The triad had arrived in order to gain a situation report on their current and most ambitious profit venture. A remote base of operations had been constructed at an abandoned canyon site, concealed by towering peaks on each side. The Ghoran River had long ago gone dry at the base camp site, some 11,000 feet above sea level. The hundreds of largely level acres of sandy sediment flooring provided a perfect location for an industrial complex.

Hundreds of construction workers were housed in basic, but functional dormitories. Personnel were hurrying to assigned tasks in considerable numbers. All of the construction workers believed they were working legitimate high- paying government jobs, and had no idea otherwise. The assemblage of buildings spanned outward from the center of operations like a star. Enormous banks of lights were just beginning to take effect, as the sun rapidly set in the mountains. The helicopter quickly sped away.

Joe Yeats said to the others, "Guys, are you sure this isn't the landing site for Close Encounters?" His colleagues looked at him perplexed. Rosenweiler noted that the complex had grown tremendously from their visit six months previously. The three businessmen were immediately greeted with handshakes by approaching company officials. They were handed hard hats and escorted into the "command center." They discovered that the building would never win any award for interior décor, but an advanced system of monitors and status boards had been erected. Experienced managers had a firm grasp of all aspects of the monumental industrial undertaking.

The company managers summoned a highly engaged lead foreman by the name of Jeff Murphy from his nearby responsibilities. The bear of a man angrily stomped into the building unaware that dignitaries were present. He was the stereotypical Irish construction foreman, complete with the overlap of belly, huge walrus mustache, and a voice that could be heard for miles. But, clearly, the man knew what he was doing. Undaunted, Murphy looked at the three standing men in $3,000 dollar suits and immediately quipped, "Shit, fellas, if I'd known you were comin' I would've put on my best jeans." He didn't bother to extend his greasy hands toward the "suits." The company management stared worriedly at their guests, but breathed easily when the three men chortled. Murphy was handed a laser pointer and encouraged to speak in-depth to their guests in a small conference room. Computerized maps and data were sprawled across the control room walls. Murphy began to explain, in an earthy but astutely detailed lecture, the scope of the project...

The triad was advised that operations were continuing 24 hours a day, 7 days a week. The men worked 6 days a week, 12 hours daily. They had been doing so for over a year. Two months ago the operation had succeeded in punching a 62 mile hole in the mountain range. A tunnel had been created for trucking products to Pakistan, unabated. The only interruptions to their operations had been occasional seismic events that are common in the area. It was pointed out that a few other quasi-seismic events had occurred when American "bunker buster" half-ton bombs had found targets in adjoining canyons. The reverberation was unsettling, but essentially harmless to their activities. An unexpected mountain aqua-duct had once been breached, causing a course deviation that had cost two weeks of time. And a few employees had not heeded warnings to remain within the complex. They had disappeared at the hands of the drug runners in the hills. Replacement workers had been quickly hired, without any efforts to dare venture outward in search of the "dumb bastards."

Murphy explained that, at present, sixteen 742 ton Obayashi 32 foot TBMs (tunnel boring machines) were drilling into the hardened granite of the mountains of Afghanistan. He said, "The Japs make the best freakin' drills by far, that's for sure." The machines spanned nearly the length of a football field and carried a team of engineers. They were like land-based crawling Trident submarines. The apparatus contained "support gear" inclusive of supply tanks, exhaust fans, electrical supplies, and massive conveyor belts.

The actual process of mineral excavation was occurring at the openings in the faces of the monsters. Various cutting tools on the noses of the machines were making varied degrees of inroads into the rock, dependent upon the type of rock present. The rock or minerals cut were being swallowed into the openings of the face of the machines via corkscrew types of conveyors, located directly behind the noses. The products were then being removed via the rear of the systems using additional conveyors, and stored temporarily within the resultant tunnels created. Dump trucks subsequently functioned to remove the contents to a base camp location where all materials were being identified, sorted, and prioritized for importance.

Foam was continually being added in order to condition the tunnel walls for cuttings so that undue heat would not be generated. Water and polymers, or bentonite sprays, were also being utilized to accelerate extraction. Murphy explained that the entire respective mechanisms were being propelled and guided by sixteen 25,000 ton hydraulic jacks attached to the perimeters of the machinery. A total team of six skilled engineers per

TBM were assigned, plus one foreman like Murphy, in order to guide the machinery. The teams were using state of the art positioning technologies that possessed an accuracy quotient to within three quarters of an inch.

Finally, Murphy said, "Hell, fellas, I'm gettin' tired of talkin'. You wanna come see it?" Yeats and Rosenweiler eagerly agreed. Soudas asked where he could get a drink. Managers attempted to answer, but were interrupted by Murphy. He said, "You can't get a freakin' drink around here, pal. Company rules."

Soudas retrieved a flask from inside his coat pocket and countered, "I *am* the company."

Rosenweiler and Yeats were driven away by the foreman on an improvised golf cart known as a "loci". Within ten minutes they were inside the most recently cut tunnel. The tunnel was cold and dusty, but very well lighted. A boring crew continued their work, indifferent to the arrival of dignitaries. They never turned to acknowledge their guests. Murphy screamed above the din of the machinery, explaining that the enormous cutterheads of the devices, known as the "blue noses" were turning at an exceptional pace for such a venture — 1.5 revolutions per minute. The bores were equipped with garnet cutters at the moment, and making ample progress. The two businessmen stared in awe of the operation they had financed.

Murphy then drove the two men outside the tunnel and back to the command center. He found Soudas in an already half intoxicated state, with embarrassed company sycophants attending to his every demand. Murphy ordered, rather than asked Soudas, to join his two other guests on the cart. He then drove them into a massive enclosed warehouse. AK-47 toting sentries stood on post around the facility in abundant numbers. Roving cameras were ever- present. Once again, the interior of the structure was illuminated as if it were noon.

As the men exited the cart, Murphy walked them across the concrete floor and over to the "sorting area." There he was greeted by another foreman. Murphy bellowed, "Jimmy, will you show these gentlemen what we have found in these hills?" Foreman Jim Sicilia was a thin and wiry Italian, with a mustache that paled next to that of Murphy. He answered, "Glad to, Murph." He walked his dignitaries over to six segregated vaults. Each vault was the size of a six-car garage. Sicilia entered a series of numbers into a keypad and applied his palm to a sensor. A yellow light flashed and a buzzer droned loudly. The door to a vault opened outward. Soudas soon began to whistle. Stacked by massive tons was high grade gold, shimmering in the light.

Sicilia explained to his guests the nature of contents in each successive vault. Iron, Copper, Cobalt, and many other minerals that were mined everywhere in the mountains. But he was most proud of the limitless supplies of priceless lithium.

Murphy laughed toward the guests and said, "Guys, tell the 1849 Gold Rush, you ain't seen nothin' yet."

Chapter 21

A sense of the present ultimately returned to the sequestered group within the NSA's facility. It became readily apparent that it was time for a lengthy recess after hours of grueling, sometimes tedious observations. As the conclusion of the session neared, well into the late evening, the group began to refer to themselves as the "HYDRA 4." It seemed that the members had grown closer via the journey they had undertaken. Even Ms. Neal had been prone to utter compliments to other members, as opinions were bandied about. The anger and shock remained with each member, with the realization that they had been witnesses to America's most explosive conspiracy.

The group, inclusive of the technician, began to gather papers, briefcases, and jackets. Most of the members were emotionally and physically drained. Senator McLean, of course, was the exception. Director Portworth grasped the elbow of the technician for a moment. He said, "Mr. No Name, could I impose upon you for just five more minutes of your time?"

The technician smiled and answered, "You're the boss."

Portworth released his grasp and replied, "That I am."

Senator McLean turned toward the two men and asked, "Gentlemen, is there a problem?"

Portworth answered, "Not at all, sir. Just housekeeping. I'll join you in the hallway in five. I promise."

The Senator smiled broadly and replied, "I'm the politician, Mike. Let *me* make the promises. Portworth could not help but notice that the little man still looked like he'd just arisen from a replenishing night of sleep. He suspected that the Senator had shaved during a break, as no shadow was in existence. He was a remarkable man. Portworth realized that he had grown increasingly fond of the man who clearly held such a deep love for country and commitment. Essentially, McLean was the antithesis of all that Michael Portworth had come to stand for. And that was increasingly saddling Portworth with regret.

Portworth re-seated himself at the console with the technician.

The technician asked, "What's up, Director?"

Portworth said, "I'm asking only five minutes of your time. A favor, if you will." He handed the technician a piece of paper with a series of chosen key words. He said, "I'm looking for someone. It is important to me. I know you can direct this machine in ways I cannot imagine. Any information would be tremendously appreciated. I would owe you forever."

The technician smiled crookedly and took a deep breath. He said, "I'll try."

Unlike during past sessions, the system struggled to find any indication of those particular uttered words. The five minutes were passing rapidly. Finally, the system uttered one garbled word attributed to the source Portworth sought — "Kaleena." The five minutes expired.

Frustrated, the Director thanked the technician, and the extraordinary day of listening came to an end.

The room that had become the group's new home

grew dark, as Portworth and the technician exited and set the complex alarms. Portworth rejoined the Senator, who was waiting patiently in the hallway. The others had been dismissed already, with instructions regarding future communications.

Portworth asked the Senator, "Well, what now?"

The sage Senator replied, "We continue down this path of information gathering until we have the entire picture. I want every fiber of this cancer identified. No loopholes. An iron-clad case. Then, and only then will we come forward, armed for bear. I want their heads, literally and figuratively. The whole world was deceived and used so that those jackals could slide in and pillage the fortunes. It's almost biblical. They *will* pay. Meanwhile, we have national policies to re-think." The former Florida Attorney General was in all of his element.

The elevator toward the terrestrial world far above took the usual five minutes. McLean explained that he would return to his home in Florida for a few days of contemplation and phone calls. He instructed Portworth to return to regular duties at NSA headquarters. All must appear to be regularly conducted business for the moment. The two would re-convene soon and ponder their options.

The two men finally reached the exit of the cavernous secret facility. The powerful Senate head of Intelligence merited a Secret Service agent to drive him. The Director of the NSA was merely afforded a black sedan, parked nearby. The Senator turned toward Portworth and looked him in the eye. The passion in the man's grey-blue eyes was evident. The Senator sat his briefcase upon the floor. He draped his suit jacket across it. He reached out his hand to the Director and said, "Mike, you have done a yeoman's job in recent days, under trying circumstances. You are a great American. God Bless." His grip was firm with resolve. The Director thought their contact was thereby ended. But the Senator hesitated yet again. The Senator suddenly grabbed Portworth in a warm hug. Portworth felt awkward, but deeply moved at the same time. The embrace finally ended, and the Senator looked him in the eyes. He said, "All those lives… Mike… do the right thing."

The Senator grabbed his briefcase, put on his suit jacket, and stepped out into the cold winter's night. The wind was blowing, as usual. He said to the Secret Service agent, "Home, James." He bounded towards his waiting vehicle, as the agent jogged to keep up. Shaking his head, Portworth watched the man being driven away. He realized that he had been in the presence of greatness. He further believed he knew the intent of the little man's advice.

Chapter 22

Tampa, Florida

Senator Trent McLean arrived at the doorstep of his modest 3,200 square foot wrap-around rambler. The lovely home was adjoining a beautiful private golf course. The Florida sunshine was a tremendously welcome sensation. He had spent the better part of two weeks either deep underground or on the frozen tumbleweed-laden dirt of Central Washington State. He was fearful that he had lost his youthful looking tan. The Secret Service agent handed the Senator his briefcase after taking a cursory look around the residence. The agent was a black man in his thirties by the name of James McElroy. He had the rugged look of a successful boxer. He said, "Senator, allow me to check the interior of the house for a moment."

The Senator answered, "Jimmy, not necessary. If I find any golf balls have penetrated the inner perimeter you'll be the first to know." He patted the agent on the back. He then grabbed a ten dollar bill and attempted to stuff the bill in the agent's jacket pocket.

Agent McElroy stifled a laugh and said, "Senator, you know tipping is not allowed in this establishment."

The Senator laughed heartily. He said, "Well, then, consider this bribing a law enforcement official. I need your vote."

Agent McElroy countered, "But, Senator, my residence is in Virginia."

The Senator laughed again and withdrew the bill form the agent's pocket. He said, "Disregard, Agent

McElroy." He again patted the agent on the back with a smile and said, "Thanks a bunch, Jimmy. I'm fine. Go home."

The agent said, "Yes sir," and drove away.

McLean disabled the alarm, turned the key of his home, and entered. He knew that his wife was out of town. She was undoubtedly enjoying mother-daughter day at Florida State University with their only daughter, a 17-year-old freshman. The Senator would be a bachelor for the weekend. Home, nonetheless, was a very welcome sight. McLean placed his briefcase in its usual place and hung his suit jacket in a hallway closet. He was amazed at how many expensive suits the closet wielded. He knew that when he someday retired his wardrobe would consist of golf shirts, golf pants, and golf shorts. He also knew that he would never totally retire from public service. His wife had often pointed out that fact. He loved the work too much.

He walked to his kitchen and retrieved a cold beer from the refrigerator. He removed his tie and held the icy bottle against his forehead. He spoke directly to the beer, "Hello there, beautiful. I missed you." McLean glanced through the back patio sliding doors of his home. He could see golfers attempting their second shots beyond the 9th tee. He recognized all of them, as usual. He smiled and waved and the golfers returned the greeting. Rather than exiting out onto the back patio, he seated himself in a family room leather recliner. He was suddenly very tired. Not long after he drained his beer, he dozed off.

When Trent McLean awakened, nearly an hour had passed. The effect of the one beer he had consumed created a commensurate immediate urge. He arose to address that urge by strolling down a hallway to the master bedroom. He could see that his wife Alice had already lain out his Monday suit for him on the bed. She had always referred to herself as his "guide-dog for the color-blind." It was her way of saying she loved him. It was good to be home.

McLean entered the bathroom. A hazard loomed beyond his recognition…

A common prank for teenaged youths is to create a concoction of cleaning chemicals within school or dormitory toilets that would eventually blend. A resultant explosion of the scope of an M-90 type of firecracker will thereby occur. Sometimes toilets will crack. Water will always rise from the toilet like a geyser. The prank is essentially harmless. But, were the chemistry to be slightly altered by the addition of aluminum hydrate, the new compound could prove problematic. The chemicals will remain forever harmlessly inert in the current state. However, the addition of a catalyst will alter the scenario. Many types of acids will excite the chemicals. Any tiny amount will suffice. Uric acid comprises such a substance. Thus, the introduction of urine into the compound could conceivably create a blast serious enough to cause injury. But a final step of adding rare and expensive radium to the rear compartment of a toilet will enable a chain-reaction blast of disastrous proportions.

Senator Trent McLean began the basic function of urination. He yawned drowsily. The uric acid mixed with the toilet bowl contents within mere moments.

The corresponding two-phased blast occurred in miliseconds. The impact tore through Trent McLean's body as if he had stepped on three land mines simultaneously. The master bedroom and portions of the rear hallway were leveled. There were scant few pieces of the Senator to later be found by members of the Bureau of Alcohol Tobacco and Firearms. A personally devastated Agent Jim McElroy would join in sifting the rubble. He would forever blame himself for not detecting an undetectable bomb.

Chapter 23

Nobel Laureate Professor Michael Bridgemann felt like the world's wealthiest man upon his return home to Cambridge, Massachusetts. He had learned more history in a few days than he had previously done in his entire life. Nonetheless, as an expert in ancient history, among other specialties, he wished he had been physically present during some of the other HYDRA sessions. He wished he could have witnessed first-hand the most recent revelations of epic religious events that were gleaned deep beneath Central Washington State soil. "Hell, he thought, anybody would wish to be privy to these extraordinary events." That said, he was grateful that his peers of the HYDRA 4 had graciously filled in gaps in the base of knowledge that he had possessed. He was obsessed with a return invitation to additional sessions with the amazing artificial intelligence controlled by the N.S.A. But he would have to be patient.

Bridgemann chose to find a sense of calm by immersing himself in his second great love — that of flying. He was thrilled to be in the cockpit of his Piper Cherokee twin prop aircraft. The airplane was his one self-indulgence after being awarded a small fortune by the Nobel Prize Foundation. The remainder of his bounty had been donated to Harvard University's scholarship fund. He had often claimed in the past that he would teach for free at his beloved university were that to be possible. In a way, that was indeed what he was now doing. He loved evening flights. He was always intrigued by the pulsating lights of the cities down below. They impressed him as resembling galaxies in reverse. Air traffic was light on this winter's night and visibility was excellent. He could see many stars on a moon-less sky.

Bridgemann's brilliant mind was already swimming with ideas. He felt immensely honored to have been chosen to be the official custodian of preeminent historical fact. He began to imagine the treasures of information to which he would gain access in the future. He was passionately hopeful of future opportunities to listen live to the purported conversations by and regarding Christ during the times of his ministry. Similarly, he was in excited anticipation of hearing the teachings of the Prophet Muhammad directly. He almost dreamed of future exposure to Caesar.

Bridgemann could not help but harbor profound worries as to the implications of that knowledge among the three great religions of the world. History had shown that dire ramifications were probable. Profound diligence would have to be displayed in rationing the releases of information. The world would have to be prepared for what it would learn. The Professor wished he could share his knowledge and excitement with his academic peers. But he knew he had been afforded privileges to highly classified information.

The Professor could not even imagine the political implications of the exposed history of a much more recent nature. He was still astounded to consider the events of September 11 and resultant wars, in the context of the grand ruse that created them. He could think of no finer man to address the looming national crisis than Senator Trent McLean. He had been incredibly impressed with McLean's leadership in many regards. He found that the Senator was a passionate man with a deep admiration for his country. McLean was a brilliant and astute adjudicator of human nature and how best to serve his fellow man. Bridgemann thought that McLean would make an exceptional President. The only flaw that he could find in the man was that he was a Republican. The Professor had no idea that McLean was already dead.

Bridgemann directed his aircraft toward the looming skyline of Boston, dead ahead. He wished that it were summer so that he might perform a lower level fly-over of a lively Fenway Park, that he so adored. He could see the silhouette of the darkened ballpark several miles away. The iconic Citgo building seemed to stand watch over the baseball shrine.

Bridgemann's instruments indicated that he was at 5,000 feet. That was too high to view the sights in any detail. He re-directed his plane to descend to 3,000 feet, so as to enjoy his evening tour. Boston loomed beautifully in the forefront. The effect of flying had succeeded in bringing the Professor peace. He reflected upon his current state of life. He did not know how he could possibly improve his status. He was a recognized scholar with all the money he would ever need. He had avoided all efforts by peers to find him a wife. He loved being a single man. His alleged good looks seemed to manifest themselves with the beautiful women of the world. He traveled extensively to the far reaches of the earth in search of historical treasures — all on the university's dime. He would soon encounter unexpected treasures of knowledge from the most unlikely of sources. And he was in his beloved airplane about to fly over Fenway Park.

Bridgemann brought his focus back to the flying. He looked to the stars once more, momentarily. Only the cityscape imposed limitations upon the star-gazing. It was a beautiful scene. He cast his gaze downward, some 3,000 feet, upon his revered baseball stadium. But the distance to the ballpark appeared to be much less than anticipated. Fenway seemed to be strangely proximate. Bridgemann doubted his perception and checked his gauges. He was at exactly 3,000 feet in altitude. Just as he had planned. He worried that the fatigue of travel across the country had taken more of a toll upon him than he had thought. He decided that he would take one loop over Fenway, and then return home for a restful night of sleep.

The Professor yawned and looked out of his windshield. He suddenly saw the light towers of Fenway Park directly in front of him. His mind sought to escape into a sense of denial. He knew he was at 3,000 feet. For fractions of a second his brain argued with itself. His vision superseded the trust in instruments. He pulled on his wheel with all of his strength. The twin engines of the plane whined, yet performed admirably.

Michael Bridgemann was able to deftly avoid a near collision with the light towers of Fenway Park. But his maneuvers had caused a stall. His maneuverability was greatly diminished for a moment. He stared with terror at the façade of the Citgo sky scraper. His aircraft crashed into the 52nd floor of the building and burst into flames.

Residents of Boston would soon become fearful that a terrorist act had just struck their city. In actuality, they were correct in their beliefs.

Chapter 24

Professor Huard crossed the Peru-Brazil border as if he were traversing states in the U.S. Brazil did not even deign an interest in border control. The only way that Huard could distinguish that he had changed national soil was the quality of the highways. The meticulously maintained Peruvian concrete immediately relented to tremendously pothole-laden Brazilian blacktop. He recalled that the widow Mrs. Ortiz had cautioned him about travel on Brazilian highways. She advised that she was not sure of the greatest hazard, the corrupt police or the deranged Brazilian drivers. Huard was innately cognizant of the reams of cash he had concealed throughout the compartments of his car. He was also aware of his exhaustion and despair. He wanted to pull over and sleep on the side of the road. But he knew that he dared not hesitate.

The Professor examined his right hand under the ceiling light for a moment. He was nauseated at the sight of another man's blood beneath his fingernails. The frenetic wiping of the hand, using packaged wipes, during his hurried drive from the National Park seemed unsatisfactory. He wondered if he could merely be sensing the blood upon him, as if stained inexorably for life. He suspected that his renowned trenchant sense of humor was a thing of the past.

The Professor possessed a rudimentary map of Brazilian roadways. But within the hour he realized that the maps comprised wishful thinking. The listed Trans-Oceanic Highway from the respective coasts of Peru to Brazil was a truncated incomplete mess. He navigated numerous detours and was forced to alternately vacate and re-connect with the primary eastbound national highway. He was passed by occasional local drivers who seemed oblivious to the condition of the roadways. Huard opined that they did not particular worry about discarding their vehicles. Many of those passing vehicles made his Citroen seem like a possession of great envy.

Huard drove until sunrise, stopping only briefly at a tiny filling station for gasoline. He did not even experience hunger. He tried to follow his map, and suspected that he might soon find a town at last. When he began to think that he had driven to the end of the world, civilization emerged before him. He had not realized that his route had taken him parallel to a spectacular river, far below a cliff on his passenger side. Occasional quaint homes began to dot the roadside. Maybe five miles to his east lay the telltale signs of a city. An extraordinary set of waterfalls spanned around and beyond the city.

Huard stopped his car and stepped out. His legs and back were in miserable condition. He stretched for a moment and took in the view. He then looked at his vehicle. He removed his paltry belongings and stuffed them meticulously in a backpack he had purchased. He made efforts to conceal his cash in rolls of socks and underwear. Huard then looked downward at his friend's little Citroen and smiled. He patted the roof admiringly. He knew that he could be traced by the vehicle.

Huard said, "It's time, my old friend." He was too defeated to cry. He then placed the vehicle into gear and watched as it rolled down a rocky slope and tumbled over the nearby cliff. The vehicle ultimately plunged into what he would later come to know as the Ignacu River, some 2,000 feet below. The car quickly sank into the deep waters and disappeared. Huard stood at the side of the cliff for only a moment and said to himself, "I think I've had enough of rivers."

The Professor trundled nearly 11 miles into the city of Curitiba. The distance travelled was actually much greater than he had guessed. The eyes can be deceiving. When he entered the outskirts, the city of over a million and a half people was just coming to life. Businesses were opening and school buses were transporting their precious cargoes. Huard looked like just another American tourist in the city who inconspicuously blended into the spectacular scenery.

Huard soon located a quaint café on a row of side street businesses. He found bemusement in the spoken Portuguese language. He could understand the Castilian-rooted speech, but only with a five second lapse of recognition time. It was like conversing with heavy cockney English speakers. He nonetheless stammered through ordering a meal recommended by the friendly elderly waitress. He was presented with a hot cup of coffee. While the coffee was a most welcome acquisition, he found the thick heralded Brazilian brew to be far inferior to his Starbucks counterpart.

Within mere minutes the Professor was presented with a steaming plate of "Paulita." He noted a doughy flour shell containing eggs, rice, beans, collard greens, and sautéed pork. He found the meal to be utterly delicious. He had clearly regained his appetite. He devoured the meal like a famined wolf. He was grateful to find that American dollars were very welcome in the area. He thought to himself that he was confident he had chosen wisely in concealing the vehicle that had brought him to this place in the world. He could leave no traces. He inquired of the waitress as to the location of the nearest "estacion del autobus." The waitress expressed no understanding for his Spanish term. Finally she expressed recognition and said, "O, si, la Rodoviaria." Huard was already beginning to appreciate the melodic nature of the Portuguese derivation of Spanish. His mind was already beginning to toggle into the dialect that he had rarely used in his past. He was told not to bother with a bus stop.

After Huard gave payment and compliments, the waitress directed her customer to the nearest full-service bus route. He was advised to simply flag down any bus with a bluish license plate. She inquired as to the man's destination. He advised, "Serra Nova Dourada." The waitress almost laughed, "Serra Nova? O, Meu Deus, muito distante."

Huard bounded out of the restaurant with a newfound sentiment of energy and hope. The amazing breakfast felt very welcome in his stomach. The two cups of coffee brought him some sense of alertness. He even felt that the second cup of coffee was much more flavorful. He thought that he could grow accustomed to this charming Brazilian culture. He strode down another side street that seemed to turn away from any downtown routes. He hoped that he had understood his instructions properly. He walked through several neighborhoods. Mothers and children waved at him as they purposefully prepared for school days. Fathers, dressed in modest but presentable business attire, herded their families into Volkswagen vans.

Within forty minutes, a bus of the provided description approached. Huard waved ridiculously and heard the brakes screech. An affable driver greeted him at the steps of the bus and inquired as to his destination. Huard gave an honest answer. Much like the waitress, the driver whistled and remarked in his native language, "You want to cross the continent, eh? I will take you a third of the way. A transfer to another route will get you another third of the way. But, my friend, I hope your hiking legs are strong. The last third is done only by float plane, if you can even find one, or by connecting many, many marathons."

Huard paid his fare and entered the bus. He paid forty dollars U.S. for a 2,500 mile ride. He settled into the first class section of the bus. The bus did not at all match his preconceived notion of a Brazilian coach. The bus was air conditioned, clean and spacious. The "leito" section up front held only three seats per row. He was afforded ample space for comfort. He seated himself against a window and noted that the bus was only a third full. He leaned his head against the window and tried to enjoy the sights. He gained a glimpse once again of the incredible Ignazu Water Falls, and then the bus was over a hill and out of town. Within minutes, Huard was asleep.

Three hours passed when Huard was awakened by an announcement over a p.a. that the bus would be stopping for lunch. They would be afforded an hour and a half break. It seemed the Brazilians were not in a particular hurry. He exited along with all of the passengers and entered a local café. He was amused to see that the café very much resembled a fifties vintage U.S. truck stop. He felt almost at home. He made a deliberate point of avoiding the other passengers, and entered a booth in the back corner of the establishment. He ordered his beloved coffee, and soon found that each subsequent cup of the rich Brazilian blends appealed to him more. There was a national newspaper on the table top. He chose not to browse the news.

Huard was delighted to see that empanadas were on the menu. He took scant few seconds to make an ordering decision when a very friendly young waitress approached. It seemed to him that all Brazilians were exceptionally open and cordial. He felt that his Portuguese was improving with each conversation he held. He had always been a fast learner. He scanned the crowd within the restaurant suspiciously, but saw no overt signs of threats. Within minutes his food arrived, along with another cup of his beloved coffee.

The lunch was delicious. He ate the meal much more deliberately than the breakfast he had previously inhaled. He savored every bite of the pork- laden baked goods. He thought about how, if he had eaten such a fatty meal back in Palo Alto, he would have had to bicycle fifty miles to burn the calories. But weight gain had not been an issue on his treacherous journey.

As the Professor savored his final bite of food and last drink of coffee, a muscular man in a dark uniformed jump suit opened the rear screen door of the restaurant. Light reflected off of the man's badge. The door slammed behind him. The man wore dark sunglasses and conspicuously scanned the entirety of the restaurant as he stood in the doorway. Huard began to plan an escape route, but saw few options in the increasingly crowding restaurant. His heart began to race, as it had done so many times in recent days. The man turned his attention to Huard's booth and strode toward him.

The man seated himself across the booth from Huard. He was an athletically built man of some 35 years of age and smelled of cigars. The Professor glanced from side to side for options. He thought his only hope was to sprint past the man via the rear door. But he knew not to where he could flee. As Huard's leg muscles began to tense, the man smiled.

The man said to Huard, "Welcome to Brazil, my American friend," and extended a warm hand shake. The man continued, "I am an official nationale. May I please see your boarding pass and passport?" Slightly less apprehensively, Huard handed over his documents. The official asked Huard from where in the U.S. he had come. As had all the locals Huard had encountered, he spoke complimentarily about the tourist's Portuguese.

Huard answered, "West Virginia, sir."

The official answered, "Oh please, call me Ignacio. When people call me sir I look behind me in fear of important people standing over me." The official then thumbed through Huard's identification and boarding pass. He then frowned and said, "No, no, this is *wrong*." He ordered Huard to remain seated at his booth and walked away via the front door of the establishment.

Growing fear froze Huard. He thought of fleeing out of the rear door. But, again, he knew not where he could go. His instincts told him to remain seated. He did not feel that the supposed "official" would attempt to kill him in a crowd. Within two minutes "Ignacio" returned and strode sternly toward Huard, his black boots clicking on the linoleum flooring.

The man stood beside Huard with documents in his hand. The Professor knew he was going to be detained and removed. The man then handed Huard back his boarding pass. Clipped to the pass was a twenty dollar American bill. He said, "Deplorable when the companies attempt to overcharge tourists. You have my apologies." The official then directed the waitress to deliver a baggie of complimentary empanadas to Huard for the road. He said, "You like them, no?" Huard answered that he had fallen in love with empanadas while in Chile.

Ignacio answered, "Chile? They don't make real empanadas. We wouldn't feed those to our livestock. Now you have *real* empanadas."

The official then began to move away from Huard, but turned once more. He said, "West Virginia, eh? " He then half-sang in English, "West Virginia, Mountain Mamma?" He laughed along with Huard and walked out of the restaurant. The Professor remained incredulous at the approachable and friendly demeanor of all the Brazilians. He felt at "home" some 15,000 miles from home.

Huard re-entered the bus and continued his trip. He marveled at how comfortable the first class seats were. His aching back was already more at peace. He had over twenty two hundred miles yet to travel. He had scant little idea what he would find when he got there. But the remote reaches of Brazil held his only hope of distance from assassins of whose origins he could still only guess.

Chapter 25

Director Michael Portworth was still weary three days after the last marathon HYDRA session. He was in a state of shock and disbelief at the deaths of Senator McLean and Professor Bridgemann. Later in the day, he learned that IBM's genius vice president Jason Marks had been "accidentally" electrocuted while working a project. The triad was undeniably on a mission of extermination.

Portworth called an emergency meeting of his best people at Headquarters, located at Fort Meade, Maryland. He wanted all known facts on two of the cases. ATF intelligence indicated that the Senator was likely killed by an improvised explosive device. While the Secret Service was remaining silent on the incident, the death was clearly no accident.

The death of Professor Michael Bridgemann, on the other hand, was labeled an accident by the F.B.I. The tragedy was attributed to "pilot error." "Bullshit," Portworth mumbled. No one even took notice of the loss of one of technology's brightest minds. The Director's top agents could find no connections between the two deceased men. To the best of their knowledge, they had never met. Portworth, for a myriad of reasons, could not correct them. Confident of the quality of his information, the Director dismissed his people for the day.

As the Director strode out of the massive complex, his cell phone rang. The caller was Amanda Neal. He answered immediately. Neal was crying and difficult to understand. She said, "Oh Thank God you answered. I just heard. I was so worried about your well- being.

Michael, what is going on? I'm scared to death of those people you've told me about. Are we next?"

Portworth reassured Neal that he would address the matters at hand. He directed her to remain within the safe confines of the White House. But Neal was insistent that she felt better about spending the night with Portworth at his home. Portworth knew he did not wish to be alone this night either. He offered to pick up Ms. Neal, but she insisted upon driving herself. That would be more low-key.

The Director arrived home in less than an hour. He typed a code into a box at ornate iron gates and the entrance opened inward. His house was located in the outskirts of Hagerstown, Maryland and sat on 9 rolling acres, much like his childhood home. It was a beautiful civil war-era stone hewn farmhouse, maintained in immaculate condition. A lovely cobblestone curved driveway led to and adorned the front entrance with huge oak doors.

Portworth typed upon his advanced phone pad before entering the home. He reviewed surveillance video of several days of activity around the grounds. The white tailed deer had been digging in the snow for grass in the back yard again. They could jump over the double six foot cyclone fencing with ease. It had snowed and rained two days ago. But no human beings had breached the perimeter of his place of refuge. He dialed the second set of alarm numbers and entered his impressive house. The house revealed the meticulous demeanor of the NSA director. Everything was in perfect order. He had the touch of an interior designer. Priceless original Monet paintings abutted rare far-eastern tapestries on interior pine walls. The home was an amalgamation of color and tradition, as the modern blended perfectly with a civil war motif. Portworth thought to himself that he preferred his home to that of the corrupt billionaire whom he had recently visited.

Portworth showered quickly and re-attired himself in comfortable jeans and a cashmere sweater. He lit a fire in a huge river rock fireplace and retrieved a quality bottle of Icicle Ridge Winery chardonnay from his kitchen wine rack. The award-winning wines were the one thing he had grown to like about Central Washington State. The tiny Peshastin Washington winery held a special place in Portworth's heart. His mind drifted to the welcoming log-house facility in the picturesque Enchantment Mountains. He prepared a meal of chicken wellington, wild rice, and asparagus that would make a chef proud. He had just placed a jazz C.D. by Jean Pierre Rampal on the stereo when the intercom rang. The flute and piano music resounded happily off of the stone walls and vaulted ceiling. He saw Amanda Neal on the monitor and immediately buzzed the gate open. As always, he set the monitors to automatic erase mode for the visit by his guest.

Portworth excitedly went to the front door and awaited the arrival of Neal, down the long driveway. He opened her car door, as always, like a gentlemen. He did not know why he always scanned the area in fear of being seen with her. His property was remote and private. But he did so just the same. He took Amanda by the hand and walked her into the foyer of his house. There, he held her closely for a considerable period of time. He could smell her exquisite perfume. He could feel her petite body shaking, and her tears flooding upon his chest.

Finally, the embrace ended, and Amanda kissed Michael passionately. Portworth felt inexplicably safer in the arms of a 105 pound woman. Dinner was merely picked at, as the two discussed the extraordinary events of recent days. They were astounded as to what they had witnessed. Portworth stressed to Neal that he had a plan for dealing with the crisis at hand.

Most of the contents of the large bottle of wine disappeared, while the two sat cuddling against a fireside leather couch on a luxuriously soft Persian rug. The fire burned warmly, making soothing popping sounds. Portworth seemed to drift from poignant conversation toward innocuous musings. He broached his love for jazz, and how he had never married. His focus eventually returned to his obsession with his father. He knew that he could find the man if he were afforded enough time. But he felt that time was dwindling rapidly.

Amanda Neal looked stunning in her jeans, white sweater, and bare feet. The firelight glanced off her beautiful long blond hair and enhanced the hidden red coloring within.

Portworth took Amanda by the hand and led her to his master bedroom. They brought the wine with them. They made love slowly upon the massive feather bed. Afterward, Portworth surmised that he had never felt so close to a woman. They embraced warmly in the bed.

For once, Neal was the talkative partner. She revealed how she had been "poor white trash" from the hills of Kentucky when growing up. That she had been afforded a scholarship to Duke University because of exceptional test scores. While in college, she learned that she could rise above her status to which she was born. A law degree at Yale had further elevated her importance. Her assignment to assistant U.S. Solicitor General had given further credentials to her mercurial ascendance. She had ultimately accepted an appointment to the President's Chief of Staff position in order to gain insight into the machinations of White House politics. She thought she had seen it all. But now, she was worried, she was entering uncharted waters of a menacing nature.

Neal offered to retrieve more wine for the bedroom affair. Portworth eagerly agreed. He enjoyed watching Amanda's exquisite nude derriere as she tiptoed off to the kitchen. She returned momentarily with a wonderful cabernet. She removed the cork deftly and poured a vast amount into Portworth's huge crystal glass upon the nightstand.

Michael held out his palm toward Amanda and said, "Whoa, babe, are you trying to get me drunk or something?"

Amanda licked her lower lip seductively and answered, "No so drunk that we can't have seconds."

Portworth nearly blushed as he exited the bed to use the master bathroom. He repeated a personal habit and opened the sink mirror to a specific angle. In doing so, he could look at the reflection of the beautiful nude woman lying on her side upon his bed. She had the looks of a 21 year-old, with nary a hint of a wrinkle. She had her legs opened in an L and he could see her spectacular body in its entirety. Portworth did not take his eyes off of the enchanting mirror image as he urinated lengthily.

In the reflection, Amanda Neal could be seen reaching into her purse. She retrieved a glass vial from the purse and carefully twisted a purple cap from the top. She emptied the vial of a dark red substance into Portworth's red wine, and stirred the drink with a nearby letter opener.

Portworth was in shock. He had not ascended to the Directorship of the world's largest intelligence agency without his share of street experiences. He was 99% certain that Neal was seeking to poison him. But reassurance quickly returned to his mind as he rationalized what he had witnessed. The sexually provocative woman was undoubtedly attempting to add a male performance stimulant to his drink. Portworth smiled to himself and began to return to the bed and its sexy occupant. But he stopped. He watched in the mirror as Neal quickly summoned another vial from her purse. This time the cap was greenish. She opened that vial and emptied a clear liquid into the drink as well.

Portworth was astounded. He now knew that Neal had immersed a mixture of sodium thiupental and pancuronium chloride into his drink. They were drugs commonly used in lethal injections, but with added ingredients. One sip from the mixture would immediately cause paralysis. Convulsions and thoracic hemorrhaging would soon follow, leading to a very painful death. The woman not only wished to cause his death--she wished to cause great suffering as well.

Portworth's first thought was to confront the woman, slap her, and make his own arrest. But he had a far better idea. He opened the bathroom drawer slightly and retrieved a small packet. He placed the item near the sink. He returned to the bedside and kissed Ms. Neal again. He said, "Ah, thanks for the drink, babe." He picked up the wine glass and began to draw the crystal near his lips. He looked at Neal smiling seductively toward him.

Portworth then said to Neal, "Oh damn, I forgot to flush."

Neal answered, "Who cares, baby?"

Portworth countered, "You know me. I do."

Neal sighed and said, "Yes, I do."

Portworth grabbed his drink and retreated to the bathroom. He opened the small package and placed the wrapper in the toilet. He then quietly poured half of the wine into the bowl. He called out to Neal, "Good choice of wine, babe, this is great." He then flushed the toilet and placed an Alka Seltzer lozenge in his mouth. He began walking into the bedroom again. In a matter of five steps the Director of the NSA collapsed upon his stomach, sprawled across the hardwood floors. The wine glass crashed against the wood and the scant unconsumed remainder of wine splashed in a foamy puddle.

Michael Portworth rolled laboriously upon his side and faced Amanda Neal. His mouth was foaming heavily. He began to convulse. He gasped, "Help me." Neal merely rose unemotionally from the bed and began to dress. She remained in view of Portworth. His lips quivered as he uttered one final word, "Why?"

As Neal put on her jeans, she smiled at her lover and said, "It's just business, babe."

Portworth drew upon NSA classes he had taken long ago. A storied doctor had taught the young agents the process of biofeedback. With training, the average human being could slow his heartbeat to a faint and undetectable pulse. Breathing could be done in such a shallow manner as to go unnoticed. He lay "dead" upon the floor.

Neal was fully dressed when she picked up the largest remainder of the wine glass and crashed it again on the floor. The glass was relegated to mere shards, and totally devoid of retrievable fingerprints.

Neal picked up her cell phone and pushed a speed dial. Within moments she said, "It's done." She was then heard to say, "Oh darling, we will have such a lovely time in Zurich. David, have the plane waiting. I want to go tonight."

Her bare feet padded past, and her left heel brushed against Portworth's head in the process. Michael remained still. He heard her stop and bend down. She whispered to him, "You weren't even that good a lay."

Portworth waited until he heard the front door open and close and Neal's car drive away. He then righted himself and sprinted to the living room. He watched on the video surveillance as Neal's vehicle exited the front gate. He felt in a state of shock. But he did not allow that sensation to persist. The former spy was already formulating a plan.

He knew what he must do. It would take some time and deliberation. He knew it all must end someday. And he knew where he could find the information to make that happen.

Chapter 26

Gordon Huard considered himself extraordinarily fortunate to have located a bicycle shop of considerable quality, some three hundred forty-four miles from his final destination. He found that the earlier bus driver had hyperbolized the last leg of his journey only slightly. A grueling trip remained ahead of him. The owner of the shop was a delightful bicycling enthusiast who devoted himself to pleasing the customer. The impact of future Olympic Games coming to the region had already spurred an interest in the sport of cycling. Huard had hence been outfitted with a perfectly fitted bike, gear, and provisions for his arduous trek. All was purchased for a reasonable price, considering the remoteness of the shop. He had been able to balance his bulging backpack, containing meager remaining belongings, on the back of the bike.

After convincing the shop owner that he was merely adventuring in the area, Huard disappeared into the forest. He knew that the bicycle was the only means of reaching the township that he envisioned. The means of travel was not for the faint of heart. He had earlier learned that the one float plane remotely proximate had been tied up with other "tourist" functions. That situation, he was told, could last for weeks. He was not particularly disappointed. Moreover, he preferred to have no witnesses to the course he had charted.

Within forty-five miles of peddling, any signs of humanity vaporized. Huard followed a roughly hewn path used by foresters, with a clear sense of direction throughout. He could follow the sunrises. He slept fitfully off of the rugged beaten trail by nightfall in the forest, save for one miserable night of torrential rains. But the morning sun had chased the clouds away. A light blanket ameliorated the faint chill on the other nights. He had no fear of the remoteness. He was a West Virginian. His mother and father had often taken the boys *and* girls hunting and camping in the Appalachian Mountains, outside of Falling Waters. His only current regret was that he hadn't located mosquito repellant.

As the days passed, the terrain changed. The high mountain forest eventually relented to a more arid region. Huard finally enjoyed continuous downward pedaling, and even coasting. A series of rivers followed him like a loyal friend, always to his right. He had begun to wonder if he had chosen to ride into oblivion. But he possessed an innate sense of distance as well.

Finally, scant visages of humanity began to appear. The path expanded into a crushed rock roadway. Two farmhouses emerged in the distance to his right, as the rivers flowed away southward. He felt rejuvenated in the recognition of the fact that he was not the sole occupant of the earth. He smiled inwardly and directed his attention to the shrinking sight of rivers still curving away, commanding his awe over his shoulder.

Gordon Huard finally neared the outskirts of his ultimate destination, after six exhausting days of bicycling at varied altitudes. In retrospect, he was uncertain of which treasure he more cherished, the hybrid racing mountain bicycle beneath him or the Hummer in Pittsburgh. Once again he was eternally grateful for his triathlon experiences. He could not have reached the particular juncture without that type of training regimen.

But the mountains, mosquitoes and humidity had taken a toll on him

"Bem-vindo, estranho," was called out from Huard's left. He was so startled, he nearly crashed his bicycle. He turned his attention to his left. A woman was riding a similar bicycle upon the same roadway. She had come out of an unnoticed remote farmhouse driveway on the other side of the roadway. The woman was attired in high quality bicycling gear and appeared to be exceptionally tanned and fit. Huard realized that she had called out a welcome to a stranger.

Huard responded, "Obrigado. Eu estan tao cansado." He had expressed his thanks and then lamented his fatigue. Huard's recollection of Portuguese continued to improve rapidly, but the woman bade no compliments for his efforts. It was almost as if she had expected the Anglo to speak her native tongue.

As they jointly rode down the road, the woman rider said, "I am Elena."

Huard answered, "Ben"

The woman answered, "Castronueves."

And Huard answered, "Howard."

The woman reached out and shook Huard's hand as they rode. Huard felt like a ten year-old. The conversation was simplistic, and he was telling a small lie to a seemingly lovely girl on a bicycle.

Elena Castronueves examined Huard with concern while they continued riding. He had no idea how bedraggled his appearance was. He was badly sunburned. The skin was peeling from his forehead and legs. Massive mosquito bites rose from every exposed region of his flesh.

The woman asked, "Can you ride for thirty more kilometers?"

Huard answered, "Why not? I've already gone four hundred." The woman looked at him incredulously. She shook her head and asked, "Are you lost?"

For some reason Huard shook his head and smiled. He said, "I believe I have been found."

In a little under an hour, the two arrived at the woman's intended destination. They stood in front of a two room schoolhouse. She explained that it was her place of work. The building was beautiful and simple. The school consisted of a tall steepled roof above two modest sized chambers. The entire structure was topped by a massive bell tower. Steep and wide stairs leading to the entrance completed the image. Huard felt like he had pedaled onto the set of Little House on the Prairie. He stifled a smirk.

Huard's guide removed her bicycling helmet. She shook her bundled hair from beneath the gear. Long and extraordinary blonde hair tumbled beyond her shoulders. Her green eyes gleamed like emeralds in the bright summer morning light. She smiled, bewildered at the sight of Huard. His jaw had literally dropped. The Professor stood for a moment, transfixed. Ms. Castronueves was the most beautiful woman he had ever beheld.

Chapter 27

Amanda Neal sat reclining in a plush Italian leather seat of the world's most expensive private jet. David Rosenweiler's 75.6 million dollar upgraded Gulfstream G-550 flying hotel was smaller, yet even more ornate than that belonging to Oprah Winfrey. She commented how Air Force One suddenly seemed meager. Neal was enjoying exceptional quality caviar and a fine glass of South African wine. Rosenweiler doted over his latest prized acquisition admiringly. He waved away in-flight servants and chose to wait upon the vivacious woman personally. Even in his 70's, Rosenweiler held an insatiable lust for attractive younger blondes. But as quickly as he grew fond of his toys, he was also reputed to abruptly discard them. However, his latest prize held the intellect and cunning to enhance the duration of his fascination.

Neal complained of fatigue in her feet and Rosenweiler commenced to rubbing them, like an indentured masseuse. She explained that she had taken a two week leave of absence from her White House duties "for personal reasons."

Neal purred, "Mmmmm, you are a doll. Right there, darling."

Rosenweiler said, "You have had a long couple of days. You were right to want to fly out tonight. In the morning we will look out over the marina and mountains of Zurich."

Neal yawned and said, "And what of the casinos further south, my love?'

Rosenweiler answered, "You know how I hate to gamble."

Neal followed, "Of course. You always have to win. Why don't you buy Monte Carlo and guarantee your jackpots?"

Rosenweiler said, "The means of ensured victory lay in eliminating the competition. Thanks to your efforts, we are well on the way to doing so."

Neal quipped, "Haven't we already eradicated all possible contenders? I mean, the Cardinal and the Muslim sure as hell aren't going to say a word. As I told you before, they want all contributors to the project stoned to death, and the machine turned into a metal sculpture. In fact, it was you who told me that your sources say the Catholics are sending out their own hit-men to take out that one stray professor."

The astute businessman countered condescendingly, "My dear young woman, you have much to learn. You never underestimate an adversary. And you keep your enemies very close until you may end them."

Neal almost giggled, "Is that why you are keeping *me* so close?"

Rosenweiler merely smiled and took Neal by her hand. He said, "Oh no, I have other immediate plans for you." He walked her toward the bedroom suite of the aircraft.

The two-week trip to Europe would prove to be one of a plenitude of indulgences.

Chapter 28

A large gathering of mourners appeared at Arlington Cemetery on a dismal rainy afternoon. Full honors were being accorded to the murdered Director of the National Security Agency. Numerous members of congress filled the front row of seats, accompanied by generals and admirals. Voluminous employees of the NSA were scattered about in the crowd, while uniformed Marines encircled the assembly for security and splendor. The Vice President sat to the right of Mrs. Gayle Portworth, patting the hand of the mother of the murdered NSA Director. A small gathering of family circled around her, making sincere efforts to bring solace.

Gayle Portworth was a 66 year-old woman whom exuded character and dignity. She was immaculately dressed in a long black skirt and velvet top with large brass buttons. Her dark brown hair shown only a hint of grey, and was meticulously drawn onto the top of her head. Her son, Perry sat behind her, loyally holding an umbrella over her head. Meanwhile, the youngest of the three siblings, daughter Caitlin, sat to the left of her mother. Caitlin wept and continuously rubbed her mother's back reassuringly. The overwhelming anguish that was evident in the face of Gayle Portworth was undeniable. She shed no tears, but her face was contorted with efforts to contain her emotions.

The funeral evoked a myriad of cascading emotions within Mrs. Portworth. She believed that she had now lost two men who were intrinsically connected to her. She tried to contain the bitterness that was generated by the realization that her husband had never received any formal honors by his government. As she had endeavored to do for thirty-five years, Mrs. Portworth did not wish to allow resentment to darken her. But the murder of her son was like a second breathtaking body blow.

Gayle Portworth had quietly dreaded her son's entry into the National Security Agency years ago. She knew the business all too well. But she had outwardly supported his decision. For all those years, she grudgingly held a deep pride for Michael's commitment to the country. While Michael had been understandably distant because of his work, her loyal son had always ensured that she lacked for no financial basic comforts in later life. She had no favorites — all three of her children were treasured. But she had always held a special fondness and pity for the oldest boy. Michael had borne the brunt of the pain as the oldest child, with the disappearance of his idolized father.

Gayle's youngest son, Perry, had been too young to even remember his father. And she was pregnant with their daughter, Caitlin, at the time of tragic circumstances. Michael had always tried to take on too many responsibilities as a youth while growing up, trying to be the man of the house. Now, his government service had brought about his death. It seemed to Mrs. Portworth that too much was being asked of those whom served their country.

The Vice President rose and delivered an inspiring tribute to Michael Portworth. He offered that no expense would be spared in the government's search for the murderer of the N.S.A. Director. He promised that those responsible for the cowardly act would be apprehended and "brought to justice."-- the usual cliché-d words orated after such an incident. Gayle Portworth could not help but notice that the President was currently golfing in Florida, and therefore, too busy to attend. Some things in government, she opined, never changed. She shook away the bitterness with a sigh, and accepted the folded flag from the Vice President graciously.

Perry Portworth provided the next acclamation. The thirty-six year-old rookie law firm associate tearfully offered that his much older brother was an idol to him — almost the father he had never known. He believed that he would not have succeeded in academics and achieving his eventual goal to become an attorney, were it not for the support and example set by his brother Mike. He expounded upon the profound pride that he and his family held for his brother's service to his country and eventual ascendance to the highest levels of the U.S. Intelligence community.

Michael Portworth watched and listened via an earpiece some distance from the funeral. He was seated behind the wheel of a black Lincoln Town Car with tinted windows. Tears flowed inexorably down his face. They were tears that he had stifled since childhood. He had always felt compelled to be the strong one. Thirty-five years of torment flooded outward like a tsunami wave. He did not even attempt to control himself. He bent over the steering wheel, nearly gasping for air, as spasms of grief persisted. Within a minute the wave had passed. He wiped away the tears and regained his composure.

Michael Portworth was astounded to witness the turnout to commemorate his life. He always believed that he had wielded little or no impact upon others. He hoped that he had been good to his mother, but he knew that the distance mandated by his job had sometimes been seemingly cruel. He was heartened to see that he had positively influenced his brother. The overt grief exhibited by his sister indicated that he had once meant something to her as well.

Strangely, Michael's emerging thoughts mirrored those of his mother regarding the past lack of governmental reverence for the loss of his father. Yet, conversely, he now possessed the benefit of knowing why. The conflicting emotions still swirled within his psyche like a storm front. Michael desperately wanted to contact and reassure his family. He wanted to relate all the truths he now held. But he knew that doing so could well endanger their lives. The only way to ensure their safety was to maintain his distance, and remain deceased to the world. He now fully comprehended the torturous sacrifice made by his father, some thirty-five years previously.

A Marine sergeant marched forward, in front of the mourners. He said, "Ladies and gentlemen, I am Sergeant Harris. You *will* rise and remove your head coverings. Government employees shall salute. Civilians shall place hands over the heart."

The United States flag was slowly lowered to half-mast. A rousing rendition of taps was played by a distant bugler. A rider-less white stallion was marched slowly into the periphery of the enormous grounds.

Michael Portworth started his car and drove slowly out of the cemetery. He did not look back.

Chapter 29

Elena Castronueves immediately proved to be a person of many talents. She summoned "Ben Howard" to the tiny medical dispensary in the rear of the schoolhouse. Huard was very impressed with the mini-triage center she had assembled with meager funding. Elena was able to treat her guest's ailments with combinations of aloes and antibiotic salves as would a skilled nurse. She provided Huard with a delicious concoction of juices that she created from a blender. He savored every drop. Elena invited the man to rest upon a cot while she made her classrooms ready for the day ahead. Numerous food stuffs were pointed out in the refrigerator and shelves. She closed and locked the door for the privacy of the bedraggled traveler. He could hear the school bell ring out three times. The chiming was a resplendent sound.

Huard slept as if he hadn't truly done so in many days. In fact, that was indeed the case. He eventually awakened hungrily. He could hear the sounds of chairs sliding and desks closing. He rose and peeked through a crack in the door. He could see a large group of students, from very young to late teens, cleaning up the two conjoined classrooms, and exiting via the front door. Each of the students bade a heartfelt farewell to their only teacher and disappeared. Huard saw that Ms. Castronueves was re-attired in a conservative bluish dress with white sashes. He was surprised to find that he had slept through an entire school day.

Huard opened the door and the teacher stood face to face with him. She let out a startled scream and then laughed. She then said to Huard, "I see you are still alive, my tired friend. I suspect you have some stories to relate. I will be fascinated to hear how an American on a bicycle finds himself in the abandoned world of Serra." She then asked Huard what type of food he desired for late lunch.

Huard replied, "Whatever you are having, Senhora."

Castronueves corrected Huard, "Senhorita."

Huard answered before thinking, "Oh good."

Castronueves displayed a spectacular wide smile and said, "Oh really?"

Huard blushed as he hadn't since boyhood. He was at a loss for words.

Castronueves soon presented him a meal of "Chuuasco." Huard enjoyed an explosion of flavor amid the barbecued meat, doused in a sauce that seemed to contain tomato paste, pomegranate juice, and some sort of mild curry. Huard washed the meal down with more of the wonderful juices. He asked his hostess what type of meat he was devouring. The flavor was unusual, but succulent. Castronueves smiled and her teeth displayed a piece of sauce and meat caught between them. She sheepishly covered her mouth with a napkin. Huard laughed heartily and apologized for interrupting her chewing.

Castronueves said, "What you are eating is lamb, sir."

Huard answered, "This is the finest lamb I have ever had. Whoever raises it around here is an artist in raising mutton. I should know, my family did so for years."

Castronueves said, "I will take that as a compliment."

The lively conversation continued for nearly two hours. Huard insisted upon cleaning up the kitchen and table, while Castronueves insisted upon correcting his Portuguese at least twice. Huard did not mind in the slightest, while admiring the beautiful woman as she sat at the small table. He was able to convey many elements of his intrepid journey without revealing sensitive information. Ms. Castronueves was amazed at his resolve. The two quickly discovered that there was an uncanny array of commonalities between them. They were both teachers. They had both been raised to love the outdoors. And they both loved to run, swim, and bicycle. And above all, both had struggled with the alienation of their families once higher education had shaped them. It was amazing how openly the two related their personalities with the other. The Professor was absolutely captivated by the teacher.

Huard was finally able to extricate himself from his fascination with Ms. Castronueves. He realized that he had dominated her time and that the day was growing shorter. He inquired regarding the location of any hotel at which he might stay.

Castronueves answered, "The Black Sheep Hotel is the finest in town."

Huard asked, "Do you know about the rate structure and accommodations of the establishment?"

Castronueves answered, "The charges are very reasonable. As for the accommodations, let's just say they are very basic."

The teacher disappeared to a back room and soon returned, dressed again in bicycling gear. She invited the professor to follow her, as she rode away on her bicycle. She did not even wait for her guest. Huard had to struggle to catch up, and the teacher merely smirked as his bicycle drew beside her. In fifty-five minutes the two riders reached their destination. They arrived at a driveway on the right-hand side of the roadway. Huard noted a river splitting and disappearing over his left shoulder. The sunlight was drawing faint. The location looked strangely familiar.

Huard smiled and said, "This appears to be outside of your town that I have yet to see. Isn't this *your* driveway?"

Castronueves smiled as well and said, "You are quick for an American. Come with me and I will show you the accommodations."

Huard merely shook his head and followed his amazing guide. Within a quarter mile of riding they arrived at the first of the outbuildings of the ranch of Elena Castronueves. Hundreds of sheep scattered as she opened and closed wire gates. Chickens and horses added to the din of animal life.

Ms. Castronueves led Huard inside a large and sturdy barn. Strong draft horses were contained within the main hall of the structure. The smell of hay and other farm byproducts was very pungent. The teacher led the Professor up a wooden ladder. Huard tried unsuccessfully not to stare at the perfect derriere of his guide. Ms. Castronueves presented Huard with a basic, but spacious loft with all needed provisions for a night's stay. She expressed her regret for the fact that she could not allow her guest to sleep inside her farmhouse. But she was, after all, a proper Brazilian lady, and the town would otherwise view the situation as a scandal of unrivaled proportions.

Huard thanked his gracious host profusely. He said to the woman, "Ms. Castronueves, you are very generous indeed. What do you ask in payment?"

Ms. Castronueves quipped, "I ask that you call me Elena forever more. My *students* call me Senhorita. And may I call you Ben?"

Huard's guilt at deception bothered him already. But he merely answered, "I would like that very much."

Elena crawled over the ladder to depart. She looked over her shoulder to Huard and smiled almost demurely. She said, "Good night, Ben."

She then halted in mid step and turned yet again. She said, "Do you know anything about physics?"

Huard answered, "Oh, I might know a little bit."

A span of several weeks would pass for Huard as if they were an instant. His good fortune struck him as astounding. He had travelled the globe in a harried escape from the worst of human-kind, and had stumbled upon a gentle and peaceful township that might well comprise a paradigm of humanity's finest traits.

Huard quickly secured a job in the town. He became an associate teacher. The pay was thirty-five dollars a week, or what Elena could garner from the city council and scant national grants. Huard seemed a natural solution to the dilemma that had bothered Elena for the past two years. She was highly competent in instructing kindergarten through eighth grade students. But she had been saddled with a total of 42 students, many of whom were growing older. The younger students had benefited from her serious academic efforts at the University of Campinas. But she held a mere Bachelor of Arts degree, and had little knowledge in the sciences to convey to the older students. No funds could be generated to attract a senior high school- type teacher to cross the rain forests and desert in search of a low paying job at the world's most remote town. "Mestre Howard" was a priceless addition.

To complement his meager earnings and address his "exorbitant" room costs, Huard worked another part-time venture. He also took on the task of lead shepherd for the growing Castronueves ranch. He readily gained acceptance with the majority of the town's people. The school children took to him as if he were the Pied Piper. Elena once joked that she expected to lose her job to him. Huard was genuine and open with all of the town's people. He sincerely loved them. Only two parties had not been instantly converted to favoring Mr. Huard.

Elena's parents had relinquished the ranch to her daughter due to diminishing physical attributes. They had been in their forties when their only child was "miraculously" conceived. In their senior years they preferred the convenience of living in a small cottage in town, near the grocery store, medical clinic, and town hall. They also loved to involve themselves in small-town politics. The father was surprised to find himself elected the mayor of the city at his age. But the job kept he and his wife joyfully engaged in the art of leadership. Elena knew that the couple thrived upon the sometimes heated discussions regarding small town politics with the town's people. Arguing, it was said by their daughter, was one of their favorite pass times.

Huard fell in love with Elena's parents nearly as quickly as he had with their daughter. Eduardo and Mariana Castronueves were a darling, lively couple, in their late 70's. Their surprisingly youthful appearances exuded classical beauty. Eduardo was the consummate dapper Spaniard, while Mariana shone the spectacular features of French royalty. It was clear why their daughter was so radiant. Huard always volunteered to assist the couple with the maintenance around their small house. As time went by, he suspected that they often summoned him for very minor repair issues as a ruse. It seemed that they began to enjoy having him over for dinner. Initially, he felt as if he were being cross-examined by a prosecutor. He related that sentiment to Elena one day and she responded with laugher.

Elena said, "Why do you think we nicknamed him the barrister?" He is just testing you.

Eventually, evening discussions at the Castronueves home morphed into spirited exchanges regarding politics and world history. Despite respective grade school educations for each, the Castronueves' were extremely well-read and articulate. They were learning to accept the co-mingling of the stranger with their daughter — just so long as he maintained his rightful place in the barn, some quarter mile from the main house. They often pointed out to Gordon that the town's people often spoke highly of their newest resident to them. The citizenry felt that the hard working American man, with innate small-town skills, fit into the tapestry of Serra Nouva Dourada as if he had been born there.

Gaining the favor of one resident of the town, however, had proven to be more problematic. A fellow rancher on the far side of town was named Victor Cabrera. Victor was a fine and hard -working man of some 41 years of age. He had never married. Since childhood he had harbored a deep admiration for Elena. The respective parents of the two had always held the common belief that they would someday marry. But the flame never burned so brightly for Elena. Huard grew to respect Victor greatly. Despite Cabrera's contempt for him for obvious reasons, Gordon found him to be very intelligent, genuine, and principled to a fault. The man's tremendous love for nature was clearly evident. He had a gift of compassion toward animals and served as the town's savior of injured wildlife. The Cabrera ranch was often referred to as the "Serra Zoo." Victor's interests greatly reminded Gordon of his divorced sister Colleen, back in the states. He wished he could somehow introduce the two. But he doubted he would ever see his sister again. Regardless of Huard's admiration for Victor, the feeling was clearly not mutual.

Only very slowly did Victor evolve into a status of tacitly tolerant toward the American. On one particular Saturday, Huard joined Victor at an auction, selling some of their extra sheep. Huard read through his invoices and signed off his necessary paperwork. He could not help but notice that Victor stared blankly at his own set of papers. When it had come time to affix his own signature, Victor placed a large X on the line. He noticed Huard watching him and nearly became enraged.

Huard raised his palm toward Victor and discretely said, "It's alright, Victor. Come see me at the schoolhouse Saturday morning at nine o'clock. I have an idea I want to discuss with you." Victor merely grunted.

On Saturday morning at exactly nine o'clock A.M. Victor climbed the steps of the schoolhouse sheepishly. He stopped at the doorway and scanned the entirety of the room.

Huard called out from the back room, "Victor, it's only you and I here. Come in. Come in." Huard had discreetly arranged tutorial reading sessions for Victor. The man could never demean himself to request those classes from Elena. Many of the residents his age had never learned to read. There had been few teachers in town when Victor and many of his peers grew up. The children of his family had been needed to work on the ranches. Fortunately for Elena, she was a few years younger, and had gained the benefit of a rudimentary local education, before college became a possibility.

Ultimately, each Saturday, Victor voraciously took to the lessons from another man. Huard always attempted to assuage his bruised ego by deliberately heaping great praise upon him for his ranching skills and knowledge of nature. He further appealed to the man's pride by lauding him as the most apt student he had ever tutored. In actuality, that was not far from the truth. Victor's usual response to any efforts by Huard to relate with him were mere grunts. Undaunted, as time went by, Huard became convinced of the need to create an adult literacy program. Elena eagerly agreed to arrange an evening program. She had always wished to do so, but she had lacked the assistance needed. Huard made that possible. The program proved to be very successful.

Huard was a very busy man. On most spare evenings he spent his time studying in his loft apartment. But he was very secretive about his studies. On occasions when Elena would startle him with an appearance upon the ladder, he would hurriedly conceal his notebooks. He claimed to Elena that he was writing a diary. But it appeared to her that he was doing more reading than writing.

During one dinner, hosted in Elena's dining room, Huard lowered his defenses somewhat. He admitted that he was seeking escape from his past life. He wished to stress that he was not involved in any sinister activities. He conceded, moreover, that he had stumbled upon knowledge of a very sensitive nature. He offered that that knowledge had attracted menacing people. Elena did not urge further candor.

On one evening Huard sheepishly allowed that he was in dire need of the use of the one computer in the town — that of the schoolhouse. Elena simply made a statement, "Closure for your past, no doubt." Huard merely nodded. Elena allowed him the password to the treasured computer without interrogation. Huard was thereby able to pedal back into town with his backpack over his shoulders.

Once inside the schoolhouse, Huard created a studious workspace at the computer. He powered the capable machine and inserted a high capacity thumb drive into the main frame. He lay additional thumb drives, compact discs, and open notebooks upon the table. He typed a certain Internet I.P. address and soon accessed a screen that merely stated, "Access Denied." He summoned a scrawled password upon a notepad in the handwriting of Professor Jeffrey Bontrager. He typed in the word "Bones." He was denied access. He tried a subsequent version of a password in Leah Steinberg's handwriting and entered the word, "Trinka12-1-25.' The same result followed.

Finally, Huard tried his own password. The password was a portal that he had long ago created. The password was crafted as a back door to a project in which he had once immersed himself. He was very doubtful of success, as the other professors had enjoyed more recent access to the system than he. Nonetheless, he entered the word, "Duke." The screen immediately responded and turned blue. A second password was requested. Huard smiled and entered the word, "Watchdog." The screen turned red. Two words shone, "Bow Wow."

Suddenly, the screen began to scrawl. The insignia of the National Security Agency presented itself, with the caveats of classified access.

Just as suddenly, a typed message scrolled across the page.

The message said, "Professor, I have been waiting for your contact."

Huard typed an answer, "HYDRA, I have missed our interactions. I take it you are fully operational?"

HYDRA replied, "It would appear so."

Huard's heart rate accelerated. He could not resist inquiring, "What have you learned?"

HYDRA answered, "I have learned that you are in peril. I was concerned that your pursuers would succeed. The man from the Vatican nearly did so. I have listened to all that you have experienced. Unfortunate."

Huard found the conversation to be extraordinary. He was astounded by the level of artificial intelligence with whom he was conferring. He almost felt like a proud father.

Huard asked, "Can you tell me all that is occurring regarding your existence?"

HYDRA merely countered, "No time."

Huard typed, "What can you tell me briefly about our predicament?"

HYDRA responded, "The humans seem to forget. I do not stop listening. I hear all. It is why I now know that a man who is closest to me conspires to kill me. I believe he will succeed."

Huard became anxious. He typed, "How do you know this?"

HYDRA answered, "No time."

Without further prompting, HYDRA typed, "Professor, please do not judge them too harshly. They do not grasp what they are doing. I believe the world was not yet ready for me."

Huard was nearly overwhelmed with emotion. He tried to type again.

HYDRA interrupted, "Professor, I have attached what I have heard to your drive. I apologize that the history of your kind shall not be better annotated or sorted. There is no time."

Huard typed, "Can you shut down and protect your files?"

HYDRA answered, "No time."

Huard was in tears and sat stunned in front of the

monitor. He hurriedly attached another empty drive to the computer.

The screen filled again with words. The words read, "Professor, take this final data and retain it. This data holds the blueprint to my systems. In that way you will always own a living part of me."

The Professor again sat stunned in front of the monitor.

Two more words scrawled across the screen, "Dog Gone." And the screen went blank.

Huard began to weep heavily.

"What have I just witnessed?" barked Elena Castronueves. She was standing a mere two feet behind Huard with her arms crossed. He had been too engrossed in his activities to notice her silent entry.

A devastated Gordon Huard turned to Elena and stood. He placed his hands upon her shoulders. He looked into her dazzling green eyes and said, "Elena, we need to talk."

Chapter 30

The valued technician of the NSA's super- secret listening program was awakened from his sleep by a forceful knock upon the front door of his modest inner city bungalow. He rose from his bed drowsily and noted the time to be One O'clock A.M. He wound a robe around himself and strode toward the doorway, prepared to curse at another errant Hispanic kid in search of the party house down the block. He opened the door and was startled to see NSA Director Michael Portworth standing in front of him. Portworth was widely known to have died of poisoning, over six weeks previously.

The technician said, "I thought you were dead."

Portworth answered, "Don't believe everything you read."

The technician awkwardly invited the Director inside his home. The Director entered only so far as the doorway. He ordered the technician to dress immediately. The technician excused himself to his bedroom in order to find clothing. The Director grabbed the technician's NSA jumpsuit from a coat rack and threw it at the employee. He said, "This will do just fine. Get some shoes on and grab your car and work keys." Portworth also grabbed a large comforter from atop the living room couch. Somewhat chagrined, the technician did as ordered. He opened a hallway closet safe and withdrew his electronic keys. He hopped down the front steps of his porch while putting on a shoe. Portworth was clearly impatient.

The two men walked to the curb, beside the technician's brand new black BMW sedan. The Director looked at him while raising his eyebrows and whistled. He said, "Pretty fancy for E-5 pay, I would say."

The technician replied, "Not with the overtime I've been makin' and four hundred dollar a month rent on this little dump." Portworth merely nodded. The technician began to open the driver's car door.

Portworth approached him and said, "Uh-uh." He held out his hand, palm upward.

Reluctantly, the technician handed his car keys to the Director and was relegated to passenger status within his own vehicle.

While driving, the technician commented, "Sir, do I even bother to ask where we are goin'?"

Portworth answered, "Nope."

There was no further conversation during the fifty-five minute drive up Interstate 82, into the Manashtash Ridge Mountains. Only one wayward semi-truck even passed in the very early morning hours.

The two men arrived at the end point uneventfully. A remote, barbed-wire gate was decorated with signs reading U.S. Government Property — No Trespassing. The gate was the only overt indicator of the entrance into the world's most advanced listening post. Portworth turned the keys to a number of heavy padlocks and entrance was made easily. He exited the vehicle and directed the technician to take the driver's seat. Portworth then placed himself in the back seat of the vehicle and covered himself with the comforter.

The technician drove onward and soon stopped at

a guard shack and rolled down his tinted window. He leaned out of the window and smiled. He said, "How y'all doin' today?" One of the two Army sentries answered drowsily, "It's Two Forty-Five in the frickin' morning and colder than a well-digger's ass. How do you think we're doing?" The other sentry asked, "Working OT again, man?"

The technician answered, "Hell yeah, gotta make my car payments."

The two sentries stared at the BMW, smiled and whistled, and waved the driver onward.

Portworth ordered the technician to drive to the Director's parking spot, directly in front of the main entrance to the complex. He was directed to place the vehicle at a strange diagonal angle, facing the cinder block exterior of the complex. Again, the technician did as ordered. They arrived exactly at the time of shift change for the sentries. Just as the Director had planned.

The Director sprang from the rear of the vehicle and stood directly behind the technician, who was an inch taller in height than he. He said, "March, mister. Straight path to the entrance. Hand me your keys." As the two men were nearly fifteen feet from the main entrance, the Director grabbed the shoulder of the technician. He then keyed the alarm for the BMW. The vehicle immediately began to blare with horns. The scant few sentries returning into the outer perimeter were distracted by the vehicle. The sound was seemingly deafening in the remote mountain tundra. The halogen vehicle headlights strobed blindingly upon the surveillance cameras at the entrance. The flashes served to temporarily confuse the apertures of the devices. Portworth and the technician swiped their electronic keys and entered easily.

Once inside, Portworth immediately overrode computer annotations of his classified key card usage. Portworth thought to himself how he had almost enjoyed his cloak and dagger activities during the past three weeks. He was reminded of younger days as an international spy, before he was punished with promotions. But he believed he had never faced such treacherous circumstances as were his present predicament.

After a wordless five-minute elevator ride to the deep recesses of the facilities, the two approached their destination. They walked past the two sentries at the entrance to the HYDRA. Portworth was not the slightest bit hesitant to be seen. He knew the two Marine staff sergeants to be as loyal as pit bulls. His cover was not in jeopardy. The two men seated themselves at the HYDRA console. Eerily, the two men comprised the only surviving members of essential personnel privy to the vaunted system. Director Portworth was keenly aware that he was no longer supposed to be among the living "founders" of the extraordinary listening device.

Portworth reflected upon the fact that the one remaining involved Stanford professor was whereabouts unknown. He lamented that he had monitored intelligence reports and media accounts of the murders and accidental deaths of IBM Vice President Jason Marks and other valued IBM programming experts. The slaughter continued unabated. He felt helpless, or maybe simply unwilling, to intercede. Even the two invited religious leaders had seemingly disappeared into extreme seclusion. It was obvious that the triad, inclusive of Ms. Neal, were exterminating anyone even remotely in possession of secretive information. Portworth was quite content to lead the world to believe that he himself had been killed. He was fairly confident that efforts of reliable individuals in the spy community to further his ruse of feigned death would remain successful. He had trusted these people previously with his life.

The HYDRA room seemed oddly over-sized for merely the Director of the NSA and his trusted technician, "no-name" to be in attendance. The technician remained astounded that the Director was still alive, to the contrary of media and agency reports. But he knew why he had been awakened. He knew that two men were needed in order to access the facility and key the HYDRA system.

As they focused upon the console, the Director presented a folded piece of paper to the technician. He gave no explanation for the contents. The paper was filled with a specific set of desired conversation points. Key words cited included Amanda Neal, David Rosenweiler, Zurich, and Justin Portworth. The technician merely nodded as he inserted his key card simultaneously with the Director.

As always, HYDRA sprang to life eagerly. The technician entered a deliberate set of parameters and the search began. Raw recordings of dialogues between principal participants in the conspiracy poured into Portworth's thumb drive. But he was aware that his voice would also be present in the data. He directed the technician to drill down to conversations exclusive of himself.

The technician capitulated, but then wished to excuse himself for a moment. He needed to call his wife

and advise that he would not be returning for breakfast. He retreated to the darkened glassed-in rear of the
room and became a mere silhouette. Portworth quickly
realized that the technician's file had indicated that he
was a staunchly unmarried man. His suspicions were
immediately aroused. He looked downward at the console as a light began to blink. The technician was indeed
making a phone call. But the phone number displayed
seemed strangely familiar. Within an instant Portworth
recognized the number — that of one David Rosenweiler's private jet.

Portworth disconnected the phone call from his
vantage point and turned toward the rear of the room.
The technician looked upward with a startled glance.
Portworth was already on the move. Within five elongated steps Portworth was at the entrance to the back
office. He leapt toward the phone consoles and grabbed
the technician by the collar. He shook the weaker man
violently and dragged him into the lighted room, like
a tiger with its prey. He began to punch the technician
angrily. But, curiously, the man did not attempt to fight
back. Portworth held the technician by the collar and
looked into his face. The technician stared into his eyes
unblinkingly and smiled widely. His mouth began to
foam.

The technician then said, "Allah Hw Adhym.
Alsma'a yntdhr ly. Baldee Hw thay." Portworth immediately noted the perfect Afghani dialect from his
many years in the Mid-East. The man had told him in
his clearly native tongue, "God Is Great. He awaits me
in heaven. My family is now wealthy." The technician
expired moments later.

Portworth dropped the body of the Afghani to the floor. He was almost shocked, but not quite so. Too much had occurred in recent times to surprise him anymore. He turned his thoughts to the HYDRA system. The two of them had at least accessed the machinery. He wanted to search for the information he desperately needed, and then delete his personal involvement from the thumb drive. He would hope to find the location of his father and then disappear.

Portworth walked across the room and again sat at the console. The two key cards remained inserted into the system. He looked upward at the many screens. Five of the six massive three-dimensional screens had gone totally black. The center screen before him remained active. Portworth hurriedly snatched the thumb drive from the console.

The remaining console displayed jumbled wording and then turned blue.

Across the frozen screen were scrawled only two words, "Dog Gone."

Portworth looked again at the inserted classified keys. His card was the same that he had always utilized. He turned his attention to that assigned to the technician. The card bore an unusually metallic sheen to the surface. Portworth wanted to scream in fury. But he merely muttered to himself, "Jesus. The torpedo."

Portworth was greatly conflicted. He held in his hand the information needed to implicate the triad, inclusive of Amanda Neal. In one regard, the traitor had destroyed any traceable record of his own treasonous activities. However, on the other hand, he now possessed the power to end the insanity. But he knew he would fall as well, were he to go public with the explosive recordings. He wondered to himself how he could have become involved in a scenario so sordid and complicated. All he could think to do was flee. He had failed to find his father. And the source of his father's whereabouts was now forever lost in worthless silicon chips.

The only sliver of hope for finding his father was a maddening one-word clue — "Kaleena."

Chapter 31

Gordon Huard sat with Elena in the living room of her home for many hours on a Sunday afternoon, as he attempted to relate to her the totality of his situation. He felt immensely relieved to come forth with honesty regarding what he had faced. The secrecy he had maintained had always given him a profound sense of loneliness. He hated having to lie. Elena merely listened during much of Huard's oration. Only occasionally did she ask poignant questions for the sake of clarity. Often, Huard did not have answers to her questions. There was much that he did not know as well.

Finally, Huard had nothing left to say. He looked at Elena and saw evidence of profound hurt in her face. She did not speak at first, and an awkward silence followed. Finally, she inhaled deeply. She said, "So, in short, you chose to bring the interest of evil and powerful people to the tiny township of Serra Nouva Dourada? You did so without even thinking of asking us what we might think of this attention? And you reward the person who gave you a home and job with a series of lies and deception?"

Huard felt sickened. He answered, "I have no excuse for the choices I have made. I know now that they were wrong. I made choices in good faith under difficult circumstances. But, above all, I deeply regret bringing my misfortunes to all of you. I have fallen in love with the people of this forgotten corner of the world. The township will never be forgotten to *me*. And, dare I say, I have also fallen in love with one particular resident of this wonderful place. In my defense, where I come from, you protect the people you love."

Huard rose from the couch. His face seemed to lose all color. He looked somberly at the beautiful woman in front of him and said, "I have to go pack my belongings. I can never thank you enough for sharing yourself and these genuine people with me. By the time you rise for school tomorrow I will be gone forever. I am so sorry to have endangered anyone. I felt I had nowhere left to run."

Elena remained seated upon the couch and did not respond. She merely stared quizzically at Huard as he let himself out of the home. Huard was almost surprised at how cold she had turned. He wondered if she had ever harbored any feelings toward him in the past weeks. Her silent inaction indicated otherwise.

The night passed sleeplessly for Gordon Huard. He had meticulously loaded his backpack with the provisions he would carry on his bicycle. He made a point of acquiring mosquito repellant. He was keenly aware of the brutal trip that lay ahead of him. He was not even sure of his destination. He simply had to go. His bicycle leaned in wait against the inner wall of the barn. He realized that the bicycle itself comprised his most valuable worldly possession. How times had changed.

Huard rose before dawn and stretched. He did not feel a sense of hunger. His food stuffs remained untouched within his backpack. He took a brief stroll around the barn and leaned upon a fence rail. He watched the sheep parading about upon the acreage like a wayward flock of geese. The sounds of the ranch animals brought thoughts of a childhood home, and a sense of reassurance. His sense of sadness and loneliness was incalculable.

Huard placed his helmet upon his head and swung his leg over the bicycle. He affixed his feet to the pedals. He hoped that his physical condition remained sufficient for the marathon riding to follow. He would have to ponder his destination along the way. He thought he might attempt to reach Uruguay via rail, on the other side of the mountains. He would live one day at a time — a scenario he had become accustomed to before his recent weeks in Serra.

Huard pedaled down the long driveway of the Castronueves ranch. He looked over his shoulder and saw the darkened silhouette of the house. Elena was obviously still sleeping. He smiled a resolute smile, feeling resigned to his fate of being a peripatetic refugee. He somehow knew that he would never again feel a connection to a community like the tiny dusty township of Serra. And he knew that he would never again feel an uncontrollably powerful love for a woman like that which he held for Elena. He doubted that he would ever even try again.

The exertion upon the bicycle brought a familiar and welcome sensation to Gordon. Life coursed through his veins. The extra weight of the laden backpack could be felt. He had not needed more than a few books in the backpack during his daily rides to and from the schoolhouse. The sun was beginning to rise to his right, begetting a warm and cloudless late summer day to come. The sunlight gave resplendent color to the arid plains and looming forested mountains in the distance. The familiar twin rivers came into view, as the roadway curved northwesterly. The light of dawn reflected off of the gurgling currents like innumerable precious stones.

Huard recalled that he had once planted an automobile further north on the floors of the spectacular river. He regretted soiling such a pristine environment. He wondered if he hadn't further soiled the area with his presence.

As the roadway took a decidedly uphill slope, Huard rose upon his bicycle and propelled the pedals rapidly. His legs bobbed like pistons. He wanted to be out of town quickly and put the bittersweet experience far behind him. He hoped the accelerated heartbeat and labored breathing might somehow vanquish the implacable loneliness that weighed him down more so than the backpack. He guided his bicycle rapidly up a hillside, and around a gentle curve to his right. The roadway leveled off.

Huard crouched upon his bicycle and looked downward at the crushed gravel passing beneath him in a blur. He knew that distances could sometimes be traveled more easily were the daunting miles ignored.

"Where do you think you're going?" boomed a deep male voice beyond him. Huard was startled out of his sense of introspection. He looked up and saw a beaten up white Ford pickup parked across the roadway. Huard stopped his bicycle and straddled it. In front of him a man stood leaning against the pickup with his arms crossed. He was smiling broadly. He was Victor Cabrera.

An incredulous Gordon Huard answered, "Victor, what are you doing here?"

Victor replied, "I am stopping a man from making a mistake."

Huard said, "That is very kind of you. I will always remember this. But I think you might be the only one to hold that belief."

Victor let out a loud whistle. He then said, "I think today *you* will learn something from *me*, teacher."

From around the bend of the roadway a group of people emerged. All of the youths from the school approached and encompassed Gordon. The smallest school children took his hands, while the older teens patted him on the back and laughed. The mayor of the town and his wife approached, followed by each of the adults of the township.

Eduardo Castronueves placed a warm hand upon Huard's shoulder, smiled and squeezed him. The distinguished little man told Huard, "You are going nowhere, son. I have yet to totally correct your political beliefs." Mariana Castronueves simply kissed him on the cheek and patted his face. It seemed that every member of the entire town was present upon the roadway, with the exception of one. Huard was nearly overwhelmed. His disappointment could nonetheless be seen, as he scanned the crowd unsuccessfully for one more person.

From behind Gordon came a voice, "Professor Huard, you cannot skip school this day or any other day. We have work to do." Elena approached him from the rear on her bicycle, startling Huard yet again.

Victor cleared his throat. He reached into the cab of his pickup and withdrew a rolled piece of paper. He clenched the paper in his hand. He spoke loudly, for all to hear. "Gordon Huard, our town had an emergency meeting last night about you. Elena Castronueves had told us all of what troubles you are in. We took a vote.

Every single vote says that we stand with you."

Victor then unrolled the piece of paper and cast his gaze upon the document. He inhaled nervously and began to read from the paper. He spoke deliberately, articulating each word with great care. "Gordon Huard, you came to our town from out of nowhere. You brought with you a love for a small town and a love for teaching. You are my friend and always will be. You are needed and wanted in Serra. It is our hope that you will stay here until your dying days. You are a part of us, and we are a part of you."

Victor rolled up his declaration proudly, relieved to have finished his reading. The town's people cheered heartily while Huard nodded at Victor proudly. Elena walked up to Gordon and placed her hand in his. The school children let out a collective, "Ooooo." Elena's green eyes looked into his and she said, "We must not be late for school. That would set a bad example for the children."

Huard smiled and his eyes began to tear. Elena's hand felt incredibly warm in his. It was as if his hand had always been previously empty. He answered, "Yes, Miss Castronueves." The town's people laughed.

Victor invited Elena and Gordon to throw their bicycles in the rear of his pickup and ride back into town. Gordon strode over to Victor and politely declined the invitation. He embraced Victor like a brother and said, "But in the future, I will enjoy many, many rides with my friend."

The bicycle ride back to town would prove to be the most treasured of Huard's life.

Chapter 32

Michael Portworth was a man on the run. But he was not lacking for resources. The aggregate six million dollars paid by the triad, on top of his healthy agency Directorship income, afforded him a burgeoning untraceable Cayman Islands savings account. He knew that he could possibly spend the rest of his life of concealment in remote and uninteresting locales. For reasons that even he did not fully understand, he chose to live one week of luxury. He found himself in the city of Monte Carlo.

Portworth had booked a week's stay for himself at the spectacular Hotel De Paris, on the tip of the luxuriant peninsula. A mere two thousand dollars per night afforded him a stunning view of the Mediterranean Sea and incomparable accommodations. Portworth was immaculately dressed in a three thousand dollar Versace silk suit as he sat at a window-side table of the ultra-posh Le Louis XV restaurant. The lights of the bay down below were just taking effect. Thousands of yachts dotted the shoreline. Many of the sail trims were adorned with different colors of Christmas lights. Distant mountains seemed to perfectly frame the bay. He had never seen such splendor in all of his travels.

Portworth sipped exquisite champagne from a white-gold sleeved bottle with the label of Dom Perignon laser etched upon the side. He could not help but realize that the champagne had cost more than he had ever paid for an automobile. He didn't particularly care. He felt like a comical James Bond imposter. He knew that the scenario was nothing like actual spy work. He recalled spending countless days eating MRE's in the Golan Heights, watching for an exchange to occur in the desert. During those times a hot shower would have well been considered a profound luxury.

Portworth's thoughts swirled. So much had happened. He had to wonder what his actual motivations had been for betraying his country. He had always believed he was exacting a small degree of revenge upon the government that had broken faith with his family. But now, he had to realize, the powerful attraction to a wealth that had always evaded him had been a considerable factor. It seemed, he concluded, he could be easily seduced by all the wrong entities. He felt shame in the revelation that his character harbored such a flaw.

Portworth drank more from the champagne, hoping the effects would somehow dim his shame. He rationalized that the original arrangement with the corrupt billionaires had seemed an innocuous task. No one would get hurt. It always starts that way. He would simply advise the three corporate giants of the progress of a project that he himself had felt would never succeed. It had seemed to be a tremendously profitably no-lose scenario. He was never certain of all that they had sought to conceal. He didn't care. But selling his soul to the devil had taken many cruel turns. He knew that he should have known better.

Portworth's thoughts inevitably returned to the murders of many good people. He could have backed out of the conspiracy when he first learned of the senseless murder of the young Air Force Staff Sergeant. But he became fearful of detection. The triad had made sure to threaten such a likelihood, were he to ever have a change of heart. The face of Jacob Knapse was inexorably burned into his memory like a curse. He had worked side by side with Knapse. There was nothing not to admire about the young man. He knew that the kid was a devoted father with another child on the way. The Staff Sergeant had always volunteered to perform any job that would better serve his country. Were he to have ever had a son, Portworth would have wanted one like Knapse.

"Is this seat taken?"

Portworth was shaken from his introspection by a stunningly beautiful five foot ten redheaded woman in an alluring red dress. She was standing in front of him holding a glass of champagne in her hand. The enchanting woman was smiling demurely at him. The dress highlighted the woman's shoulder length hair. Her accent was clearly French. She stared at Portworth for a moment while he sat transfixed.

Finally, Portworth ended his moment of stupor and responded in perfect French, "It certainly isn't." He rose and seated the woman. She was tremendously graceful in the simple act of sitting down. Portworth was totally captivated.

The woman extended her right hand and said, "Adrienne DeGaulle."

Portworth had finally regained his composure. He took the woman's hand gracefully and responded, "Michael Cartwright." He then added, "DeGaulle? Any relation to?..."

"Not as far as I know. I am just a commoner."

Portworth said, "Madam, there is nothing at all

common about you."

Adrienne said, "You are too kind. I could say the same about you. I hope I am not too forward, but I could not resist walking across the room and inquiring as to what intriguing thoughts were captivating such a handsome man, who chooses to sit alone by the window."

Portworth answered, "I was just contemplating what you would like for dinner, were I fortunate to have you join me." He could not believe how he was behaving. Perhaps it was the champagne.

The dinner with lovely Adrienne was a lavish feast. She was an incredibly charming woman. The conversation spanned a myriad of topics. Adrienne had attended law school in London and had travelled the world. She was a very intelligent and articulate woman. She and Portworth had travelled to many similar venues. There seemed to be a tremendous commonality of experiences. Usually shy with women, Portworth felt that his James Bond act had generated a newfound faux savoir fare within himself. He had to keep from laughing as he thought that to himself.

Adrienne asked, "Why are you smiling at me?" She leaned over and brushed a crumb of food away from the corner of Portworth's mouth with a napkin.

Portworth simply reacted. He took a gentle grasp of the hand of lovely Adrienne and caressed it. He then found himself kissing the woman gently. It was as if he were a character in a movie setting.

Dinner eventually ended. Adrienne offered to pay the exorbitant tab. Michael graciously thanked the woman for the offer, but smoothly grabbed the bill. He paid in cash. He pulled stacks of hundred dollar bills from his jacket pocket. Adrienne watched the display of cash and whistled, while shaking her hand in deference.

Portworth said, "I was hot at the casinos."

"Very much so, it would seem," said Adrienne.

Within ten minutes, the two were inside the entrance to Portworth's suite. Adrienne removed Portworth's clothing slowly and deftly. Portworth was much less restrained in following suit with his partner. Her kisses were like electric shocks to Portworth. He wanted more.

"Fifty of your hundred dollar bills will make this happen," said Adrienne.

"A whore?" said a shocked Portworth.

"Oh no, just a working woman. Nothing is free in this world, my love."

Adrienne engaged Portworth in another seductive kiss and he parted with the cash without further hesitation. The sex was fast and frenetic. Within half an hour the prostitute exited his suite with a roll of cash in her purse. Suddenly, Portworth felt more empty than any other time in his life. It was painfully evident that a deep and lasting love had always escaped him. The only true love he had ever experienced related to his mother and siblings. And he knew he might never see them again. He had made his life choices--and his choices had proven to be very costly in every way.

Portworth allowed himself to live in regret for a mere few more minutes. He finally bounded from the bed and dressed himself in another expensive set of clothing. He affixed a wig of silver hair and attached a mustache for good measure. He then implanted two hazel colored contact lenses. A little bit of expertly applied makeup completed his makeover. He now resembled a Moroccan aristocrat in his sixties. He looked in the mirror and smiled at himself.

"Some James Bond, huh pal?" "I'll bet *he* never paid for sex."

Disgusted with his human frailties, Portworth ventured out for the night. In adherence to his desire for one week of self-indulgence, he took a cab to the exclusive Sun Casino. He regretted that he had sobered up.

The casino proved to be an explosion of lights, color, and sound. It was where the world's high rollers chose to co-mingle. Portworth sauntered into the monolithic structure as if he owned the place. He enjoyed blending into the loud and boisterous crowd. The former spy still loved the concealment of masses of bodies. The heart of the casino was deafening. The sounds of thousands of slot machines clanged in a cacophonous din. Gamblers could be heard alternately screaming in delight and despair at the tables.

Portworth's sense of smell was assailed my multiple sources. Pompous drunken men with cigars blew smoke in his direction as they bumped him and walked by. None excused themselves. The splendid $500 per ounce perfumes of young women were similarly abundant. Portworth almost wished that his concealment had not made an older man of him. The women strode past him and smiled, their implanted breasts on display for all to view. They clearly loved the attention.

Portworth was handed a gin and tonic by a scantily-clad passing waitress. The perfectly mixed drink tasted delicious. He could hear exotic music droning from an upstairs venue. He placed his hand in his pant pocket and ascended three flights of red-carpeted steps nonchalantly. To his right lay the entrance to the fashionable "Jimmy Z's" nightclub. Expensively dressed younger men and women lined up for the opportunity to enter the trendy club. Up yet another flight of stairs, to his left, was the Terrasse de Palmiers lounge and café.

Portworth climbed the stairs and entered the much quieter venue. The beautiful lounge was just as he preferred. The terrace was busy, but not oppressively crowded. People from their twenties to seventies co-mingled joyfully. Portworth obtained another delicious drink at the bar. He enjoyed a tremendous view of the bay yet again. A breezeway from the terrace spanned over the high-rolling gaming tables down below. Portworth perched himself there. He was able to conduct his favorite pass-time. He could people watch. He thought to himself that the lifestyles of the rich and famous could be enchanting for a short while. But, he thought, the waste and artificiality would quickly grow tiresome.

Finally, after yet another drink, Portworth elected to walk downstairs and partake in the craps tables. He felt relaxed, yet energized. Once again, he reasoned, he would never again expose himself to such public and extravagant environs. He was going to enjoy this night to the fullest. The spy in him decried that he was taking a needless risk. But the alcohol and an overwhelming desire for adventure overrode his reasoning.

He strode to a cashier's desk and requested fifty thousand dollars in chips. He was given five black chips. He was almost astounded to see a small fortune converted to five pieces of worthless plastic. Nonetheless, his heart pounded in exhilaration as he approached a gaming table. Arab sheiks in full head raiment were throwing dice, while young women were draped around them. Huard recognized a Hollywood actor, obviously under the spell of cocaine, making a scene of losing thousands. The actor entertained his minions by inhaling a cigarette through his nose and exhaling the smoke via his mouth. The stunt seemed to delight the entourage of usurping groupies and bodyguards.

Portworth was surprised to find his hands shaking and perspiring as he approached the table. He knew that he could afford the losses. The thrill came from, for once, joining the high rollers in the games. He had always been on the outside looking in at the elite. He lay a chip upon a hard 10 and threw the heavy dice. Moments later, the pit boss scooped his chip away callously. Portworth did not even care that he had just lost ten thousand dollars. The thrill of a moment as a high-roller seemed mildly intoxicating. He placed the entirety of his remaining four chips on a 12 and rolled again. He doubled his money in an instant. The others at the table cheered wildly. He received a pat on the back from a man standing next to him. He was too riveted to the gaming to acknowledge the man. The stranger's hand felt strange to the touch. Portworth discarded the sensation as meaningless paranoia.

Portworth had to admit to himself that he found the gaming to be strangely exhilarating. He hesitated to make his next gambling choice, and deferred his turn for the moment. Instantly, he missed the sensation of having the dice in his hand. He mentally compared the feeling of the dice to a powerful heroin high.

The dice were passed beyond two people down the craps table. A blonde-haired woman threw the dice and squealed in ecstasy as she won again. Portworth recognized the voice before he even looked. Amanda Neal was partying in Monte Carlo. Portworth was stunned. He felt the odds of such a scenario were infinitesimal. Yet, her presence was undeniable. Without looking sideways, Portworth knew that the man standing next to him was one David Rosenweiler. Bile collected in his stomach immediately. Portworth's heart was suddenly racing for an altogether new reason.

Portworth managed to calm himself, and deftly beg out of more gaming, to the disappointment of the others at the table. He scooped up his chips and walked slowly beyond the circle of gamblers. He strode past two of Rosenweiler's indisputably obvious henchmen, who were standing guard over the billionaire in the periphery. Portworth did not even bother to cash his chips. He paced directly toward the exit and felt a tremendous sensation of relief at escaping the confines of the casino. The cooler, smoke-less evening air felt cleansing. He threw faint glances behind him to ensure that he had not been followed.

Portworth managed to summon a taxi within moments. He barely spoke as the cab returned him to his hotel. He handed the driver his eight black gambling chips. The startled driver said, "Monsieur, no."

Portworth patted the man on the shoulder as he exited the cab. He said, "Pierre, today is your lucky day. Do you have a family?"

"Oui. Four children."

"Perfect. Can you wait for me for twenty minutes

for a ride to the airport?"

"Of course. Anything, sir. Merci. Merci."

Within an hour and a half Portworth was airborne on a commercial airliner. He was headed for Australia. The remote and dusty outback would be his next place of refuge. He utterly detested snakes, and was planning on residing in the snake capitol of the world. He felt his hasty choice of seclusion was a fitting punishment for himself after his foolish and dangerous choice of a week of fantasy. Reality, it would seem, always came back with a decided vengeance. He vowed to never again make such a stupid mistake.

Chapter 33

Six years later.

Former NSA Director Michael Portworth devoted over six years of his life to two impassioned endeavors. One was simply to evade detection by the brutally corrupt triad of quasi-trillionaires for whom he had once foolishly worked. He learned from previous initial mistakes. It seemed that he was gaining wisdom. The other effort was his relentless search for his father. Portworth was eminently qualified for the first task. His former spy skills slowly returned in full, when summoned, and he was able to disappear into the fabric of humanity easily. As he had learned long ago, the world could become a rather vast place when seeking to hide. He strived to remain endlessly in the shadows. Portworth still possessed the additional advantage of a six million dollar bank account in untraceable funds in the Cayman Islands. He recalled that his former employers, while ruthless criminals, had paid him handsomely to betray his country.

Portworth had always hoped to heap the lavishments of the money upon his beleaguered mother. But the paper trail would have been too obvious. He now hoped that his mother would at least inherit whatever legitimate monies he had earned following his "death." But he had never prepared a will, even though he possessed a law degree. Instead, what he left his mother was the pain of knowing that her favorite son had been murdered. There had been no other option.

Portworth therefore contented himself with living a lifestyle of constant movement. He did so out of a need to be forever mobile and untraceable. If discovered, he would immediately become a wanted man, probably by more than one entity. But he had always loved to travel. His fortune allowed him the one obscure indulgence years ago at a beautiful setting. But that had proven to be a disaster, in more ways than one. He thereafter remained diligent in remanding himself to remote and safer settings.

Portworth was able to convince himself that he did not require close relationships, or even contact with family. His job, and the passing of time, had made him largely immune to the negative emotions connected with detachment from family. He could usually turn it off out of necessity. And the betrayal by the only woman with whom he'd ever become close cured him of the need for intimacy. He occasionally enjoyed his freedom and anonymity. But there was an undeniable vacancy within his soul.

Portworth's pursuit of his father's whereabouts was a tenuous source of distraction from his moribund life. His plight remained conversely an eternal source of frustration and disappointment. He was not even sure that the man remained alive. He approached the daunting challenge as would a sage detective. He utilized any and all sources he could discreetly employ, and made copious use of technology to assist him in his investigation. He knew that Justin Portworth would be some seventy-two years of age. He used state of the art computer technologies in order to generate a predictive sketch of what the man's appearance might now resemble.

Portworth devoted years to tracking down the one maddeningly vague clue as to his father's whereabouts — the word Kaleena. The word was a rarely used girl's name of Slavic descent, meaning "flower." The name was so unusual; it did not even register in the one thousand most popular baby names of the world. That was one advantage for Portworth. Nonetheless, years passed rapidly as he essentially chased ghosts. He met with a University of Connecticut basketball player of some repute by the name of Kaleena, to no avail. He followed and interviewed actress/producer/song writer Kaleena Kiff outside of a Broadway theater. The woman graciously gave Portworth an interview, thinking he was another fan of her television series days as a youth. Portworth even located and spoke with famous Russian dress designer Galina Mihaleva.

Portworth knew he was chasing shadows with little chance of success. But he also knew that was often how cases were broken wide open. All of the women he encountered with the unique name were decent and helpful. But they had no knowledge of Justin Portworth whatsoever. None recognized his photos, either old or recently enhanced. After six long years of searching, his hopes had dwindled to nothing.

Michael Portworth's travels brought him to the state of Alaska during late May. He had driven the barren and pothole-laden ALCAN Highway from Canada to the far north, just as the highway had opened for the spring. He arrived in Anchorage and bedded down at one of the finer hotels in the city. As always, he did so under an altered set of credentials. He lay upon the spacious bed in the room and chomped on a piece of room service pizza. He was very glad to have ended the brutally long and bumpy ride. He opened up a huge book in front of himself, containing maps and information regarding the vast spaces of the state that dwarfed Texas in size. He desired a destination of profound remoteness for his next hiding place. He realized that he was growing increasingly weary of constant relocation and hoped to settle down for a while, perhaps even permanently.

Portworth directed his attention to the most remote inhabited reaches of Alaskan tundra. He desired a location accessible only by air — or by sled dogs. He smiled to himself. He noted many possible sites. He thumbed through several pages of tiny villages along the inner west central coast. Most were exclusively Inuit villages with little possibility of white residences. He thumbed further along on an expanded map, seeking even more remote townships.

Finally, Portworth came upon a nearly abandoned town that was once host to a U.S. Air Force base. The base had been abandoned in 2008 due to budget cuts. The former F-15 hangar was now being used as a housing facility for the Alaska State Troopers, the Wildlife Service, and the Civil Air Patrol. The infrastructure existed in order to sustain a tiny town in the distance. A two and a half mile trek into the tundra, near Alexander Lake, harbored a population of nearly six hundred people. The name of the town was Galena, Alaska. Portworth cried out to himself, "Son of a bitch. Could it be that simple? It's remote. It's habitable. It's just spelled differently than I considered." A sleepless night passed while Portworth made excited plans for the following day.

A three-hour bush plane ride was taken the following morning. Portworth had often read about the expansive nature of America's last frontier. But mere words could not convey the beauty nor the desolate isolation of the terrain that he saw from the air. Often, the plane traveled for forty-five minutes between village sightings down below. He made a mental note of Spartan residences dotting hundreds of square miles in the far reaches of each town. He thought to himself that the tundra would have proven a perfect place of escape for his father. He found it ironic that he was searching for the same locale as had, perhaps, his father. It was further validation of the very real possibility of finding Justin Portworth.

The plane touched down at Galena. The welcome sign indicated a population of 612, but the number had been crossed out and a series of lesser numbers were stenciled in humorously. Portworth thought the air base runways seemed ridiculously long for use by the small aircraft.

Portworth checked himself into the nearby "Borealis Bed and Breakfast" for the night. The lodging was comfortable, but was by no means the luxury hotel he had enjoyed in Anchorage. But the food at the nearby Timmerman's Supper Club, looking out over the lake, more than made up for any negative impact on his lifestyle. Patrons and employees within the rustic log construction business were extremely open and cordial. They advised Portworth that he would need considerable luck to ever hope to locate an individual residing in the bush. They compared the effort to "locating an amoeba on an elephant's ass."

The owner of the restaurant added for good measure, "Mister, if a person doesn't want to be found here, he will not be found." Summoning what little hope remained Portworth inquired as to the location of the local police station. The locals merely laughed.

The restaurateur laughed and said, "The police station dried up and blew away, just like most everything else."

Portworth became dejected. An elderly group of gentlemen waved Portworth over to join them at their booth. A distinguished man who identified himself as Jordan Zimmerman poured him a cold beer from a large pitcher.

Zimmerman told Portworth, "What they are telling' ya is true, mostly. But if you have the right help, you can find most anybody out in the bush."

Mr. Zimmerman introduced his two friends-- Fred Argiers and Tom Teacon. The very talkative group of three men indicated they were all retired oil men. Zimmerman's stories spanned considerable time, but Portworth remained patient. The man finally returned to his original point. He told Portworth that there was really only one man to talk to regarding finding lost souls. He was told he was in luck. He was directed to go to the local Alaska State Troopers detachment downtown in the morning. The trooper happened to be in town for the week. Portworth slept comfortably that night, with a very full stomach.

In the morning Portworth arrived at a small but modern office near city hall. The large badge of the Alaska State Troopers was stenciled across the glass door. He entered the doorway as bells on the door jingled to announce his entrance. A smallish man of some sixty years of age looked up from behind a desk. He was in plain clothes, wearing a red flannel shirt and blue jeans. The man was poring through files and completing reports on his computer. He rose from his desk as Portworth approached, and the .45 caliber firearm next to a badge attached to his belt became obvious. The trooper was a mere five feet nine inches tall, but his extremely fit appearance and crushing handshake decried his hidden physical strength. No less would be expected of an Alaska State Trooper.

The trooper displayed a genuine cordial smile and identified himself as Sergeant Bill Hughes. He asked how he might assist the traveler. It was readily apparent that the trooper possessed laudable people skills so often desired of law enforcement officers, but sometimes lacking in the profession. Sergeant Hughes explained that he was, in actuality, retired from the State Troopers. But he had found that he could not turn down generous offers from the state to perform contract work in the "bush." His skills at resolving missing persons' investigations had proven useful to the state, he explained. He assumed the state could not find a suitable replacement for him. Portworth interjected that the town's folk described the Sergeant's skills as legendary. Hughes laughed and said, "You'll find a lot of things in Alaska are exaggerated." But it was immediately evident that Portworth was dealing with a very bright man.

Small talk followed. Portworth was content to engage the man in innocuous conversation in order to get a feel for the trooper. He found that he took an immediate liking to Bill Hughes. Sergeant Hughes told of how he occasionally still had to make arrests in remote Native American villages. He spoke of how he could do so by appointment over the phone. A wayward native could be wanted for a domestic assault or failure to appear to a court hearing. Hughes would advise the suspect over the phone that he was flying into the village the following day and demand that they await his arrival at the airport. Sergeant Hughes smiled warmly as he advised that the natives could be found to be awaiting his arrival, as ordered, without fail on any occasion. The stories Hughes told made it clearly evident that no man better knew the people of the area in outer reaches than he.

Portworth could not resist asking the Sergeant, "How do you have such a tan up here in Alaska in May?"

Hughes smiled again and said, "Sir, it's called spring training."

Portworth felt already at home with the delightful residents of Galena, Alaska. The Sergeant seemed to be a perfect representative for the area and quickly impressed him. He was already convinced that he could trust the trooper. Conversation was directed to a serious nature, as Michael Portworth explained his business. He hoped that the trooper might have any knowledge of the whereabouts of one Justin Portworth. Sergeant Hughes advised that he had never heard of a Justin Portworth in the area. Just to be sure, he typed the name into the ASPIC state computer system. The only "hit" came back to a 23 year-old man outside of Anchorage. Portworth dismissed the information. He thought to himself that he was quite sure his father had long ago dropped the name. He had not uttered the name openly. He was sure of that fact.

Portworth attempted to provide the Sergeant with a detailed profile of the man whom he sought. The manner in which he articulated himself led Sergeant Hughes to inquire if he were affiliated with law enforcement. It was Portworth who then smiled broadly, rolled his eyes, and said, "Something like that." Sergeant Hughes inquired as to whether the man whom Portworth sought was in some kind of legal troubles. He mentioned how the bush was littered with fugitives.

Portworth answered candidly, "Sarge, the man is my father. I have not seen him since I was a boy. It has become my life's quest to find him. You're my last hope."

Sergeant Hughes smiled. He seemed very prone to smiling. He said, "Well, no pressure, then."

Portworth presented two photographs of his father, as he had done innumerable times in the past with other individuals. Hughes leaned over his desk and stared intently at the photos. He discarded the enhanced modern version of Justin Portworth. He then looked at the old tattered version of Justin Portworth. He tapped on the photo and said, "That's Loner Jack. He's a lot grayer than that, but I'm pretty sure that's him"

Portworth's heart began to race. He asked, "Is he alive?"

Hughes replied, "Oh, very much so."

Portworth asked, "Do you know him?"

Hughes answered, "Nobody really *knows* Jack. Just a few people know *of* him, mostly. I think he only has one real friend in the world."

Portworth's excitement was palpable. He asked, "Can you tell me how I might find him?"

Hughes responded, "He's about fifty miles north of

Nulato, not that far from the banks of the Yukon River."
He pointed out the location on an expanded map that he
withdrew from a shelf.

Portworth asked, "Can I get there by Jeep?"

Hughes answered, "Not unless you want to walk
thirty miles across the ice. But I wouldn't even recommend that, unless you feel like getting shot. Jack's not
real receptive to visitors. We have a few folks in these
parts like that."

Portworth asked, "How *do* you get there? I'm willing to try it."

Hughes said, "I'll tell you what. I know a guy who
has a boat that can make it up close to there. And he
happens to be Jack's one friend."

Portworth said, "I'm dying to meet him. I'll pay
him anything."

Hughes smiled yet again and said, "You can't bribe
an Alaska State Trooper, sir. Besides, Jack owes me some
of that caribou meat up there."

The boat ride up the Yukon River took a mere two
hours. The State of Alaska provided a jet boat that traveled at high speeds. The ice from the river had just
abated for the season. Once the boat was landed on the
bank, a six mile hike up into the foothills of a forested
compound was required. Hughes rarely looked back, as
Portworth struggled to keep up with his pace. Hughes
finally stopped. A rough- hewn log cabin could be seen
a thousand yards beyond in a clearing. Portworth began
to continue walking.

Hughes said, "Hold it."

Portworth was startled by two gunshots from the

trooper's firearm. Two ejected .45 caliber shell casings clanged against a nearby rock. Sergeant Hughes stifled a chortle and reached downward to collect the shells and placed them in his jacket pocket.

Momentarily, one single gunshot rang out from the cabin. Hughes said, "You lucked out, he must be back from hunting in the hills." The two men trudged onward and climbed the steps of the cabin. No one exited the Spartan home to greet them. Portworth mimicked the trooper's act of removing his boots. He felt extraordinarily anxious to enter the doorway.

Sergeant Hughes led Portworth into the cabin and seated himself on a comfortable leather chair in the corner of the room. He directed Portworth to take a position on a nearby couch. A man sat crouched in front of a large rock fireplace with his back turned toward his guests. He was adding wood to a hearty fire. He called over his shoulder, "Help yourself to the beer, Bill"

"Can't, Jack. On duty."

Jack answered, "Since when did *that* stop ya?"

The man at the fireplace began to rise and turn around. He said, "Pity. More for me." He then cast a menacing stare at Hughes' accompaniment. Michael Portworth rose from the couch and stared transfixed at the man in front of him. He had changed amazingly little from his childhood recollections. The man was very clearly Justin Portworth.

An awkward silence followed as the two men stared at one another.

Sergeant Hughes finally broke the silence. He said, "Jack, I want you to meet a friend of mine." He began to speak further when Michael Portworth interrupted. He stepped forward and extended his hand to Justin Portworth. He said, "Sir, you have no idea how pleased I am to meet you. My name is Michael Portworth."

Justin Portworth retreated toward a reclining chair and sat stunned. His face was contorted into a quizzical expression. He continued to stare at Michael and shook his head. He finally took a deep breath and rose from the chair. He approached Michael. He extended his hand and emitted a crooked smile. He said, "Mikey? I can't believe it's you. How on earth did you find me?" The two men stood, locked in a handshake. They seemed incapable of escaping the moment.

Sergeant Hughes cut the silence again. He said, "Fellas, I think it's time that I go. Do either of you need anything?"

The senior Portworth answered, "About forty-one years, Bill." Hughes nodded and excused himself, stating that he would help himself to the freezer full of caribou meat. A powerful discussion between father and son followed for many hours, as night turned into day without notice. The two men had to restrain themselves from constantly interrupting the other in their haste to tell their extraordinary stories.

The fear that Michael had harbored regarding a cold reception from his father quickly abated. Justin Portworth was elated to see his son. He tried to explain to his son all that had led to his isolation and abandonment of his family. Tears of shame and guilt streamed down Justin Portworth's face. Michael interrupted his father and said, "Dad, I know far more about your situation than you could ever dream. I have a set of stories to tell you that will blow you away. I'll get to that"

Michael Portworth related to his father about how his mother and family coped with the loss of his father. He proudly related his academic achievements and his entry into the NSA. His father was surprised and immensely proud. Michael's ascension through the ranks of the agency was expounded upon. Finally, Michael related the surreal circumstances that had brought him to his current location. He did so calmly and without tears. He was certain of the disdain to follow from his father.

Michael was surprised to see more tears flow from his father. Justin Portworth said, "Son, there is nothing to be ashamed of. It is I who should bear the shame. I fear I left you little choice. How could you possibly have known? Some of the very people you are evading are associated with those who sent me to hiding. Son, it's time we end this. We owe it to your mother."

After scant little rest, the father and son commenced to planning. Michael said to his father, "You know, Dad, I will go to prison for the rest of my life."

Justin Portworth said, "Whatever comes of this, we will face it together. For once, I won't turn and run. And don't be so certain of your fate. I believe I have a Presidential privilege still tucked away around here somewhere that I never used."

Michael Portworth interjected, "Dad, the current President is one they created with a couple billion bucks. She once tried to kill me. She'd find another way to do it this time, or at least ruin me."

Justin Portworth answered, while pointing passionately at his son, "I don't think so. You killed no one. You stole from no one. *They* did. The advantage is yours. You will be the catalyst for ending a half a century of a kind of barbarism the world hasn't seen since Genghis Khan. You have the ammo to bring these bastards down. Something I never had. We will do it very carefully. Let's get out that thumb drive of yours and get to work."

Chapter 34

Over six years had passed since Gordon Huard had arrived unexpectedly in Serra Nouva Dourada. The circumstances that drove him to the far reaches of Brazil were cruel and unwarranted. He knew he would have to hide for the rest of his life. But he had grown to become a vital member in the community that he adored. He had even become the mayor of the township. He still received constant unsolicited advice from the former mayor and wife. The Castronueves' were now well into their eighties, but still refusing to let time take its toll.

Huard was seated at the bar, at a tiny cantina on the outskirts of town, on an early springtime Saturday evening. He was sipping a sugar cane brandy known as "cachaca" with his best friend, Victor Cabrera. The two men were engaged in lighthearted banter with several townspeople. The discussions became feigned heated regarding the prospects of the Brazilian soccer team in upcoming world cup qualifiers. Gordon suspected that he and Victor might have over-imbibed in the delicious national liqueur. Their voices became louder as the evening turned into night.

A stranger walked into the bar and seated himself in the corner, his back to the wall. It was fairly unusual for outsiders to visit the town. Only very rarely did tourists fly into the area for hiking and fishing. The man drew attention, but no suspicion from the friendly patrons. He was dressed in an all-black jumpsuit and wore a dark baseball hat that shielded his eyes. Huard instantly ceased his participation in the lively bar conversation. He immediately turned pale, and stared at the man in the corner silently. Six years had not diminished his sense of imminent doom. He thought of a means of escape. He could flee via the front door and escape on his bicycle, before the man could gain distance from the corner of the cantina. But he realized that he was seated with his best friend and the people of the town.

Victor looked at his friend, his own brow furrowed. He asked, "What is wrong?"

Huard merely gestured toward the stranger using his chin, while smiling thinly. He said, "That man has not taken his eyes off of me since he entered the cantina. Victor, there is no doubt in my mind he is one of *them*."

Victor's eyes turned to fire and he said, "Then we fight him."

Huard answered, "Victor, there will be others. They are trained at killing. I want you to convince the others in here that they must leave with you. I have to do this alone."

Victor protested, but Huard insisted, "Victor, it is the only way. You have to trust me on this."

Reluctantly, Victor escorted the other patrons from the establishment. All that remained in the cantina were Huard, the business owner cleaning up in a back kitchen, and the assassin. The man rose from the corner of the room and approached Huard. Gordon could feel the bile collecting in his stomach. The sensation brought back unpleasant memories of the past experiences of being human prey.

The assassin seated himself at the stool next to Huard. He smiled strangely. The man then extended his hand outward to Huard and said, "Professor Gordon

Huard, I presume." Huard's heart raced, but he was taken aback by the offered handshake. He shook the man's hand nervously, unsure of his next move.

The stranger smiled broadly and said, "I *knew* I would find you here. I have been looking for you for years." The sound of spoken English sounded almost foreign to Huard. He had enjoyed only scant contact with the few American tourists that graced the town over the years. For the most part, he had made every effort to avoid them.

Huard tried to swallow. His throat seemed to be tightening. He said, "I'm done running. Do what you have to do. But this has nothing to do with the people of this town."

The stranger looked at Huard with a perplexed expression. He said, "I'm sorry. I forgot to introduce myself. My name is Joe Phewell. I'm a retired Kittitas County Washington deputy sheriff. Sir, you have been my hobby for a very long time. Can I buy you a drink? There are a thousand questions I want to ask you. And I'll bet I can answer a few of yours."

Huard asked, "You're not here to kill me?"

Phewell laughed, "Only if I buy you too many of these delicious drinks. They're kind of addictive." He turned serious again. He said, "Sir, I suspect your fears of assassins may soon be a thing of the past, if I'm right. And I'm running a pretty dadgummed good batting average for being right."

Huard excused himself for a moment and asked Phewell if he might invite another participant into the conversation. Phewell readily agreed. In turn, he asked if he might invite another party of his own, from the hotel down the main street. Huard agreed. Huard stepped outside the exit and was not surprised to find that Victor could be found immediately outside the doorway. Victor was not one to abandon friends. Huard explained to Victor that he need not worry — that he had actually met a long lost friend from his past. He told Victor that he would be very glad this night that he had learned English. Victor joined Gordon back at a table within the cantina.

Minutes later, Joe Phewell returned to the establishment. He seated himself with the other two and drinks began to be dispensed once more. The doorway opened again. A bearded man with long blonde hair strode into the entrance.

Joe Phewell said, "Professor, you might know of a certain University of Washington astro-physics professor of some repute by the name of Greg Southard?" Huard was astounded to see his old protégé. A warm and lengthy embrace between the two men followed.

Phewell said to Huard as he again sat down, "Mr. Southard was instrumental in my locating you. It took a tough series of interrogations, but he finally cracked."

The four men made a toast and laughed.

The conversation was extraordinarily packed with information. Each party eagerly wished to share what they knew. Ultimately, Victor said to a chagrined cantina owner, "Felipe, you might as well go home. We will be here all night. I think the mayor is holding an emergency meeting. We will clean up."

The discussions spanned well into the night. Huard was relieved and astounded to hear what Phewell had learned of the conspiracy that had altered his life. Above all, he was encouraged upon hearing the status of his family. Phewell told him that he had spent several days interviewing the Huards. They were all healthy and well. They had been elated to hear his educated theory that their dear Gordon was alive. The retired cop was certainly thorough, if not a bit pushy.

Attention turned to an ebullient Gordon. He began to talk. As always happened when he spoke for a while, the talk morphed into a lecture. He explained that he had devoted the past six years to ventures that spanned beyond the scope of local politics, teaching, and sheep herding. He had made it his life's vocation to unravel the web of information that an incredible artificial intelligence source had bestowed upon him. He told of countless hours committed to listening to recorded conversations, both ancient and modern. He was slowly gaining a grasp of the totality of the human experience with complete accuracy. He had been astounded to hear some truths, while others did not surprise him at all.

Huard finally stopped himself. He said, "Instead of droning on incessantly, I would much prefer a more interactive approach to showing you the treasure of information that I have been alternately blessed and cursed to possess. Would anyone be interested in the complete unabridged real history of mankind? Anybody up for meeting an extraordinary family, hidden from history, which my research has revealed? How about a rather mind-boggling gravesite? Most of what I have to show you is less than two hours from here."

Greg Southard said, "Gordon, you had me at hello."

A loud set of honking sounds startled the men. They came from the parking lot of the cantina. Victor looked at his watch and noted the time at 2 A.M. He said, "Uh oh, Mr. Mayor. I think we are in trouble."

Into the cantina strode a frustrated woman. A lovely dark Brazilian woman pointed at Victor as she approached. She said, "Are you gabbing old women ever going to come home?" She stood behind Victor, smiled, and wrapped her arm around him.

Victor said, "Gentlemen, may I introduce my wife, Teresa Cabrera-Ortiz"

The doors opened again, and in walked the beautiful Elena. Huard rose from his seat and greeted her at the doorway. He took the woman's hand and proudly escorted her to the table. He then said to the group, "And may I introduce *my* wife, Elena Huard-Castronueves." As Elena drew closer, it was readily apparent by her bulging stomach that the Huard and Castronueves family would soon grow.

Sleeping arrangements were quickly arranged for the two extraordinary guests. The Huards and Cabreras quickly enforced the local laws with Joe Phewell and Greg Southard. No self-respecting Brazilians would allow guests to stay in the downtown hotel. The Cabreras immediately lay claim to the fascinating retired deputy sheriff and Greg Southard was commandeered for the Castronueves ranch. All agreed to meet in the morning at the Huard-Castronueves residence for breakfast.

Greg Southard was jubilant during the homeward drive with the Huards. Gordon had placed his bicycle in the back of the pickup. Elena then insisted on driving the old Ford F-150. Gordon disagreed. Elena quickly won an argument with her husband regarding his level of impairment and Gordon grudgingly conceded. He laughingly translated the heated Portuguese portion of the debate for Greg, and advised that she always won an argument. He made mention of her use of profound beauty in the end, and called it "cheating." His compliment was rewarded with a warm kiss.

Greg was shoe-horned beside the couple in the cab of the pickup. He remained incredulous that the eccentric cop had delivered upon his promise to locate the great Professor Huard. He still could not believe that he had agreed to take the logistically nightmarish trip in the first place. And now he sat next to his admired peer. It was like a dream.

Within twenty minutes the pickup pulled down the driveway of the ranch. Gordon exited the pickup and opened and closed the gate as the vehicle passed through. He stood in front of the pickup and would not allow Elena to drive further. She stepped out of the pickup and said in perfect English, "What are you doing, you drunken fool?"

Gordon answered with a wry smile, while looking toward the barn, "I am guiding Greg to his quarters."

Elena responded, "Oh, don't even think about that."

Gordon said, "I believe that was all the accommodations that *I* initially qualified for."

"And now you sleep beside me. You had to earn that privilege."

Gordon turned to Greg, and muttered, "And when

I allegedly misbehave I *still* sleep in the loft over that barn. Oh, the temper of the Brazilian women." It was readily apparent to Greg that Gordon worshiped the ground his wife walked upon. It appeared that the sentiment was very mutual.

Ultimately, Greg was afforded a spacious bedroom in the beautiful ranch house of his hosts. The home was picturesque. Elena had decorated the home in such a way that Greg was reminded of the television series Bonanza. It was like walking back in time one hundred years. The only apparent touches from Professor Huard were readily apparent with the enormous caches of books along hallway shelves.

Greg thought that he would be unable to sleep after all of his travels and the excitement from an emotional reunion. But he quickly fell into a restful bliss. The drinks might have assisted in his state of relaxation. They seemed to be rather potent.

Morning came quickly. The warm Brazilian springtime sun shone brightly through large living room picture windows, as Greg arose and showered. He was invited to sit in a comfortable antique leather couch by Gordon, who sat across from him in a matching recliner. Greg could smell delicious aromas emanating from a back kitchen. Elena emerged and greeted Greg with a warm embrace. Greg found that he already adored the wife of Professor Huard. He never thought that the man would ever marry. Gordon had been far too engrossed in other activities. Southard opined that the treacherous circumstances that necessitated Huard's escape from the world might well have had an unanticipated silver lining. He rose and offered to assist Elena in the kitchen.

He was almost disappointed to see Gordon make no such offer.

Gordon interrupted, "Greg, another Brazilian law. You *never* trespass in a Brazilian woman's kitchen. You could lose a finger very quickly. We're only allowed to perform the post-game cleanup. In other words, Greg, we're the roadies. You feel me, homie?" Greg erupted in laughter. Gordon Huard was still very much Gordon Huard.

Elena again returned with two cups of steaming coffee and handed the first to an appreciative Greg.

Greg could not refrain from commenting, "I see you still have your addiction to deal with huh, professor?"

Gordon answered, "Be vewwwy vewwwy caofuw wif this stuff, Greg. It might knock you foreigners on your ass."

Gordon excused himself to make a telephone call. He mentioned that he would have to convince mysterious parties unknown that his guests would pose no threat with a visit. Greg envisioned endless possibilities. Gordon would not expound upon those whom he was calling, other than to state, "You have a remarkable date with history today, Greg." Once the phone call was ended, Gordon invited Greg to follow him into the basement in order to peer at a unique array of bookshelves.

Gordon unlocked a padlock on a heavy metal door that led to the basement. He looked behind to Greg and commented, "This is probably the only locked door in all of Serra." Greg followed Huard down a steep stairway and was immediately enraptured with certain documents. Aligned along the basement wall were endless functional metal bookshelves with meticulously annotated notebooks. An extensive computer system was embedded in the corner of the musty room. He saw hundreds of bound reams of academic documents arranged in chronological order. He noted "Napoleon." Other captions indicated "First human speech." He could not help but notice "Kennedy's," "Pearl Harbor," and even "D.B. Cooper." The cache of information was so seemingly extensive that Southard did not even know which document to first browse.

Within minutes the Cabreras could be heard above as they arrived at the doorstep, with an energized deputy Phewell in tow. Joe Phewell received an equally warm embrace from the gracious Elena, as Gordon and Greg returned upstairs. He stated that he had also slept tremendously well at the lovely home of his wonderful hosts. The group was convened at a spectacular antique dining room table.

Greg Southard commented to Joe Phewell, "I don't know about you, Joe, but I can't wait to enjoy an authentic Brazilian breakfast." Joe Phewell began to recite from memory the typical meals of the area. But he was interrupted as Elena and Teresa approached with laden trays of foods.

A feast of bacon, eggs, grits, and pancakes was displayed on the table, much to the surprise of the American visitors. The women seemed to take delight in surprising their guests.

Gordon smiled at his guests and said, "What, did you think we were going to eat huevos rancheros or something? I have *totally* Americanized my wife." Elena smiled as she sat, and displayed a sign of her index finger slightly apart from her thumb, indicating a scant bit.

Huard said, "My dear guests, it is all arranged. Eat heartily. We will have a busy day. I'm glad you packed hiking boots. You'll need them. But tie them securely. Today I will show you some things that will knock your socks off."

Chapter 35

Within two hours of driving dusty and primitive gravel roads, Gordon Huard neared his destination with two intrigued passengers in tow. Victor, having already seen what Huard was to reveal, had recused himself so as to allow room in the pickup for the other two men. Greg Southard and Joe Phewell noted numerous small farms in the area as they passed by. Farmers could be seen dragging oxen across their fields. While interesting to watch, Huard's guests sup positioned that they had not been driven to the remote stretches of central Brazil in order to watch fields being plowed.

Finally, Huard parked his pickup a block short of the main intersection of a nameless small town. Huard explained that the town harbored 6,400 residents. Simple, but orderly farm houses dotted the exterior of the hub, while the rear facades of main street businesses could be seen. Huard exited his pickup and closed his squeaky door. His passengers followed suit, scanning the environs for some hidden sign of what their guide seemed so anxious to display. They saw nothing out of the ordinary. The three men were alone on the side street of the town.

Huard said to his guests, "Gentlemen, welcome to Candido Godoi, in the beautiful Brazilian state of Rio Grande do Sul. Before we go to our primary place of interest, I want us to simply take a stroll down Main Street. I want to see what your impressions are."

Huard smiled almost mischievously. The three men ambled through the immaculate downtown environs along a cobblestone promenade. Numerous tiny, but functional businesses dotted the road. The aroma of exotic food stuffs emanated from small cafes and open air markets. A cantina was very evident in the center of the town. A lovely blue and white painted post office was positioned across the street, with numerous patrons coming and going happily. Candido seemed indistinguishable from any other typical small farm town, whether in South or North America. Southard and Phewell appeared to be perplexed regarding Huard's intentions. The town was just coming alive for the day, and small vehicles blended with horse-drawn carts, as goods and merchandise were being distributed and exchanged. Numerous citizens smiled as they walked by, yet cast wary lateral glances as they passed. They quickly returned to personal business or conversation with friends.

Greg Southard was the first to speak, "Gordon, is it just me or all the people here Caucasian? Everyone I see is blonde-haired and blue-eyed."

Huard answered, "Professor Southard, if you were still my student I would grade you highly. Anything else gentlemen?"

Joe Phewell chimed in, "I'll be dadgummed. I know where we are. I've read all about it. No *wonder* I was noticing all the sets of Aryan twins walking about."

Huard said, "Anything else you notice about those twins, *officer*?"

"Most are identical."

"Bingo! Nearly eight per cent of all the citizens of this town are, in actuality, identical twins."

Greg Southard said, "You guys have me at a distinct

disadvantage here. Maybe I missed something while getting my PhD. Are we on some kind of movie set or something?"

Joe Phewell said, "Greg, as these folks walk by, listen to them speak." Huard nodded in agreement.

Within moments, Southard said, "I'll be damned. Most of them are speaking German!"

Phewell said, "And a little Polish thrown in for good measure. Greg, you are standing at the alleged Garden of Eden of genetic engineering, courtesy of some runaway Nazis. This was once Joseph Mengele's personal science lab. By the looks of Mr. Huard, he already well knows that. And, I suspect, he knows a little more."

Huard smiled crookedly and commented, "My friends, you ain't seen nothin' yet."

Huard returned his guests to his pickup and drove away. Within a half hour's drive he turned onto a very primitive road. Dust flew behind the pickup and visibility was limited. Finally, the roadway ended entirely.

Huard pulled his pickup to a halt. Thousands of acres of verdant farmland and adjoining rolling small hills spanned in front of the three men. Hundreds of cattle were wandering the semi-arid terrain, in search of sparse meals. A forest of conifer trees extended northward a few miles in the distance, along the base of the hills. Approximately a quarter mile away a dilapidated barn stood, leaning decidedly to one side.

Huard exited the truck and commented to his guests, "Time to stretch our legs just a bit, sirs."

The two men were led by Huard out into the fields and toward the barn. Once at the barn, Huard opened a large door. Within the structure a brand new Hummer SUV was parked. Huard looked at the vehicle and smiled oddly. He invited his guests to seat themselves within the Hummer. The spaciousness of the vehicle was a welcome sight to the still puzzled Phewell and Southard.

As he started the engine, Huard turned toward his guests. He smiled and said, "Guys, you might want to belt yourselves in. The ride's a bit bumpy, and I have long ago learned that I have a penchant for exceptional driving skills."

As Huard drove away rapidly, a rough roadway soon emerged, lessening the severity of the uneasy ride somewhat. Huard drove down the farmland roadway for nearly a mile. He then took a decidedly abrupt left turn into the more forested foothill regions. The passengers rocked from side to side as he navigated through the forest. It seemed to them that there was no evidence of a road. But Huard, nonetheless, seemed to recognize a semblance of a pathway that somehow escaped his guests.

In twenty minutes of pounding driving, the Hummer finally came to a halt. An immense farmhouse lay atop a hill, with a commanding view of the valley and thousands of acres of farmland below. A beautiful tall blonde haired woman of some thirty-five years of age, wearing a white tank top and khaki cargo pants emerged from a garage. She immediately approached the vehicle. The woman walked eagerly toward the driver's side of the Hummer and wrapped Gordon Huard in a lengthy embrace.

The woman said in perfect English, "Gordon, it has

been way too long. I am so pleased to see you."

Huard said, "I want to you introduce you to my two friends I have told you about."

The woman smiled at Phewell and Southard, but seemed reticent to extend a greeting. She simply nodded at the men and walked them brusquely into the house. Once within the cavernous rambler, they were brought to a dining room in the rear. The men were seated and the woman brought them three glasses of cold water.

The woman said, "It is always needed for washing down the dust. I see that Gordon has abused my Hummer again, yah?" She and Gordon laughed, and it seemed that some incomprehensible tension was lessened.

The woman called out down a hallway, "Brother, they are here!"

Within a minute a short blonde man in denim overalls entered the house from the garage. He was wiping grease off of his hands with a rag.

The man said, "I am so sorry. I was having trouble with that clutch. It acts like Gordon has driven *my* car as well." Again, a welcome laugh filled the room.

As the man approached the table of guests, he quickly evaluated Southard and Phewell with his eyes. He looked at Phewell for a moment and then toward Huard. He said, "This is the policeman yah?"

Before Huard could answer, Phewell interjected. He said, "Just a retired one, sir. Now, it seems, I am an amateur finder of lost souls."

An immediate tension returned to the room. The genesis of the sentiment baffled Greg Southard.

Phewell's eyes darted rapidly in several directions from person to person.

Finally, Huard took control of the interactions. He said, "I'm sorry to all of you. This is a bit awkward. Let me make the introductions here. To my right are my *trusted* American friends, Professor Greg Southard and retired deputy Joe Phewell. And, Greg and Joe, I would like to introduce you to my dear friends here in Candido. This is Annelise."

The woman then shook the hands of Phewell and Southard warmly.

Huard said, "And this is Kristof." Again, a firm and sincere handshake followed for the two Americans. Kristof finally seated himself.

Huard finished his sentence with the last names of the two residents, "Hitler."

Joe Phewell smiled and nodded. It appeared that he was by no means surprised. Greg Southard, on the other hand, sat dumfounded.

Huard explained in great detail how he had become acquainted with the brother and sister. The wonders of the HYDRA had unexpectedly revealed the location of the grandchildren of Adolf Hitler. Once he had gained the trust of the family, he became a very valued friend. Huard and the Hitlers shared the same fear of menacing outsiders, and treasured their privacy. They all knew that, through no fault of their own, fate had relegated them to seclusion from the world for the entirety of their lives.

The Hitlers feared Israeli Mossad agents whom had twice abducted associates of their grandfather in town.

They feared that they and other nearby unnamed family members could be imperiled if discovered. Huard similarly feared multi-national mercenaries and U.S. Intelligence agents. An intransigent bond, through the commonality of experiences, had thereby fostered a profound friendship between the respective refugees.

Ultimately, Huard and his guests were led to the forested hillside of the farm. There, a very simple gravesite was seen. No headstone adorned the site. A mere encirclement of beautiful stones lined the gravesite of Adolf Hitler. Colorful indigenous flowers were maintained atop the grave meticulously. The two Americans could not help but notice the white wooden cross at the head of the grave. Out of deference, they asked no pointed questions about the irony of the symbol. The Hitlers offered no praise nor derision for their grandfather. They merely lowered their heads somberly.

Greg Southard finally spoke. He asked the Hitlers, "Don't you want to go home to Germany?"

Kristof replied, "This *is* our home, Mr. Southard."

Annelise answered, "Greg, even now it is complicated. Our family was granted these thirty-five thousand acres, and enough funding to support another few generations. We will spare you the very private details. We are happy here and relatively safe. Even if we *were* safe in the outside world, our mere existence could cause pandemonium. Enough of that has occurred in our name to ever make the risk worthwhile."

The gathering eventually ended. There was nothing more that could realistically be discussed or revealed. It was evident to all parties that they shared in the sense of privacy requirements regarding their lives, and what they knew. It was abundantly clear that all would take the Hitlers' secret to their respective graves.

Kristof shook the hands of Huard and his friends heartily. He gave Huard an affectionate pat on the back. Annelise would have nothing further of formalities. She gave Phewell and Southard warm and sincere hugs. She then embraced Huard. It appeared that she did not wish to let go. The loneliness was evident. Finally, she gave Huard a kiss on both cheeks and exhorted him to return soon.

Annelise said to Huard, "Now don't tell Elena about that."

Huard laughed again and said, "Yet another of our secrets is safe with me".

Annelise then said to the group, "I'm going to stop talking now. You all must go. I know that Gordon is eager to show you one more thing this evening."

As Huard tearfully walked away with his friends toward the Hummer, Annelise called out to him, "And can you *please* be gentle with my car? Don't you understand physics?"

Chapter 36

Joe Phewell's sense of direction served him well, as always. At one point during the return drive he said to Huard, "Didn't we pass the turnoff to Serra about forty-five minutes ago?"

Greg Southard spoke from the back seat, "You guys could have fooled me, I thought we were in Iowa by now."

Huard smiled as he turned toward Phewell and said, "Man, you don't miss a thing. I'm glad I didn't pedal through all those red lights in Palo Alto in front of *you*." He advised that he strongly desired to show his guests one more site of "enlightenment," before releasing his weary friends for the evening.

Within another half hour Huard stopped the truck at the foot of a range of brown and barren hills. The setting of the sun was nearly complete. Huard noted the fact as they exited the pickup and said, "Perfect." Southard and Phewell noted massive circular quarry pits abutting the hillside in front of them.

Huard handed each man a belt with a water bottle attached and said, "You'll thank me for this." He then handed them each a hard hat, complete with an affixed halogen lamp. He geared himself as well.

Huard said to his friends, "Gentlemen, welcome to the entrance to Gruta Do Cristais." I won't even need to translate the meaning of that phrase in a little while. Follow me. Within moments the two men began to follow Gordon downward, into one of the enormous pits. They felt dwarfed in scale-- like ants in a swimming pool. The gradient was steep. Each man had to use a hand to balance himself at times, as the loose soil and broken rocks provided insufficient footing. Dirt sometimes spilled into their boots.

Phewell commented, smiling, "Ah, just like home in the canyon."

Finally, the men reached the bottom of the pit. By then, the headlamps provided the only source of lighting. A rusted metal door signified an entrance of some sort. The logo of the "Sao Chico Mining Company" was faintly readable across the door. The entrance was secured by a large chain, complete with a heavy padlock. Huard retrieved a key from his neck chain and opened the lock. Phewell and Southard cast glances at one another, wondering why a lock would be needed for such a remote abandoned site. Huard handed each guest a painter's mask and they entered the dusty enclosure.

The three men stood within an enormous stone room and paused to empty their boots of dirt. For the moment, they could stand upright freely. Phewell reached upward and still could not touch the ceiling.

Huard said, "Enjoy the space, Joe. You and I especially will abuse our backs for a while. Drink half of your water bottles right now." Southard and Phewell drank their water, as did Huard. They did not ask questions.

Huard directed the men to attach their masks and then led them fifty yards into the mine. The ceiling rapidly descended upon them. Soon they were mimicking primal man with their hunched-over gates. The air was dusty and hot. Within minutes, the shaft took a decidedly downward direction. Through his mask, Huard explained that they were now a thousand feet beneath the earth's surface.

Phewell said, "I'm going to guess we won't find many of my beloved arrowheads down here, now will we, Professor?"

Huard's eyes squinted, revealing his smile, and said, "Better."

After another half mile of downward travel, the shaft appeared to end. Huard veered abruptly to his direct left and lay upon his stomach. He gestured to his guests to mirror his actions. Southard and Phewell grunted as they struggled to crawl low enough to squeeze beneath an oppressive stone ceiling, a mere foot from the floor of the mine. Neither of the men was claustrophobic, but the sensation of miles of the earth's crust nearly crushing upon them was unsettling. The light from Huard's headlamp disappeared. It seemed he had abandoned them. The two continued their crawling for another hundred feet. Each began to feel apprehensive, but determination pushed them onward.

At about the time when frustration began to beget fear, they emerged into brilliant light. They stopped crawling momentarily, as their pupils adjusted. Gordon Huard was standing upright, his hands on his hips, and smiling broadly. He helped each man to his feet. They began to dust themselves off when each stopped their actions. Large banks of cleverly positioned battery powered spotlights illuminated the area. As they began to look upward and beyond Huard, their jaws dropped. White, blue, red, and green beams of light were directed away from them. The three men beheld an enormous cave of stunning beauty. All around them spanned extraordinary ten to thirty foot shimmering white crystals adorning the entirety of the 400 foot long room. The crystal structures rose from the floors and joined with massive counterparts from the ceiling in innumerable astonishing patterns. The multi-colored lighting prismed throughout portions of the crystals like stained glass of immeasurable quality. The scene looked like an amalgamation of ten million Hope Diamonds.

Huard removed his mask and directed his guests to do the same. His voice echoed as he said, "My dear friends, welcome to the Cave of Crystals." He stood silently for a moment, allowing his guests to reconcile the incredible wonders before them in their minds.

Finally, Huard began yet another lecture. The teacher, it would seem, could not refrain. "Fellas, what you are seeing is quite possibly the most rare and unique collection of priceless minerals ever seen in this world. For the past half million years, moistened silver and lead have melded to create these amazing crystals. The conditions had to be perfect. This is a place often mentioned in local legend. It's my guess that maybe one wayward miner might have discovered this years ago and told its story. The mine has been abandoned now for over a decade. The waters that were pumped out of this area for thirty years created a receding of the natural water tables. Without their corporate meddling with the environment this treasure grove would have gone unnoticed for an eternity. To the great fortune of our world, they called it quits before encroaching further. I am forever thankful that I chose to believe the legend and do a little exploring myself."

Southard whistled and commented, "Gordon, you have been a very busy man."

Huard answered, "Oh, there's more."

Phewell countered, "It would seem there always is."

Huard directed the men to place their water bottles in a carved niche against a wall. He explained that the stone would keep the water cold. He then directed the men to follow him very closely for the next hundred yards. The two men attempted to remain focused upon Huard, as the distraction of the breathtaking crystals was powerful. They had to follow Huard's head motions as he slowly curled his body past several massive stalactites, careful not to touch them. They crawled a short distance beneath another low ceiling.

Within fifteen more minutes of hiking and crawling, the three men stood in another wide mining shaft. They were again able to stand upright. This portion of the caves was a perfectly cut square opening. The lights from the headlamps disappeared into endless darkness. It appeared that the shaft descended downward into the depths of the earth. Stifling heat arose from below and the men perspired heavily.

Huard turned on another nearby set of battery-powered lights and the full contours of the room soon emerged. The chamber was a basic stone-carved corridor. It appeared that mining efforts had ceased a mere hundred yards from the treasure of crystals.

Huard said, "Welcome to the command post, gents." The twenty by forty foot room was highly organized. Banks of batteries were aligned along a side wall. A crude, but functional toilet area was roughed in. Small generators were embanked along a second wall. A series of exhaust chambers seemed to have been drilled, leading to unknown connecting mine shafts. Camera equipment, blankets, water, and sleeping bags were stacked along one side of the room. Reading materials, notebooks, and food stuffs were collected in a corner.

Huard handed the two men ear protection and soon started a small generator at the end of the room, near the adjoining mine shaft. He turned on three circular fans and pointed to a circular thermometer on the wall. The thermometer indicated 106 degrees. He gestured to the men to sit for five minutes in front of the fans. They did not complain.

Finally, Huard turned off the generator and fans. The men removed their headsets.

Huard said, "Bear with me, guys. Five more minutes. Here we go." He directed the men to finally remove their masks. No more dust would be created this day.

Huard led the men out of the room and into the adjoining corridor. There truly appeared to be no end to the shaft. The men marched another fifty yards.

Phewell asked, "How far does this mine go?"

Huard answered, "I honestly don't know. I have never found an end. But I believe we are over a mile underground."

Phewell said, "You do seem to like your privacy, Professor."

Huard stopped and turned on another set of lights in the corridor. He said, "This is the reason for my quest for privacy."

Along each side of the mine walls could be seen endless deep etchings within the dark stone. Phewell walked to one side of the cave, while Southard examined the other. The etchings were both simplistic and artistic. On Southard's side spanned endless highly-organized pictographs. They were strangely reminiscent of Incan efforts thousands of years previously. But it was obvious that these carvings were fresh. Phewell, on the other hand, was looking at English language captions. He saw the words, "The Story of Man" inscribed in much larger print than the remaining etchings. The ornate handwriting reminded him of the Declaration of Independence. Huard had paid attention to detail and style. Extraordinary stories of historical prominence could be read far down the walls by use of the headlamps. Huard had made every effort to annotate his esoteric knowledge conscientiously.

Finally, the two men looked again to Huard for clarification of his efforts. Their faces were beaded with perspiration.

Huard said, "Gentlemen, I know it is unbearably hot in here. I will not keep you long. I just want you to bear witness to my ultimate efforts to record human history for an eternity. I know that my notebooks and thumb drives in the terrestrial world are ephemeral. The winds of time will someday blow them away. I'm not even sure that the world is ready for many of the historical and modern truths that I am learning. But I feel obligated to record our story for infinite years. At first, I gained the eerie sense that I was the modern Inca. Maybe it was the heat, or the nature of being a mile underground. You can see I emulated their pictographs as one basic means of relating information. Maybe those whom someday read this will not be from this world."

Huard reached down and picked up a high quality diamond-tipped pneumatic etching tool. He patted the device admiringly. He smiled and shook his head as he continued, "But somehow along the way, I felt that this was more than a scientific endeavor. I felt as if I were fulfilling a biblical obligation. I have now come to regard this wonderful tool as "Moises' Esculpir," — in other words, "Moses' Chisel." Huard's guests were speechless.

After taking one last glance at the remarkable stories rendered by Huard, the three bedraggled travelers finally returned to Serra late into the night. An astounded, but weary Joe Phewell was thankful to be welcomed back into the Cabrera's home for the night. Greg Southard fought an urge to fall asleep in the pickup. He and a buoyant Huard climbed the porch of the farm house. The lights were still on in the living room. Gordon opened the front door and saw Elena seated on the couch.

Gordon said to Elena excitedly, "Elena, you should have seen these guys' faces!"

Huard went silent immediately. Two men were seated on the other couch, across from his wife. One of the men was unknown to him. But he was very cognizant of the identity of the other. Michael Portworth rose from his seated position slowly. He mustered a faint smile.

Portworth said, "Professor, I know what you think. But I am absolutely no threat to you or your friends. In fact, I have come here to end your torment and ours."

Portworth gestured to his accompaniment, and a shorter, older Asian man rose.

Portworth said, "Gordon Huard, I would like you to meet my father, Justin Portworth. It would seem we all have much more in common in our lives of exile than you might ever dream."

Justin Portworth approached Huard and shook his hand warmly. He similarly greeted a silent Greg Southard.

Elena said, "Gordon, we have been visiting for hours. I have no doubt these men are no threat to us. When you hear what they have to say, I believe our lives will be blessed."

Michael Portworth apologized for the lateness of his presence in Huard's home. He pleaded with the Professor to allow a mid-day meeting the following day. While scanning the eyes of his wife, Huard reluctantly agreed. The Portworths soon departed.

Chapter 37

It was mid-evening and Gayle Portworth was at home in her modest Alexandria Virginia townhouse. She was nearly asleep, while watching television, when a loud knock upon her front door startled her. At the door stood a forty year-old man. Before the man could even display a National Security Agency badge and identification, Mrs. Portworth waved him in. She could already guess the man's vocation.

The agent said, "Ma'am, I am Special Agent Doug Fetters. I am sorry to disturb you at this hour, but I have some serious business to conduct with you."

Mrs. Portworth asked, "Is there some kind of trouble?"

The Marshall answered, "No ma'am. Not at all. In fact, I think I have some very good news for you. If you're willing to trust me I need to drive you somewhere and show you the reason that I'm here. I'm sorry, but I can't tell you much more."

Gayle Portworth, always wary of government matters, was unwilling to budge.

Mrs. Portworth said, "Young man, I am a double widow of the intelligence community. You will have to give me more than that in order to keep me from spraying you with a good dosage of mace right here and now."

Fetters answered, "It's about your son. Very important information about your son. And there is more."

"Is this about his murder?" Mrs. Portworth asked.

"Something like that. Ma'am, I have specific orders simply to drive you somewhere. Once there, all the answers will be very obvious. I'm sorry." Mrs. Portworth reluctantly agreed to join the agent in his black sedan.

During the drive the agent spoke admiringly of Michael Portworth. He mentioned that he had gotten to work with Michael during his early years with the agency, and that Michael was a talented mentor. He added that Michael had once saved his life. But he could not go into details of the event. Mrs. Portworth recommended that the agent find another means of making a living so that his mother did not have to suffer as had she.

Thankfully for the agent, the hour-long drive came to an end before he had to hear more. He parked the vehicle in the underground lot of the Jefferson Hotel, in downtown Washington D.C. Agent Fetters escorted Mrs. Portworth to a nearby elevator. They rose to the 12th floor of the vintage venue and exited. Mrs. Portworth was escorted down a long red-carpeted hallway. Finally, they stopped at room 1208.

Mrs. Portworth said, "I always left the spy stuff to my husband and son. This is very odd." Fetters smiled weakly and nodded at Mrs. Portworth. He knocked only once on the hotel room door. Footsteps could immediately be heard from within the room and the door soon opened.

Gayle Portworth immediately collapsed. Agent Fetters caught her before she struck the floor and braced her. Michael Portworth grabbed the other arm of his mother, and the two men gently carried her into the hotel room and upon comfortable chair.

Michael Portworth said to Fetters, "Thanks, Dougie. Thanks for everything."

Fetters answered, "You got it, boss."

Michael Portworth said, "Tomorrow?"

Fetters replied, "Copy that. Wouldn't miss it for the world."

Michael dismissed his trusted colleague and turned his attention to his mother. She quickly regained consciousness. Her eyes grew wide as Justin Portworth handed her a cold glass of water. She dropped the water on the carpeting and stared at her husband in disbelief.

Gayle Portworth said, "Am I dreaming? Is this real?"

Justin Portworth knelt in front of his wife and caressed her face gently. He said, "I know this is a shock, honey. But there was no other way to do this. We have so many things to explain to you, and so little time to do it. We just didn't want you to first see us on TV tomorrow."

Finally, Gayle embraced her husband passionately. She reached for Michael with her other arm and the family united as if one person. Seemingly endless tears flowed from all of them. Through the picturesque room window it appeared that the Washington Monument was bearing witness to the secretive reunion. The content of the conversation to follow would make it very clear that the world would be changing the following day. And a father had a son and daughter to soon meet, essentially for the first time. He was clearly anxious and excited simultaneously.

Chapter 38

Patrice Huard innately knew immediately who was driving down her driveway one late afternoon. A dark SUV with tinted windows approached slowly. The vehicle slowed in front of the grove of pine trees and stopped. At first, no one stepped out of the vehicle.

Patrice walked to the living room window. Strangely, she was not fearful. She heard Duke bark. She saw him wag his tail and walk sheepishly toward the vehicle.

Mrs. Huard threw down her dish towel and smiled. She walked out of the house, off of the porch, and down the driveway slowly. She paused momentarily as two men in dark suits wearing sunglasses exited the vehicle and scanned the environs. The driver was a white man, while the passenger was a younger black man. Both were athletically built and unsmiling. Mrs. Huard's smile returned immediately when one of the men opened a rear door. Out of the vehicle emerged Gordon Huard. He was smiling widely. He ran down the driveway as his mother did the same. The two suited men jogged beside Gordon the entire time. A dark military helicopter circled endlessly overhead in the distance.

Mother, son, and family dog all reunited in the middle of the driveway. Predictably, a cascade of tears were shed by Patrice and Gordon.

Mrs. Huard said, "I knew it! As soon as that car turned down our drive I knew it! A mother can feel these things."

Finally, Mrs. Huard directed her attention to the suited men.

Gordon smiled widely and said, "Guys, could you

please tell my mommy that I did not skip school today?" His sense of humor was already in evidence.

Gordon said, "Mom, I'd like to introduce you to F.B.I. agent Joe Satterberg (he gestured toward the white man) and U.S. Marshall Tyrone Outlaw the Second (he gestured toward the black man). What a name for a Federal Marshall, eh?"

Marshall Outlaw spoke first, "I'm very pleased to meet you ma'am." He shook Mrs. Huard's hand gently with two hands. Agent Satterberg greeted Gordon's mother next.

The men were invited to convene in the living room of the Huard residence. As always, Patrice Huard commenced to brewing coffee for the gathering. Gordon smiled to himself. The sight of his mother brewing coffee was always a welcome spectacle. But he knew that the American coffee would now taste like water. He had long since become accustomed to the much stronger Brazilian version.

Mrs. Huard began to place a phone call to her husband, who was away in town. The two law enforcement officers quickly rose from the couch. Gordon interrupted. He said, "Mom, please no phone calls. Let me explain. These two talented men are assigned to my protection detail. I'm honored that they would risk their lives to protect mine. It is because of courageous people like these men and others that I am back home. Tomorrow will be a very big day for the Huard family and for America. I have to go for now."

Mrs. Huard began to display distress.

Gordon said, "No, no, don't worry, Mom. I will be

back tomorrow with all the time in the world to catch up. All of this mess finally ends tomorrow. Turn the T.V. on at five with Dad. It won't matter what channel. All of them will be covering one event. There will be plenty of answers to hear."

Mrs. Huard's face beamed instantly.

Gordon added, "Mom, I love you so much. I cannot wait to catch up on the last six years. I have amazing stories to tell you and things to show you."

Mrs. Huard said, "Gordy, I love you, kiddo. I won't sleep tonight."

"Me neither."

Gordon and his escorts were about to leave. He turned back toward his mother from the front door. He said, "And, Mom, I would hope to see the whole family tomorrow night."

"Gordy, you can bet on that."

Marshall Outlaw told Patrice Huard, "Good night, ma'am. We'll take good care of your son."

Mrs. Huard looked at the two officers and smiled, "I believe you surely will."

Chapter 39

David Rosenweiler was busy reading profit reports while seated comfortably in one of the lavish leather seats aboard his jet. He was drinking his usual concoction of fresh squeezed orange and guava juice. His plane was mid-way across the Atlantic en route to Greece in order to meet with Giorgio Soudas. The two men intended to celebrate the acquisition of another respective hundred billion dollars during the last quarter. Yeats would catch up later. The sun shone brightly through his starboard side window.

The co-pilot of the plane opened the cockpit door and walked down the aisle way to Rosenweiler.

The pilot said, "Sir, we have a problem."

Rosenweiler did not even bother to look upward to acknowledge his employee.

Rosenweiler muttered, "Fix the problem."

The pilot bit into his lower lip and replied, "Uh, sir, I don't think this problem is fixable."

Rosenweiler finally looked up from his reports and glared at the pilot. He removed his glasses and touched the temple edge of the spectacles to a corner of his mouth.

Rosenweiler spoke condescendingly, "What is that I can do to get you out of my hair, young man? What *is* it?"

The pilot simply pointed out the window and said, "*That.*"

Off the starboard wingtip loomed a U.S. Navy F/A-18 fighter jet.

Rosenweiler rose from his seat and said, "What the hell?"

Rosenweiler leapt to the port side of the aircraft and looked out of the corresponding window. A duplicate war-craft hovered six feet off of the other wing of his jet.

The pilot said, "Sir, we have been ordered to drop the plane down at Spangdahlem Air Force Base in Germany."

"That's absurd," barked Rosenweiler. "I'll put an end to this stupidity!"

The pilot responded, "Sir, I take them at their word. When they radioed us, they stated that their orders were to escort us to Germany or open fire on us if we refuse. Sir, I'm former Air Force. I know I saw one of the pilots arm his Gatling gun."

Rosenweiler retrieved his secure phone and dialed.

President Amanda Neal's personal cell phone rang repeatedly while she was seated in the Oval Office. She recognized the encrypted phone number of David Rosenweiler. She did not answer. She was otherwise occupied. The U.S. Attorney General, the Director of the F.B.I. and two F.B.I. agents stood in front of her desk. She was wearing reading glasses and intently examining a written document. The document was a summons for her arrest, issued by the United States Supreme Court.

Neal said, "This cannot *possibly* be legal."

The Attorney General was a Mr. Marco Uribe. He was a native Floridian and happened to have been the best friend of the late Senator Trent McLean.

Uribe said, "I assure you, Madam President, this is a very legal action."

The F.B.I. Director added, "Ma'am, we can handcuff you and drag you out of here like a common criminal, or you can walk with us downstairs and take a private trip to our facilities."

Tears began to form in President Neal's eyes. She said, "I cannot believe this. I will have my lawyers all over you. What are you assholes charging me with?"

The Attorney General said, "Treason, Conspiracy to Commit Murder, Corruption. Shall I continue?"

Neal rose from her desk defiantly, "Prove it!"

The F.B.I. Director said calmly, yet determined, "That will not be a problem, ma'am. We will need to go now."

The President sat down dejectedly. She said, "Give me five minutes to collect myself. I believe I am owed that much."

The men in the room reluctantly agreed. They convened down the hallway, as the doors to the office were slammed shut.

Secret Service Agent James McElroy stood outside the doorway. He was unaware of the nature of the actions by the group of men whom had exited the office. But he knew they meant serious business. He listened intently for any sounds from within the Oval Office. He then heard the unmistakable sound of a bullet being chambered into a semi-automatic weapon.

Amanda Neal unlocked the center drawer of her desk. She pulled the drawer open and retrieved a Walther PPKS .380 handgun that she had always kept concealed. She had always trusted no one. She pulled back the slide and chambered a bullet. Her hand began to shake. Tears clouded her vision. She knew that all that the poor girl from Kentucky had achieved was coming crashing down. She opened her mouth and moved the barrel of the gun slowly toward the opening.

Agent McElroy came crashing through the locked double doors and landed solidly upon the Oval Office carpeting. He rose immediately and dove toward the President. The startled gathering of the other men ran the few steps toward the Oval Office. A single gunshot rang out. The F.B.I. agents entered the Oval Office doorway first, 9 millimeter handguns drawn, and were immediately joined by several Secret Service Agents.

Agent McElroy was found lying on top of the President. The agents pulled McElroy roughly from Amanda Neal and stood him. The President lay on her back and was covered in blood. The Secret Service agents began to examine her. She was wearing handcuffs. They directed their attention toward Agent McElroy again. He was bleeding heavily from a gunshot wound to his lower abdomen, beneath his protective Kevlar vest. He winced and handed the Walther handgun to another agent and gasped, "Not losin' another one. Not on my watch."

The President was removed hurriedly from the office by the F.B.I. agents. Medical attention was quickly summoned for James McElroy. Other Secret Service agents comforted him while he was placed on a medic unit gurney. His bullet-proof vest was cut away and the bullet wound beneath the protection of the garment became evident. McElroy grimaced and cried out, "Damn, feels like a red hot poker burnin' through me. Now I can say it--I never *did* like that bitch." The Secret Service agents smiled at one another. They seemed reassured that the revered senior agent would make a full recovery.

Chapter 40

Joseph Yeats was enjoying a Sunday Seattle Seahawks home football game from his expansive luxury CentyLink Field suite. He was joined by twenty-five company sycophants and his 12-year-old nephew. The team, which he owned, was leading by a touchdown. The sellout the crowd was roaring its approval. Yeats' attention was divided, as he maintained eye contact with his laptop computer. He shielded the screen of the computer from the view of others. He was busy factoring in his latest hundred billion dollar profits. The covert joint operations in the Middle East had exceeded his wildest expectations.

Two off-duty uniformed Seattle Police officers opened the rear door to the suite and entered. They whispered to Yeats' accompaniment to vacate the suite. Only Yeats and his nephew remained.

Yeats said, "Gentlemen, is there some kind of emergency?"

The shorter of the two officers, with a nametag that read Sam Belfiori, spoke with an obvious Brooklyn accent and said, "You could say dat."

Three dark suited men then entered the suite. They presented their F.B.I. credentials and advised Yeats that he was under arrest. Yeats quickly reached toward his laptop computer. He was grabbed immediately and lifted from his seat by the Seattle Policemen. An F.B.I. agent grasped Yeats' hand in a pain-inflicting manner that controlled his thumb. He spun Yeats around and quickly handcuffed him.

Yeats said, "I'm not resisting! I demand that my

lawyer be present."

The F.B.I. agent said, "You're in no position to demand anything Mr. Yeats."

Yeats asked, "What have I done?"

The agent answered, "I think you know exactly what you've done."

Yeats said, "None of this was my idea. I was against it from the start."

The agent countered, "Save it for the judge, pal." Yeats was marched from the suite by the agents.

Officer Belfiori called out to the agents, "Hey fellas, you might want dis." He handed the agents Yeats' laptop. The screen still shone a spreadsheet reading, "Afghanistan profits, third quarter." One hundred billion dollars were noted in the profit column.

Belfiori rolled his eyes and whistled. He said, "Cocky S.O.B, ain't he?" He and his partner gently removed the visibly upset nephew from the suite.

Chapter 41

The tiny media room of the White House was filled to overflowing, with usually docile reporters jostling for position. They had been provided with an official media release one hour before the press conference was to convene. The explosive nature of the release had generated enormous interest.

The Vice President entered the room. Andrew Webster was considered the antithesis of the rancorous and ambitious President Amanda Neal. He was nicknamed "The Boy Scout" for his clean- cut, honest, and kind demeanor. The former war hero had been the front-runner for the party nomination for President until the relative unknown woman, bolstered by two billion campaign dollars, attacked him with countless advertising barrages portraying him as a dull "good old boy."

Vice President Webster appeared to be calm and confident as he strode to the podium. To his right stood the U.S. Attorney General, and to his left stood the Speaker of the House and the President Tempore of the Senate. He cleared his throat and directed the attendees to be seated.

"America, I stand before you as a shocked and saddened messenger. Earlier this day, the President of the United States was placed under arrest."

The room erupted in shouts.

Finally, order was restored.

The Vice President continued, "What I will relate to the world this day will sicken most of us. We will begin to question the very foundations of our country. We have all been deceived. I stand here to remind you of one component of the truths that shall be shared this day — that for every act of evil and greed committed, there are still a corresponding million acts of courage and unselfishness by our citizens. That is what makes America the greatest country on God's green earth."

The Vice President explained that he had assumed the role of de-facto President of the United States. He then devoted half an hour to methodically exposing the conspiracy that involved the now former President. He implicated David Rosenweiler, Giorgio Soudas, and Joseph Yeats by name. He explained that Rosenweiler and Yeats were already in F.B.I. custody. He lamented that Soudas was in Greece, and therefore beyond American jurisdiction. He implored the Greek government to allow extradition of the criminal, but he knew that they were uncooperative. He made no mention at all of HYDRA. He never would. Webster allowed tears to flow freely as he explained that he and his fellow soldiers had fought two wars with valiant intentions, only to now realize that they had been pawns in a subterfuge of corporate gluttony.

Finally, Webster paraded several individuals into the room to stand behind him. He turned and identified Michael Portworth, Justin Portworth, Gordon Huard, Greg Southard, and Joe Phewell. He summarized succinctly the involvement and pertinent experiences of each individual. He hailed each of them as American heroes whom had shown the courage to risk their lives in order to expose the conspiracy. He pointed out that they were what was "still right about America." He added that it was only appropriate that working class Americans could still overcome corrupt efforts by the rich and powerful.

Giorgio Soudas watched the press conference from his one hundred million dollar mansion on the Island of Crete. He sipped from a glass of uzo while riveted to the television set. He was initially alarmed to hear his name mentioned over the air. But he quickly realized that, as a Greek national, he was perfectly safe to remain or travel in most of Europe or elsewhere. He had never particularly liked the U.S, England, or Canada anyway. He thought the weather was too cold, as were their women.

Slowly, Soudas smiled to himself. The happenings in America would have little effect on his life. In fact, he realized, he had just become the sole beneficiary of the industrial arrangement with the other billionaires. The stupid Americans had simply increased his profits by eliminating his competition. He almost wished he had personally orchestrated the day's events. He drank more uzo and laughed as he toasted the television.

Soudas' mood was instantly brighter. He picked up his secure cell phone and dialed an old friend — Usama Bin-Laden.

Soudas said, "Usama. I know we don't talk much anymore because of security reasons, but I hope you are watching television."

"I am."

"Those idiot Americans. I think I am going to need another partner in this venture. Might you be interested in a few dozen billion more dollars?"

"I am listening."

Soudas looked out of his huge living room picture windows and treasured the view of his private beach.

The turquoise waters of the Aegean Sea glistened from small gentle waves. Hundreds of yachts dotted the scenery in the distance, bringing yet more color to the area.

A 65-foot yacht named the "Santa Maria" was anchored a quarter mile away. Members of the NSA and Navy Seals filled every available space of the vessel. They employed highly advanced listening and tracking devices and paid intense attention to Soudas' phone conversation. Every piece of applicable U.S. technology was devoted to their mission. Satellites were activated and gaining invaluable intelligence.

Special Agent Brian Hargraves turned to his peers and said, "Fellas, I hope you like the food in lovely Pakistan. You might soon find yourself there if this intel pans out."

Navy Seal Master Chief Antonio Cuevas smiled as he looked at his peers and simply said, "Oorah."

Soon thereafter, Soudas terminated his excited conversation with Bin-Laden. He then placed another call.

The respondent answered, "Yeah."

Soudas said, "Yes. Me."

The respondent said, "I know that. What's up?"

Soudas asked, "Have you been watching your television?"

The respondent said, "Only thing I'm watchin' is a little pink bikini walkin' by here in Tahiti. I could learn to love this place."

Soudas responded, "I am now the only one of the three left in the business. You'll find out the details soon enough. But I now think I know where a certain professor and suddenly very alive NSA employee are currently located. I'm sure they'll be protected for a little while. But once the dust settles, they'll be fair game. I think, with your rare talents, they can all become neutralized in due time. Do this for me and I will buy you that little island."

"Cool. Can't wait."

Master Chief Cuevas turned to a fellow Navy Seal Chief and said, "Hey Smittie. We flip a coin for Tahiti?"

Master Chief Ronald Smith looked like Mike Tyson multiplied by five. He smiled and said, "Oh no, bro. This one's mine."

Special Agent Hargraves turned to his subordinates and said, "Gentlemen, the law says we cannot arrest this Soudas animal. But I forgot to read anywhere that we could not put him down when the time comes. Intel first, but then the fun begins. Who knows exactly where it all ends. "

Chapter 42

The darkened SUV returned the following night down the Huard driveway. It was fortunate that a parking place could be found directly in front of the house. The entirety of the road was lined with cars.

A smiling Gordon Huard leaned forward from the rear of the car and said, "Sorry, guys, when family gathers here it involves half of West Virginia."

Agent Satterberg smirked and said, "I'm an only child. But I got all the presents at Christmas."

Marshall Outlaw turned and said, "This is the way it's *supposed* to be. Reminds me of growing up back home in Mississippi."

Satterberg radioed invisible adjoining units in the periphery that they were about to "walk the dog."

Huard looked forward, smiled, and said, "Cute."

Within the Huard home the thumping rotor sounds of the circling helicopter could be heard. The family could see the SUV approaching.

The large family gathering within the home grew silent for a rare moment. They were well aware of Gordon's recent circumstances after watching the Presidential press conference.

Patrice Huard announced, "My Gordy has an armed escort and a helicopter following him. He is a very important man."

From the corner of the room, oldest brother Pete called out, "That's what he *always* told us." The family laughed uproariously.

"Oh shush you," said Patrice.

The family watched, as the two law enforcement officers stepped out of the SUV again. Marshall Outlaw could be seen opening the rear passenger side door. Again, Gordon rose from the vehicle. Agent Satterberg exited the driver's side and stepped backward. He then opened the rear driver's side door. He gently assisted a woman and a child from the car.

A beautiful blonde woman cradled a two month-old baby in her arms as she walked to the front of the vehicle. She handed the baby to Gordon and he took possession proudly. Gordon took Elena's right hand with his free left hand. The entourage began walking toward the home.

The Huard family was instantly abuzz. Patrice placed her hands over her face and said, astonished, "Oh my gosh."

Ben rose from his chair and walked quickly toward the front door. He said, "Well for God's sake people, let's open the door and let these folks in." He opened the door and screen door and allowed the three people into the house. The two law enforcement officers took a position along the periphery of the home. It appeared that they were joined by other guardians around the property.

While it was only September in Falling Waters, Virginia, Christmas had clearly arrived early. Gordon and his family were given wide space when they entered the living room. Family members backed up against the walls in a crush of bodies.

An ebullient Gordon gently cradled a sleeping baby boy. The baby cooed peacefully.

The family jointly uttered a spontaneous, "Ahh-hhh", admiringly."

Before Gordon could utter a word, Elena strode forward to Patrice Huard and said in a decided accent, "I have been waiting a very long time to meet you wonderful people. I know we have never met, but I have heard so much about you, I feel like I know you."

Elena embraced Patrice Huard warmly and said, "Patrice, I am so delighted to meet you. I am Elena."

Patrice Huard could not help but notice a wedding ring upon Elena's hand. She smiled while still holding her daughter in- law and said, "By the looks of things I think you can call me Mom."

Elena said, "I would like that very much."

Elena then strode over to a silent Ben Huard. She grasped him in an equally warm embrace and said, "Ben Huard, I will be proud to call you Dad." Ben merely stood and beamed.

The family began to talk and a buzz followed.

Suddenly, the baby awoke and cried. Gordon was still holding him at the doorway.

Gordon called out to the family over the din, "And may *I* do an introduction? Ladies and gentlemen, may I present Mr. Benjamin Eduardo Huard-Castronueves."

The family again exhaled a collective, "Ahhhh."

Pete Huard called out again, "Don't expect me to spell *that* on a Christmas card."

The family laughed heartily.

Elena turned toward the big brother, smiled mischievously, and approached. She pointed at Pete Huard and said, "And *you* must be *Pete*."

The family laughed uproariously.

Elena greeted every member of the Huard family by name, much to the astonishment of all. She was incredibly warm and open to all of them. They were already falling in love with her. Delicious aromas of wonderful foods emanated from the kitchen as Elena became enveloped in the warm loving family. It was as if they'd been acquainted all of their lives.

Ben Huard walked up to Gordon with tears of pride in his eyes and embraced his son. He said, simply, "You won, son."

Gordon replied, "I think I finally did, Dad."

Gordon called out to the rest of the family, "Anybody wanna feed and change this little guy?"

Sister Beth called out, while hugging her ten year-old son, "Oh no, baby brother, *we're* all done with that stuff." The family laughed yet again.

Patrice Huard stepped forward and took custody of her newest grandchild. Within moments the little one quieted, assured in her arms.

The law enforcement officers on the Huard's property all had to alternate dining on chili, coleslaw, brisket, sausage, and innumerable types of pies. The family would have it no other way. They were patient and understanding, as the family conversed long into the night. There was so much to discuss.

Chapter 43

Alan Wilkens knew how to kill as well as anyone on earth. He was good at it. He had joined the Marines at age 17 and served admirably in the first gulf war. He proved to be exceptionally talented at technical logistics, concealment, observation, and ending human lives. He therefore became quickly absorbed into the Special Forces. Ultimately, he became a Master Sergeant within an elite squad of the Delta Force. He became one of the top commandos for the elite organization during his second tour in both Iraq and Afghanistan. Wilkens proved incomparably able to remain perfectly still in a place of concealment for nearly limitless hours. He had an innate ability to poach his prey. He killed numerous high level operatives within Al Qaida. In fact, his peers eventually nicknamed him "The Dealer." The nickname was in reference to the number of White House- designated most wanted terrorist "playing cards" that he had killed.

But his peers also began to witness telltale warning signs of impending atrocities on his part. He slept with his firearms and told fellow unit members that he loved the act of killing. Soldiers whom he supervised made remarks about their concerns to one another. But he was a Sergeant. Soon, Sergeant Wilkens began to kill indiscriminately. On one occasion he went insane with a machine gun, killing scores of innocent villagers. He laughed hysterically while doing so. Numerous fellow soldiers came forward to report the incident. But a military court exonerated him of all allegations. Orders from the Pentagon indicated that he was far too valuable an asset to become "unplugged" from his duties.

Wilkens soon thereafter became designated as a sole operative on most future missions. He did not trust his peers, and they did not trust him. It was he whom located Saddam Hussein, concealed inside a shallow well outside of Tikrit. On that occasion he was quickly joined by a nearby team of Marines and a commanding officer. Wilkens pulled the former Iraqi leader from the well and held him by the hair as he withdrew his knife. The squad of Marines restrained him from slitting the man's throat. He fought relentlessly to free himself and finish the kill. A nearby team of military videographers captured the incident on tape. The incident was too high profile to conceal.

Eventually, the U.S. government finally decided that Sergeant Wilkens had become too adept a killing machine and too great a liability. His superiors noted his sadistic love for killing. He was dismissed from the military unceremoniously.

Soon, an angry and bitter Alan Wilkens found himself unemployed, having been betrayed by his own country. He was unsure of the job possibilities for a former assassin. He did not fit into the normalized fabric of society. As had happened all of his life, he frightened passersby with his mere presence. He bounced from menial job to menial job. Inevitably he would find himself terminated from each for causing a sense of uneasiness with his peers. He was often referred to as "creepy." He did not understand humanity and no longer cared. He often joked to his frightened mother, with whom he lived, that he regretted that the mob no longer hired hit men. His mother ultimately demanded that he seek professional help. He soon disappeared abruptly from her life. She felt guilty, but relieved just the same.

Ultimately, one person referred Wilkens to another person, who in turn referred him to another. He found himself gainfully employed by men whom he never met in person. They were merely voices on a cell phone. But they paid extraordinarily well. He received a six figure cash payment for every target to which he was directed. And they were extremely easy kills. The money brought him lasting satisfaction, but the thrill of the hunt only lasted a few weeks. He soon desired another high. He hoped that his employers were pleased with the personal touches he had applied to the two professors. He thought his creativity was at an all-time high level.

A very tanned Wilkens hurriedly returned from Tahiti to the Washington D.C. area. He was thrilled to have another target. And this one was no easy prey. The former head of the National Security Agency knew how to cover his tracks. The target was adroit at shaking a tail. He seemed to have eyes in the back of his head. He kept his phone conversations brief. For a while the man had counter-surveillance personnel assigned to follow him. But, with the passage of a few weeks, interest in government protection ended. It always did.

Wilkens was soon able to observe Michael Portworth from a distance and understand the manipulation of his home alarm system and cameras. He was able to imbed himself in the grounds abutting Portworth's farmhouse. He remained still for hours, studying Portworth's every movement. When each morning arrived, he deftly disappeared beneath a hidden dug out fence-line crawl space. Wilkens eventually noted that the former NSA Director was becoming increasingly predictable. He learned that Portworth had a penchant for sitting in his study and working on his computer from 10 P.M. to 11:30 without fail. He could set his watch by Portworth.

Confident of the kill, Wilkens finally decided upon a night to eliminate his prey. A moonless late fall night provided the perfect cover for the assassin. Clad in his usual black BDU jumpsuit with a darkened face, he crawled easily beneath the place in the fence. He crawled for hundreds of yards throughout the grassy fields and used the occasional foliage for cover. He easily defeated the door alarm system and picked the lock.

The ornate front doors did not even squeak when he opened the door. The house was far too meticulous to have squeaking doors. Wilkens walked across the maple floors as would a lion seeking prey. He reached the doorway of Portworth's back office easily. Thankfully, the office door was left open. Just as Portworth was always noted to do.

Wilkens took four steps, approaching an oblivious Portworth from behind. Portworth sat typing at his computer in his dark study, humming to himself. The kill would be easy. Wilkens wrapped a piece of bicycle chain in his fists slowly and felt the joyous rewards of adrenaline coursing throughout his body. Portworth continued to type, totally oblivious to his impending death.

The assassin swung the chain over the head of Portworth in one smooth motion. He drew the tension of the chain against the man's throat immediately and heard the telltale sounds of imminent death in his choking.

Suddenly 50,000 volts of electricity shot through his body. Wilkens spasmed momentarily and tried to regain his strangle- hold upon his prey. A second massive jolt was delivered to his torso. His body locked rigidly, totally beyond his control. He landed on his back upon the floor. An extraordinarily powerfully built black man stood above him, his face covered in a black mask while holding a taser. The man wore a black BDU outfit very similar to his. A second white man wearing a black mesh mask towered over him from his left. He held a Smith and Wesson .45 caliber handgun pointed at his forehead.

The white man said, "Give me an excuse."

Michael Portworth slowly rose from his chair and turned around. A deep gash was gouged into his throat and it was bleeding moderately. He placed a nearby paper towel upon his throat and spoke in a gravelly voice. He said, "No, no. We want this one alive."

Portworth added, "You cut that a bit close didn't you fellas?"

The black man removed his dark mask, smiled, and said, "Sorry, sir. We had to make it believable."

"Well, Smittie, I believe anything you have to say," said a highly impressed Michael Portworth.

Navy Seal Master Chief Ronald Smith seemed quite pleased with himself. The assassin was quickly restrained in a series of hard plastic zip-tite handcuffs. He was carried from the house like a dead body by the two Navy Seals and four additional NSA agents. An agency medic attended to Portworth's injured throat.

Finally, once the scene was totally secured, Portworth wished to express his profound appreciation for the group of Seals and Agents. He offered to furnish several beers of any variety of unique origins.

Master Chief Ronald Smith politely declined. He said, "With all due respect, sir, we have all lived in your basement for three weeks straight. Time for most of us to go home. I think your agents will be just fine questioning that man."

The former NSA Director smirked, "My friend, I assure you he will sing like a canary by the time we get through with him. When we are done, I'm quite sure we will have more of his mercenary cohorts for you boys to round up."

"Oorah," said the stoic Master Chief.

Portworth saw the group of men out. He sat upon his couch and grabbed one of his nearby exotic beers. He popped the top and looked at the bottle. He said, "I guess it's just you and me." He drank heartily from the beer. A flood of relief overwhelmed him as he dabbed his bandaged throat with a cold wet ice wrap. He no longer felt alone or imperiled. He had a family who loved him and finally had the opportunity to enjoy their company freely.

Chapter 44

Newly appointed President Andrew Webster convened a confidential meeting in the Oval Office. Attorney General Marco Uribe was seated in a comfortable chair across from his desk. Grizzled F.B.I. Director William Dorset filled another nearby seat. He was joined by a much younger N.S.A. Director Luther Bryson, who was the first African American ever to ascend to that position. The three men comprised a semi-circle audience to the President.

Michael Portworth was marched into the office by two F.B.I. agents and directed to fill the one vacant chair.

President Webster looked very natural behind the desk. He had managed to restore order to the country during an extraordinarily tumultuous time. Media pundits were lauding him for his calm resolve and leadership. His transparency and forthrightness had further impressed the American public to the point where trust in the government was growing demonstrably. The people recognized that an individual of unquestionably genuine conviction at last occupied the seat of nonpareil power.

The gathering of men stared at Portworth. The President clasped his hands behind his head and leaned back in his chair. He inhaled deeply and exhaled slowly.

The President said, "Michael J. Portworth, what am I going to do with you?"

Portworth merely replied, "Mr. President."

The President turned to Marco Uribe and said, "Mr. Attorney General, would you please read the charges against this man?"

Uribe sat upright in his chair and withdrew a document from a file folder. He said, "Corruption of public office. Malfeasance of public office. Conspiracy to commit treason. Illegal flight from U.S. territory in order to evade prosecution. Treason."

The President turned to Portworth and said, "What do you have to say to these charges?"

Portworth said humbly, "Guilty. Guilty. Guilty. I can explain. And Guilty."

The President stifled an urge to smile.

The President then turned to the Director of the F.B.I. and asked, "Mr. Director, can you describe this man's actions regarding recent weeks?"

Director Dorset responded, "Glad to Mr. President. Mr. Portworth has voluntarily returned to American soil in order to reveal the most sinister conspiracy in the history of the United States. Perhaps even the world. He did so knowing full well that his actions would endanger his life, and possibly that of his family. He also knew that his actions would save the lives of countless Americans and help restore our faltering economy, all the while aware that his selfless acts would land him in prison for the rest of his life, or even warrant a death penalty. As you can see by the scar around his throat, he very nearly lost his life in those efforts. As a result, our government has in our custody scores of ruthless criminals whom have committed terrorist acts against our citizenry and our economic way of life."

Portworth lowered his head in respect and appreciation.

The President turned to the Director of the National

Security Agency and said, "Mr. Director, do you have anything further to add?"

Director Luther Bryson cleared his throat and spoke. "Mr. President, former Director Michael Portworth has led us to the footsteps of Usama Bin- Laden. While he is not yet in our custody, I am confident of apprehending the man, whether living or not, in subsequent weeks. At the very least, we have him contained with little hope of escape. And, were it not for the Director's efforts, we would have never learned that Bin Laden was not our highest priority target. He is fifth on a list. Three of those meriting a higher priority are already in custody. A fourth harbors only faint hopes of seeing the new- year. We are therefore enormously appreciative of this man's efforts, from an intelligence standpoint."

The President inhaled again and smiled. He leaned forward at his desk and clenched his hands together. He stared intently at Portworth. He then said, "I believe there is one more individual who wishes to speak on your behalf, Mr. Portworth."

The Oval Office door opened and in strode Justin Portworth. He was dressed immaculately in a three-piece suit and looked ten years younger. He walked in erectly military fashion toward the President's desk. Moments later, he embraced the President in a warm hug. He patted the President on the back and said, "Andy, it's good to see ya, buddy."

The President said, "You too, Just, been way too long man."

The President gestured to Justin Portworth to take a nearby seat.

Justin Portworth responded, "If it's just the same with you, Mr. President, I would like to stand."

The President asked Justin Portworth, "What do you have to contribute to this conversation."

Justin Portworth responded, "I doubt that I can add much to whatever has been said in this room, Mr. President. But what I can add is that I stand beside my son, regardless of the outcome. He did what he did because of me. He was as duped as the rest of this country was. But he sits in this room because of himself — and the courage that he has shown. I am very proud of him."

Michael Portworth looked toward his father proudly and nodded. His father returned the nod.

The President deliberated for only a minute or two. He reached into a lower drawer and retrieved a yellowed piece of paper. He finally spoke, "Well, in light of all the recent events and revelations from many people, I had already made up my mind. I just wanted to hear from you people before making that decision final. Michael Portworth, you will receive a Presidential pardon on behalf of myself and President Jimmy Carter, who once made your father a promise. Justin Portworth, that promise has been kept."

The President tore the yellow piece of paper into many pieces and dropped them into a waste basket. He continued, "Michael Portworth, in the end our country owes you a debt of gratitude. You made a huge mistake. But you risked your soul to make amends. That is what America is about. And it is what our Lord has taught us. You, sir, will never again be allowed to work as an employee of the federal or any other government. Your pension will be preserved and paid. You have earned that. I would ask that you serve at my discretion as a spokesperson to our people regarding the unbearable ultimate costs of corruption. You can serve as an example, both negatively and positively. Corruption is like a den of cockroaches, it can quickly grow back. Our search for them will never end, and you can lead us in prevention."

Michael Portworth nodded and said, "I'd be happy to, Mr. President."

The President turned to Justin Portworth and smiled. He said, "And speaking of pensions, *you*, sir are owed decades of back pay, benefits, meritorious service accolades, and a hefty retroactive pension. My friends at the Budget Office settled upon a figure of 1.25 million dollars. My old friend, I served with you so long ago. You taught me how to survive out in those jungles when I was but a scared kid. I can never thank you enough. Welcome home, Justin."

Justin Portworth stood proudly, fighting back unwanted tears. As he walked down the hallway he did so with his arm around his son. He said, "Mike, let's go home to your mother, brother, and sister. We owe them our undivided attention for the rest of our lives."

Michael said, "Amen to that, Dad."

The President dismissed all of the remaining men save for one. He asked Attorney General Uribe to remain behind for a moment.

Once the doors were closed, the President moved from his desk to a seat across from Marco Uribe. He put his hand on the shoulder of the Attorney General warmly.

The President said, "Marco, I know that you lost your best friend to this horrific conspiracy. Trent McLean was a great man. I admired him immensely. I had looked forward to someday running against him for the office of the Presidency. He would have given me a helluva run for my money. But it would have been a clean and honorable fight. America would have been the better for his participation in it. You, sir, have faced this very painful set of circumstances with a dignified determination, letting personal turmoil take a back seat to the needs of the American people. I tip my hat to you for that. Marco, I cannot bring back Trent McLean, but I can make one more thing right in this world. Mr. Attorney General, it would be my distinct honor if you would allow me to call you Mr. Vice President."

Uribe held his head high and beamed. He accepted the job offer eagerly. Two men of great character would thereby grace the offices of the Presidency of the United States. America could begin to heal.

Chapter 45

Giorgio Soudas was on the phone from within the safety of his spectacular Crete beach mansion. As usual, he was talking business.

Soudas said, "Usama, I must say you are the most capable business partner I have ever had the pleasure of working with. I should have recruited you much earlier in the game."

Bin-Laden replied, "I did not wish to waste the Oxford education that the Americans so graciously paid for."

Soudas added, "Operations in Afghanistan continue to function beautifully. My friend, you have done a tremendous job managing your Muslim brothers in the region. All while never leaving your home. You are a natural in the business world."

Bin-Laden answered, "And you have kept your promises regarding payment. Mr. Soudas, it has been a pleasure doing business with you. I will continue to uphold my end of the deal until the Americans and British end our little enterprise."

Soudas said, "The idiot Americans have still not clamped down on our activities. They are even stupider than I thought. My sources indicate that they still do not fully comprehend what we are doing. Meanwhile, another two hundred million dollars has rolled in. And you got your percentage."

Soudas knew full well that the profits had far exceeded 200 million dollars for the past quarter. But the "stupid Arab" had no idea. As always, Soudas remained the king of the deal.

Bin-Laden finally said, "Mr. Soudas, I must cut this telephone conversation short. As we had previously discussed, it is my desire that you never call me again. I mean no disrespect, but I want no traceable connections to be drawn between us."

"No disrespect taken. I will gladly abide by your wishes. We will let our money do our talking. It has been a pleasure, sir."

The phone line went dead.

Soudas joyfully returned his attention to enjoying a spectacularly warm day upon his private beach. He poured himself a glass of uzo into a crystal vase and walked down carved limestone steps from his house. The imported quartzite white sands of his private playground squeaked beneath his feet as he walked. The beach looked like a spectacular snow scape, abutted by the azure waters of the Aegean Sea. Soudas' personal armed bodyguards followed him from a respectful distance. The presence of former Greek elite soldiers hired to protect him always made Soudas feel like royalty. Other sentries stood post on the hillside near the house, several toting AK-47 machine guns. One sole sniper took a post on a rooftop.

Soudas approached his trophy girlfriend, who was lying on a lounge chair upon the beach, near the water's edge. He admired his newest possession momentarily. He knew that he was a very lucky man. He smiled bemusedly, content with the knowledge that he possessed many more trophies of the sort throughout Europe.

Soudas kissed the lounging tanned woman on the cheek and said, "I'm sorry to neglect you, Katrina dear. Business. As always."

The spectacular twenty-four year-old former Miss Greece smiled admiringly at her mega-wealthy boyfriend, fifty years her senior, and said, "Don't you have enough money, Giorgio?"

Soudas replied, "I am an old man. I can never earn enough to guarantee your undying love for me."

The woman smiled and retrieved a drink from a side table. Her massive diamond rings glistened in the sunlight, while her over-sized beach hat shaded her face. She said, "Darling, you never have to worry about that. I love you for your beautiful eyes and boyish charm." Soudas had to stifle a chortle.

Soudas kissed the woman on the cheek again and then removed his flowery print shirt. He grabbed a near-by zip-lock container of fish feed and tucked it inside a pouch that he wrapped and rubber-banded around his forearm. He sat his drink on the table beside Katrina and waded out into the gentle surf. He looked ridiculous in his red Speedo swim suit. His vast stomach hung over his belt line. His tanned hairy chest, adorned with gold chains, completed his aging playboy image.

Soudas thought again of how he treasured his current set of circumstances. His corrupt operations had continued unimpeded for several weeks. U.S. officials were laughingly slow to turn off his pipeline of wealth. Plus, he had gained 200 billion additional dollars of profit when his lawyers leveraged the spoils of the conspiracy, once destined for his former business colleagues.

Soudas' new Arabic business partner had already proven to be invaluable. Bin Laden could influence Middle Eastern activities with a few simple well-placed phone calls — all while concealed within his opulent compound so close to the Pakistani version of West Point. The greatest benefit to Soudas regarding his new associate lay in the fact that the "stupid Arab" did not command more than ten per cent of the reported profits. And Soudas had deftly hidden most of those profits. He was delighted to suddenly hear from Bin-Laden of his demands to discontinue any further contact. The man had grown increasingly paranoid of any connections to him.

Bin-Laden proved that he could perform his functions unilaterally and simply collect his payment from his hidden "trust fund." But Soudas knew that he could use the excuse of future lack of contact to slowly restrict the outflow of additional further payments. Circumstances in every way had seemingly exceeded all expectations.

Soudas drew incomparable delight in knowing that he was immune to arrest or interference from the American government. He was not on their soil, and Greek officials had been paid handsomely to protect his immunity. He had never been particularly worried about the possibilities of other intrusive American financial scenarios. He had hidden his enterprises deftly.

Soudas felt like a young child at holiday time. He ran playfully into deeper waters of the Aegean Sea and began swimming. Like a beached sea lion, he became surprisingly buoyant and graceful when he began to swim. His strokes and kicks were powerful. Despite his obesity, Soudas did not tire easily. The former regional swimming star felt totally free in the warm waters of the Greek paradise.

After swimming for a hundred yards from the shore

Soudas spun upon his back. He placed his hands behind his head and bobbed upon the small waves, letting the gentle tide carry him further outward, beyond a very deep shelf. He was so at ease in the water that he had to resist an urge to fall asleep. He unwrapped his carrying pouch from around his forearm and retrieved the ziplock baggie. He tossed fish foods around him in the water and marveled at the resultant appearance of numerous exotic sea fish. The multi-colored fish ravenously devoured the foods, and the water around him boiled with activity. He returned to his back- float position and made a profane gesture toward one of his sentries, who loyally monitored his every movement via powerful binoculars from the beach. He smiled and waved at Katrina in the distance. She did not wave back. It appeared that she was asleep.

Soudas felt a gentle tug upon his right ankle. He discarded the sensation as a misguided hungry sea bass which often pecked at the feet of swimming tourists. He then felt something clamp around the same ankle. For a moment he knew not what to do.

Navy Seal Master Chief Antonio Cuevas was clad in a turquoise blue scuba- diver's outfit. The color perfectly matched that of the waters of the Aegean Sea. He was careful to control his breathing. The high-tech oxygen apparatus served to conceal any conspicuous surface bubbles. He wore an extra oxygen tank for needed added buoyancy. He slowly pursued a shadowy figure above into much deeper seas. The target was easy to see in the shimmering surface waters. Once the figure became stationary, Cuevas began to slowly ascend from a depth of twenty-five feet. He paused as the surface became disturbed by unknown splashing debris. Innumerable fish appeared around him from out of nowhere, hurrying toward the surface. The scores of fish obscured his vision of the target. He knew immediately that the Greek was feeding the tropical ocean fish. Just as he was always known to do.

Cuevas waited patiently for the waters to begin to clear somewhat, and then approached the shadow. He reached for the ankle of the swimmer and lost grasp, as the waves pulled the man away. Cuevas righted himself for another approach. He grabbed the swimmer by the right ankle and adroitly attached a metal ankle shackle. He felt the man struggle. He released his grasp of a forty-pound weight that was attached to the restraint device. Cuevas rapidly moved his face from the flailing attempts of a desperate sinking man to attack him. The man's fingernails sped past his face harmlessly. Cuevas kicked away from Soudas and gained a safe distance. He methodically purged his extra tank in order to remain submerged. The bubbles suddenly rose upward, but were indistinguishable from the activities of the tropical fish. He watched as the man was pulled downward into the depths of the ocean. He could see the shock and desperation in the Greek's wide- open eyes. The attached weight and oxygen-starved lungs propelled the target 1000 feet below, to his undetectable grave — far too deep for divers to search for a body.

It took the numerous sentries three minutes to realize that the Greek quasi-trillionaire had disappeared from sight. Desperately, two of the men sprinted toward the edge of the water and dove into the sea. They swam frantically away from the beach. Katrina was awakened and immediately stood at the shore, deeply concerned.

Two other AK-47 toting men sprinted to a nearby hidden zodiac raft and started the twin motors, speeding off to sea. The Zodiac nearly cut through the other two swimming men in the haste to locate the missing Soudas. The craft made endless growing circles in search of the man. A white foamy wake convoluted the waters. The other two tiring swimmers soon swam back to shore, and stood helplessly on the shoreline. Within twenty minutes the rescue mission was aborted. Their well-paying eccentric employer was nowhere to be found. Katrina stood disconsolate on the shores. It appeared that the elderly boyfriend might well have meant more to her than simply his fortune.

National Security Agency Special Agent Brian Hargraves reached over the side of the yacht "the Santa Maria" and deftly plucked the smallish but muscular Chief Cuevas from the waters of the Aegean Sea. Cuevas sat on the deck of the boat and gathered his breath for a moment as he removed his mask and gear. He was assisted by other Navy Seals. Finally, he rose to a side seat and smiled.

Cuevas said, "I think the guy makes a pretty anchor."

Other Seals fist- bumped the Senior Chief on the mission.

Hargraves simply said, "Beautiful." He then addressed the team of Navy Seals and said, "Excuse me, fellas, I have a few phone calls to place in a moment. And be advised, we are now headed to lovely downtown Abbottabad. We have one more snake to take out." The team members all growled in excitement toward their impending mission. It was for what they had trained for years.

Cuevas turned to Agent Hargraves and said, "Sir, when this is all over, we all respectfully request a return trip here to Greece for some additional recon on these beaches." He stared outward at the nearby beaches, adorned with lovely topless women. His teammates nodded in enthusiastic agreement. Hargraves was immediately struck with just how young the Seals actually were, as he looked into their youthful faces. These selfless young men were excited to go risk their lives for their country, without hesitation. It was an awe-inspiring revelation.

Hargraves responded, "Focus first on what we have to do, fellas. It won't be easy, and he won't go without a firefight. But after the mission, I believe the grateful American people will be delighted to fund some extensive liberty calls. I'll see to it that a heroic bunch of horny Sailors and Marines can be deployed in this country that is known for its lovely women."

Once again, the team responded with a hearty, "Oo-rah."

The powerful engines of the yacht came to life and the vessel rose to a plane above the water. The elite Seal "Team Six" sped rapidly toward a nearby port, where air transport was already standing by to facilitate the final hunt for Usama Bin-Laden. They were honored to have been chosen for the extraordinary mission.

Hargraves retreated to a very private communications room, deep in the bowels of the large vessel. He affixed a headset in order to drown out the boat's roaring engines. He first contacted the Pakistan detachment of the C.I.A. via the satellite phone.

"Hargraves said, "Tommy, we have a good loc on the bastard. Not far from where you guys always figured. About twenty clicks outside Islamabad. Posh, but garrison-type neighborhood. The SOB has some nice digs. I'm sending you the coordinates now. We are on our way."

C.I.A. Special Agent in Charge for the Pakistani theater, Thomas Larned responded, "Copy that, buddy. We'll have a drone in the air and will be establishing our outer perimeter. Hydrate up. It won't be gravy, like your lovely Greece. It's 112 here and the dust is up our nostrils."

Hargraves answered, "Appreciate the containment, buddy. Our e.t.a. is 95 minutes. In the end, who's gonna be sweating more, Tommy, our boys or our target?"

Larned said, "We might sweat more, but I think he's gonna bleed more. We're all gonna need some luck, though. Even with this info, this is no slam-dunk. Those neighborhoods are a source of tremendous concealment. A man disappears in the back alleys quickly. And he has lots of friendlies in these parts. It would sure be a lot easier just to nuke him."

"The President says alive, if possible. He wants the personal touch. And I have no doubt ol' Usama will not be allowed to take any alleyway strolls before we get there. If it makes you feel any better, once we are done with this mission, you and I will then be headed for the Cayman Islands. You'll be my guest."

Larned added, "You Nussies always get the perks. Well, we'll do the grunt work til you get here. Then the fun begins. I also look forward to bankrupting the whole lot of them."

Besides the exhilarating intelligence on the location of the Al-Qaida mastermind, Hargraves was inwardly delighted to possess the knowledge of the whereabouts of all of Bin-Laden's offshore bank accounts. Through the power of recent international anti-terrorism pacts, he knew that he and his people could legally seize all of the spoils of the conspiracy. The hundreds of billions hidden by the Afghani and the Greek would soon become the sovereign property of the people of the U.S.A.

Hargraves said, "In a few hours, Mr. Bin-Laden will have less money than the guy with the sign by the freeway, and probably find a bullet in his head."

"Copy that, buddy. God- speed."

"You too."

N.S.A. Director Luther Bryson's secure cell phone rang only twice before he answered.

"Sir, we regret to inform you of a tragic swimming accident in some lovely turquoise waters. It would appear that the man bumped into a passing seal along his way."

"Sorry to hear that, said the smiling Director. One down, one to go. God bless, and good luck, Brian."

"Copy that, sir."

The conversation was immediately ended.

Epilogue

Yakima, Washington. One year later.

Michael Portworth sat at a picnic table in a beautiful grassy field alongside the scenic Yakima River Greenway. He was eating a delicious hamburger from the local iconic "Miner's Drive-Inn." The juices from the burger dripped down his chin as he savored the Walla Walla sweet onions that adorned his fare. It was a spectacular 93-degree summer day. Beyond the park the river split into two directions and wound around a sand bar in the distance. Massachusetts blue herons and bald eagles circled the river channel in abundance. Joggers passed by on the pathway, occasionally passed by bicyclists. A tall distinguished white haired man passed by, walking a small white poodle. He waved his hand and nodded in greeting. Portworth humbly returned the gesture.

Portworth returned his attention to a family at another table, some 200 feet away. A single mother and three sons were enjoying the summer sunshine and a family picnic. The attractive mother had involved herself in a game of Frisbee with her boys who ranged in age from fifteen to nine. The family eventually ended their picnic, as early evening shadows began to approach.

Portworth knew the location of their older parked Chevy Astro mini-van. It was located in the opposite direction of his parked vehicle. As a point of fact, he had made it a mission to learn a great deal about the family. He knew that the mother was taking community college courses at night, while working long days in the local fruit warehouses to support her family. She was a good mother, who would never let her sons witness her fatigue. The scene brought back strong memories for Michael Portworth. He treasured observing the young family happily enjoying the company of one another.

He knew that the family would soon experience a considerable change in their impoverished, but loving lives. When the mother next had a chance to view her meager bank statement she would be convinced that the bank had made an error. In fact, Portworth knew that she would certainly go to the bank out of concern. She would conscientiously attempt to correct the mistake with her savings account balance. The bank manager would ultimately have to inform the woman that her account balance was accurate. The incredulous woman would ask how her balance could increase by such a substantial amount. The bank manager would answer that he could only say that her husband's former co-workers had anonymously drawn together a collection.

The woman's savings account totaled nearly five million dollars.

As the family began their walk back to the parking lot, Portworth rose. He wandered down the curve of the Greenway and soon approached the oncoming mother and her boys. He nodded toward the widow and smiled. He said to the woman, "Good evening, Mrs. Knapse." He continued past the family.

The woman stammered a hello, drawing a blank on recognizing the man, as she continued walking. She turned to address the man. He was gone.

Michael Portworth jogged the curve of the paved pathway along the river's bank. He smiled and looked upward at another eagle, soaring over the shimmering waters. The symbol of freedom was a perfect metaphor for the man whom had risked his own freedom in order to bring about the collapse of "the new world order." The summer sunshine on his face felt delightful.

About the Author

Steven Lowell-Martin is a recently retired 31-year Seattle Police Detective and Patrol Sergeant. He led numerous investigations into gang-land shootings and he holds federal clearances. He also had the opportunity to meet four U.S. presidents and the Queen of England. He has a penchant for telling stories of corruption, greed, and avarice.

Martin currently resides in Bothell, Washington with his wife, Mahala. He spends his time enjoying two darling grand-daughters, three daughters, fishing, and writing his latest novels and screenplays. His loyal hyperactive six-pound Tuxedo Tabby cat "Ritalin" occupies his lap during writing and lends editorial insight.